SHADOWS OF ETERNITY

BOOKS BY AMANDA ASHLEY

Anthologies
After Twilight
Blood & Moonlight
"Born of the Night" in Stroke of Midnight
"Darkfest" in Midnight Pleasures
"Music of the Night" in Mammoth Book of Vampire Romance

Bound Series
Bound by Night
Bound by Blood

Brynn Tor Series
Donovan's Woman
Quinn's Lady
Quinn's Revenge

Children of the Night Series
Night's Kiss
Night's Touch
Night Night's Master
Night's Pleasure
Night's Mistress
Night's Promise
Night's Surrender
Night's Illusion

Everlasting Series
- Everlasting Kiss
- Everlasting Desire
- Everlasting Embrace
- Everlasting Collection

Morgan Creek Series
- As Twilight Falls
- Twilight Dreams
- Twilight Desires
- Twilight Destiny
- Twilight Longings (coming soon)

Vampire Trilogy
- Shades of Gray
- After Sundown
- Desire After Dark

Standalone Titles
- A Darker Dream
- A Fire in the Blood
- A Whisper of Eternity
- Beauty's Beast
- Beneath a Midnight Moon
- Dark of the Moon
- Dead Sexy
- Dead Perfect
- Deeper Than the Night
- Desire the Night
- Embrace the Night
- Enchant the Dawn
- Enchant the Night

Books by Madeline Baker

Apache Runaway Series
　Apache Runaway
　Chase The Wind

Reckless Series
　Reckless Heart
　Reckless Love
　Reckless Desire
　Reckless Embrace
　Reckless Destiny
　Series Collection

The Lightning Books
　Chase the Lightning
　When Lightning Strikes
　Follow the Lightning
　Find the Lightning

Time Travel
　A Whisper in the Wind
　The Spirit Path
　The Angel and the Outlaw
　Feather in the Wind
　Under a Prairie Moon
　Unforgettable
　Shadows Through Time

Forever in Darkness
His Dark Embrace
Hold Back the Dawn
Immortal Sins
In the Dark of the Night
Jessie's Girl
Maiden's Song
Masquerade
Midnight and Moonlight
Midnight Embrace
Midnight Enchantment
Moonlight
Sandy's Angel
Seasons of the Night
Secrets in the Night
Shadows of Eternity
Sunlight Moonlight
Surrender the Dawn
The Captive
The Music of the Night

Standalone Books
- Apache Flame
- Beneath a Midnight Moon
- Bohanan
- Callie's Cowboy
- Cheyenne Surrender
- Comanche Flame
- Dakota Dreams
- Dude Ranch Bride
- Every Inch a Cowboy
- First Love, Wild Love
- Forbidden Fires
- Hawk's Woman
- Heart of the Hunter
- In the Shadow of the Hills
- Kade
- Lacey's Way
- Lakota Love Song
- Lakota Renegade
- Love Forevermore
- Love in the Wind
- Love's Serenade
- Love's Sweet Embrace
- Loving Jake
- Midnight Fire
- Prairie Heat
- Renegade Heart
- Spirit's Song
- Under Apache Skies
- Warrior's Lady
- West Texas Bride
- Wolf Shadow
- Zane

Shadows of Eternity

Amanda Ashley

Shadows of Eternity

Copyright © 2024 Amanda Ashley

All rights reserved.
This edition published 2024

Cover by Cynthia Lucas

ISBN: 978-1-68068-386-8

The characters and events portrayed in this book are fictitious. Any similarity to real persons, living or dead, is coincidental and not intended by the author.

No Artificial Intelligence (AI) was used to generate any of the text of this book.

No part of this book may be reproduced or stored in a retrieval system, or transmitted in any form or by any means, electronic, mechanical, photocopying, recording or otherwise, without express written permission of the publisher.

This book is published on behalf of the author by the Ethan Ellenberg Literary Agency.

You can reach the author at:
Email: darkwritr@aol.com
Websites: www.amandaashley.net and www.madelinebaker.net

Dedication

For William Grayson
The 5th William in the family tree
Love you bunches!

Table of Contents

Chapter One · 1
Chapter Two · 7
Chapter Three · 14
Chapter Four · 19
Chapter Five · 28
Chapter Six · 36
Chapter Seven · 42
Chapter Eight · 52
Chapter Nine · 55
Chapter Ten · 65
Chapter Eleven · 73
Chapter Twelve · 81
Chapter Thirteen · 87
Chapter Fourteen · 94
Chapter Fifteen · 102
Chapter Sixteen · 104
Chapter Seventeen · 114
Chapter Eighteen · 122
Chapter Nineteen · 131
Chapter Twenty · 135
Chapter Twenty-One · 139
Chapter Twenty-Two · 148
Chapter Twenty-Three · 150
Chapter Twenty-Four · 160
Chapter Twenty-Five · 168

Chapter Twenty-Six · 180
Chapter Twenty-Seven · 186
Chapter Twenty-Eight · 194
Chapter Twenty-Nine · 202
Chapter Thirty · 209
Chapter Thirty-One · 221
Chapter Thirty-Two · 223
Chapter Thirty-Three · 230
Chapter Thirty-Four · 239
Chapter Thirty-Five · 245
Chapter Thirty-Six · 252
Chapter Thirty-Seven · 253
Chapter Thirty-Eight · 265
Chapter Thirty-Nine · 272
Chapter Forty · 274
Chapter Forty-One · 284
Chapter Forty-Two · 294

About the Author · 309
About the Publisher · 311

Chapter One

Leia Winchester watched in awe as the Indian who had been introduced as Shadow Dancer dipped and swayed to the haunting music of flute and drum. His well-muscled, copper-hued body bent and twisted in ways she would have thought impossible, each movement masculine, sensual. His bare feet made no sound as they executed the intricate steps. Long, black hair fell like a river of silk almost to his waist, now flowing around his broad shoulders, now whipping around his face in time to the beat of the drum and the rhythm of the dance. She yearned to run her fingers through that masculine mane, trace the well-defined muscles that bunched and flexed in his arms.

He was, in a word, the most beautiful, exciting thing she had ever seen.

Unlike the other dancers who had performed earlier, adorned with colorful bustles and headdresses and beaded moccasins, Shadow Dancer wore only a breechclout. A single white eagle feather fluttered in his hair. A narrow slash of bright red paint ran from the outer corner of his left eye to the curve of his jaw; a handprint in the same bright red was painted on his chest over his heart.

She applauded wildly when his dance was over. Then, hoping to get him to sign her program, she practically ran out of the auditorium to the stage door.

Gradually, the other dancers emerged in groups of two or three or four. Half an hour later, Leia was still waiting.

She had just decided he must have gone out another way when the door opened and he stood there. He had looked magnificent in Native dress. He looked equally impressive in a pair of black jeans, boots, and a dark gray sweatshirt that said, "Go Native."

One dark eyebrow went up inquisitively when he saw her. "Are you waiting for someone?" His voice poured over her like melted chocolate, deep and rich.

"Um, yes," she murmured. "I was waiting for you."

"Oh?"

She held out her program and a pen. "I … could I please have your autograph?"

To avoid this very thing, he generally left the venue after the crowd had gone, but he was glad he hadn't waited tonight, he mused, as his gaze ran over her. She had hair like flame and eyes the color of new grass. "My pleasure," he said, reaching for the pen and her program.

Leia shivered as his cool fingers brushed her own. For an instant, in her mind's eye, she saw a flash of images—a tipi, a herd of running buffalo, a calico pony, a freshly-turned grave. Before she could make sense of the images, they were gone.

"Are you all right?" he asked, frowning.

"I … yes, of course."

Opening the program to a page featuring his photographs, he scrawled *Shadow Dancer* across one of the pictures, and below that, he wrote *Rohan,* and handed it back to her.

"Rohan," she murmured. "That seems like an odd name for an Indian."

"Shadow Dancer is the name I was born with. I use it as my stage name."

"Then where did Rohan come from?"

He shrugged. "It's easier to use in everyday life than Shadow Dancer."

"So, what's the name on your driver's license?"

"Rohan Stillwater."

"Well," she said, "it was nice to meet you. I thought you were wonderful."

"Thank you," he said, returning the pen. "What would you say if I asked you out for a drink?"

"I don't know."

"Are you married?"

"No."

"Engaged? Going steady? Gay?"

"No, no, and no," she said, with a laugh.

"Just not interested, huh? Well, it was nice meeting you."

"I didn't say that," Leia blurted, surprising them both.

"Well, good. There's a little club around the corner. We can walk, if you like."

She nodded. Her mother hadn't raised any stupid daughters. As fascinated as she was by Mr. Shadow Dancer, Leia wasn't about to get into a car with a complete stranger, no matter how gorgeous and talented he might be. Leia wasn't usually tongue-tied around handsome men. After all, with both parents working in the entertainment business, she had met more than her share. But she couldn't think of a thing to say on the short walk to the nightclub.

The nightclub was small, dark, and intimate. Rohan guided her to a vacant table in the back, held her chair for her before settling into the seat across from hers. "So, you know my name," he said, "but I don't know yours."

"Leia."

He arched one brow. "Leia?"

"My mother is a huge *Star Wars* fan. She named my older brother Luke Skywalker, even though my Dad didn't care for the idea. But Luke loves it."

Rohan chuckled softly. "So, Princess Leia, what is it you do when you're not watching Native dancers?"

"I'm a kindergarten teacher."

"Really? I'd say they didn't have any teachers like you when I went to school, but you probably hear that all the time."

She nodded. Mesmerized by his voice, she didn't care what he said as long as he kept talking.

"What do you do when you're not teaching?"

"I enjoy going to plays and concerts, taking walks in the park, going out to lunch or the movies with my friends." She shrugged. "The usual things women do. What do *you* do when you're not dancing?"

"Drink. Sleep. Hunt." He winked at her. "The usual things that men do."

"Hunt?" she asked with a grin. "You don't use a bow and arrow, do you?"

"Not anymore," he said cryptically.

"Well, you certainly don't hunt in the city, do you?"

"You'd be surprised."

Feeling suddenly like prey, Leia shivered as his dark gaze moved over her. Before she could think of anything to say, the waitress approached their table.

"What would you like?" Rohan asked.

"I'm not much of a drinker," Leia confessed. "What's good?"

"The house wine here is excellent." Turning to the waitress, he said, "We'll have two glasses of your finest Cabernet Sauvignon."

The waitress batted her eyelashes at him. "Yes, sir," she said in a deep, throaty voice. "Will there be anything else?"

Rohan looked at Leia, one brow raised.

"No, thank you." She rolled her eyes as the waitress walked away from the table, hips swaying seductively.

"What's that look for?" Rohan asked.

"I think she was hoping you'd ask her for more than a drink," Leia muttered, wondering why she cared. "Much more."

Rohan laughed, a deep rumble that made her toes curl. "You think so?"

"I know so. Women can always tell. I think she'd give you anything you asked for."

He leaned forward, his gaze caressing her face, lingering on the hollow of her throat. "What about you?"

"What about me?" she asked tremulously.

"Would you give me anything I asked for?"

"No." Pushing away from the table, she stood up. "Sorry."

His fingers curled around her wrist. "Don't go."

"Let go of me," she whispered, not wanting to make a scene. "This was a mistake. If you're looking for a one-night stand, you'll have better luck with the waitress."

"Hey, I'm sorry. I shouldn't have said what I did. Stay, please."

Leia hesitated. He sounded sincere, and she'd been having such a good time up until now, did she really want to leave? "I'll stay, on one condition."

"What's that?" he asked.

"I want to know how a Lakota Indian got a Romanian name."

"I'll tell you, when I know you better."

Leia hesitated a moment. Then, wondering if she was making a huge mistake, she sat down again, her hands tightly folded in her lap.

"I'm sorry," he said again. "I guess I'm just used to women throwing themselves at me. It comes with the territory."

Leia flushed, suddenly embarrassed because she had acted like such a fool. "I really should go. I have to work tomorrow."

"Can I see you again?"

"I don't think so. Good night."

He stood as she left the table, stared after her as she hurried out the door. "Leia," he murmured, suddenly determined to see his shy princess again.

He grinned as the waitress arrived with their drinks. He would have preferred to share a glass of Cabernet with the lovely Leia, but he had other thirsts and the waitress would serve those very well.

Chapter Two

Leia woke after a restless night. Usually, she fell asleep as soon as her head hit the pillow and she didn't wake up until her alarm went off. Any dreams she had while she slept were usually forgotten by morning.

But last night...last night, she had tossed and turned. Her dreams had been fragmented with scenes of Indians attacking homesteads, murdering men, women and children. Surprisingly, one of the warriors had looked like Shadow Dancer. Or perhaps not so surprising, she mused, since he had stayed in her thoughts long after she returned home. Interspersed with those nightmare images set in the Old West had been visions straight out of an old Dracula movie, with a dark, handsome vampire bending over the slender throat of some helpless woman clad in a flowing white nightgown.

Slipping out of bed, Leia headed for the shower, hoping it would clear her head and chase away the last remnants of her odd dreams.

After showering, she dressed, ate a quick breakfast, made sure she had everything she needed for the day, stopped at a nearby Starbucks for a latte and then walked to school, which was only two blocks from her apartment.

It was Friday, always an easy day in her class. A short lesson first and then they had storytime until their parents came to pick them up.

All thoughts of Indians and vampires fled her mind as her students began to arrive.

Leia kicked off her shoes, dumped her handbag on the coffee table and collapsed on the sofa. Fridays might be easy days in the classroom, but her work day didn't end there. She had to plan next week's activities, plus she had to arrange for several parent-teacher conferences.

She had no sooner sat back and closed her eyes than her cell phone rang. One ring. Two. Three. Shoot. She delved into her purse, pulled out her phone, and said, not very nicely, "Hey, Janae."

"Wow, rough day?"

"It's Friday."

"Right. Listen, I've got an extra ticket to that Native dance thing. Trent was supposed to go with me, but he has to work tonight."

Leia grunted softly. Janae Frumusanu was her best friend. Leia wasn't exactly sure what Janae's husband did for a living, but whatever it was, it was very hush-hush. Sometimes Leia wasn't sure Janae knew, either. The only thing Leia knew for certain was that he worked nights, was often gone for days at a time, and never discussed his job with Janae. "I don't think so."

"What? Why not?"

"I went last night." An image of Shadow Dancer flashed across Leia's mind—coppery skin, long black hair, mesmerizing eyes, a deep, sexy voice that made her toes curl. She shook it away.

"How was the production?" Janae asked.

"It was great."

"Then why don't you want to go again? You know what these tickets cost! I asked my mom and she can't make it. Come on, girlfriend, you don't even have to pay me for the ticket."

Leia blew out a sigh. After last night, how could she go back? No doubt Shadow Dancer would think she'd come just to see him again. And he'd be right. "Janae…"

"I'll take you out for a Belgian dark chocolate sundae afterward."

"You're not playing fair now," Leia complained, already mentally going through her wardrobe.

"I'll pick you up at seven-thirty," Janae said, a note of triumph in her voice.

⚜ ⚜ ⚜

Leia fidgeted with the strap of her handbag as Janae pulled into the parking lot. This was a mistake. She should have said no.

"What's wrong with you?" Janae asked. "You're as nervous as a bride. Don't tell me one of the Indians made a pass at you."

"What?"

"It happens everywhere we go," Janae said, and then she stared at Leia, eyes wide. "*That's* why you didn't want to come with me tonight, isn't it?"

Leia nodded.

"I'll make it up to you somehow," Janae promised. "Maybe dinner at your favorite restaurant tomorrow night or a massage at our favorite spa."

Feeling as if she was going to a massacre, Leia followed Janae into the auditorium, muttered, "I don't believe it," when their seats were front row, center.

Ten minutes later, the lights dimmed and the first dancers were announced.

Leia grew more and more nervous as the evening went on and then, all too soon, *he* was on the stage.

"Wow," Janae whispered. "He's gorgeous!" When Leia didn't respond, Janae glanced at her, then whispered, "He's the one, isn't he?"

"Yes."

"Times like this, I wish I wasn't married."

Leia tried not to watch him, but try as she might, she couldn't look away. He was beautiful to watch, his movements intricate and precise. She had the oddest feeling that he was dancing just for her, that every sensual movement was meant to entice her, arouse her. And, damn his hide, it was working.

She breathed a sigh of relief when he left the stage amid thunderous applause.

"That was great!" Janae exclaimed.

Leia was relieved when, at last, all the dancers came out for a final bow.

Shadow Dancer stood in the center of the stage, directly opposite her seat. She flushed as his gaze moved over her.

And then, as the other dancers took their leave, he leaped agilely from the stage and landed lightly in front of her. "Leia, how nice to see you again."

Janae tugged on her arm, silently begging for an introduction.

"Rohan, this is my best friend, Janae. Janae, Rohan."

"I'd love to have your autograph," Janae said, thrusting her program and a pen at him. "If it's not too much trouble."

"Anything for a friend of Leia's." He was speaking to Janae but he was looking at Leia, his dark eyes caressing her.

She felt the heat of his gaze all the way down to her toes.

"Perhaps I could take you ladies out for a drink?" he suggested as he returned Janae's program and pen.

Leia started to shake her head, but it was too late.

"That would be terrific," Janae gushed. "Wouldn't it, Leia?"

Yes," she said. "Terrific."

Rohan was wonderful company. Thoughtful. Polite. He listened to Janae babble about her twin sons, Mark and Mike, as if he was really interested, answered her questions about how long he'd been dancing and where he'd learned.

"My father taught me," Rohan said. "He was a Lakota medicine man, able to see into the future."

"A medicine man?" Janae asked. "Like a doctor?"

"No. He was a shaman. A holy man. They possess some mystical powers."

"That's fascinating," Janae said. Then, glancing at her watch, she said, "Oh, shoot! I was supposed to be home half an hour ago. I'll be right back, Leia. I need to call my babysitter."

When they were alone, Rohan said, "I was surprised to see you here tonight."

Leia shrugged. "Janae's husband couldn't make it and she didn't want his ticket to go to waste."

He nodded. "Any chance I could take you out some evening? I know we got off on the wrong foot last night, but how about giving me a chance to prove I'm not a jerk?"

She wanted to say no. She intended to say no. But something in his voice had her saying, "Yes. I'd like that."

"How about meeting me after the show tomorrow night? We could go out for drinks and dancing."

"All right. I'll meet you at the stage door."

His smile warmed her from head to heel.

"Here comes Janae," Leia said, pushing away from the table. "I'll see you tomorrow night."

Rising, he took her hand in his and kissed her palm. "Until then, Princess."

"You're going out with him!" Janae exclaimed as she pulled out of the parking lot. "Do you think that's wise? I mean, he's sexy as all get out, but you just met the guy."

"I meant to say no, but..." Leia shrugged. "Somehow it came out yes."

"Well, you be careful. Call me when you leave and the minute you get home."

"Yes, Mother."

"I mean it," Janae said. "The guy is drop-dead gorgeous. There's no doubt about that. And sexy as hell. But... I don't know. I don't trust him."

"Are you having one of your psychic warnings?"

"Not exactly. But... this is going to sound weird, he's a lot older than he looks."

"What are you talking about?" Leia asked, frowning. "Do you think he had plastic surgery, or something?" The very idea was ridiculous. No plastic surgeon could have molded the masculine beauty of Rohan's face.

"No. No, nothing like that. I don't know how to explain it. I mean, he looks like he's in his late twenties, early thirties, but the vibe I got from him was older. A lot older."

"It's just one date, girl." She appreciated Janae's concern, but sometimes she went a little overboard.

"Well, you be careful," Janae said again as she pulled up in front of Leia's apartment. "I've got a bad feeling about this."

"Now *you're* quoting *Star Wars* movies," Leia muttered as she stepped out of the car. "Good night, Obi Wan."

" 'Night."

Leia waved as she opened her apartment door and stepped inside. Older than he looked? What did that mean?

Rohan strolled the dark streets of the city, his thoughts focused on Leia. There was something about her, something rare that called to him. Even now, he could smell her scent—the flowery fragrance of her hair and perfume, the unique scent of her skin, the enticing scent of her blood that was hers alone. He had been sorely tempted to steal her away. Perhaps he still would. He wanted to know her better, touch her, taste her, arouse her until she begged him to take her.

It had been years—perhaps decades—since he had been so attracted to a woman.

Years since he had gone back home to where it all began.

Chapter Three

Leia was by turns excited and apprehensive on Saturday night as she dressed for her date with Rohan. She hadn't been this jittery since her first date back in high school, she mused as she applied her lipstick. Maybe she was just a little nervous because she'd never had a date with a man who exuded so much raw masculinity, or who was so blatantly handsome, or one who was famous. She told herself there was nothing to worry about. Janae knew she was going out with him and would sound the alarm should Leia fail to report in when she got home.

When it was time to leave, she took a last look in the mirror, called Janae to let her know she was on her way, and left her apartment.

It was a short drive to the theater. She parked her car, then walked to the stage door. Unlike the other night, he was the first one out.

Rohan smiled when he saw her. "I was afraid you wouldn't come."

"Oh?"

He nodded. "I sensed your hesitation last night. If it will make you feel safer, we can take separate cars." He lifted one brow, waiting for her answer. "Leia?"

She hesitated as Janae's warning drifted through her mind, then shook her head. Janae was making her paranoid. Smiling, she said, "All right."

"I was thinking we'd go to Manchester's. Do you know where it is?"

"Yes."

"See you in a few minutes."

Leia felt foolish as she walked back to her car. If she didn't trust him enough to be in a car with him, why had she agreed to go out with him? Still, better to err on the side of caution. It seemed there were always stories on the news of women disappearing without a trace. Better safe than sorry, she told herself as she drove to the nightclub.

Manchester's was an upscale club and restaurant with a large dance floor and live music on the weekends.

Rohan was waiting for her at the entrance when she arrived. "Have you had dinner?"

"Yes." Warmth spread through her when he reached for her hand.

They bypassed the restaurant and found a table in the bar. A waiter came to take their order. Rohan opted for a glass of red wine. Leia asked for a Sea Breeze.

"So," Rohan said, "tell me about yourself."

It was hard to think when he was looking at her. His eyes were dark and beautiful. "There isn't much to tell. I was lucky enough to find a job teaching as soon as I graduated from college and I love it. My parents live in Hollywood. My mother is a script girl. She's crazy about movies, especially *Star Wars*. My father is head of security for one of the major studios."

"Interesting. I guess you're a big movie buff, too."

"Oh, yes. Growing up, the walls in my bedroom were lined with posters from blockbuster movies. I have three autograph books, all filled with famous signatures."

"I would have thought you'd follow in the family footsteps."

"I wanted to be an actress when I was a little girl," she confessed. "I even had a few screen tests, but…" She shrugged. "No discernable talent in that area. What about you? How did you get into Native dancing professionally?"

"Dancing is natural to most of my people. The steps have been handed down for generations. War dances, friendship dances, rain dances, dances to ensure a good hunt."

"Are both your parents Lakota?"

"Yes."

"They must be very proud of you."

Rohan nodded. Perhaps they would have been.

"It must be exciting, traveling around the country," Leia remarked as the waiter delivered their drinks.

"It's getting old," Rohan said. His gaze caressed her. "I'm thinking of taking a long vacation."

"Oh?"

"I'd like to spend part of it with you."

It was suddenly hard to think, to breathe.

He reached for her hand, his fingers linking with hers. "Would you like to dance?"

At her nod, he led her onto the dance floor and took her into his arms. He was tall, so tall. He slow-danced with the same lithe grace he used onstage. She had no trouble following his lead. He held her close, making her feel safe, protected, as if nothing could ever hurt her again.

Rohan frowned as he caught snatches of her thoughts. No wonder she was leery of strangers, he mused. She had been kidnapped when she was four years old. Although she had few actual memories of the event, it had haunted her as she grew older, which led to a year or two of therapy, which had helped considerably.

He spoke to her mind, assuring her that she had nothing to fear from him, felt her relax in his arms.

They danced and talked the night away. It was late when he walked her to her car. "Any chance you'd give me your phone number?"

She hesitated only a moment, then quickly recited the number. "Aren't you going to put it in your phone?"

"I won't forget it." His gaze moved over her as he drew her into his arms. When she didn't resist, he lowered his head and kissed her good night. "Call you soon."

Murmuring, "Good night,"

Leia unlocked her car door and slid behind the wheel. She smiled all the way home. It had been heaven, dancing with Rohan. She had loved being in his arms, the sound of his voice, the way his gaze caressed her, the way he listened to her. By the end of the evening, she knew she was in danger of losing her heart.

She called Janae the minute she got home. "You can stop worrying now. Mother. I'm safely home, my front door locked."

"Hey, what are friends for if not to worry? How was your date?"

"Wonderful." Leia closed her eyes, wishing she were still in Rohan's arms.

"Are you going to see him again?"

"I hope so."

"Well, I'm glad you had a good time. Keep me posted."

"Will do."

"You've got it bad, don't you?" Janae said, sounding resigned. "I can hear it in your voice."

"Good night, Janae."
"Sweet dreams."
"For sure," Leia said, and ended the call.

Rohan strolled through the dark night searching for prey. But it was the woman, Leia, who occupied his thoughts. She was young, untouched, innocent, beautiful. And vulnerable.

After the kidnapping, her parents had kept a close eye on her. She had been tutored at home until high school, not allowed to date until she was sixteen. Her parents had enrolled her in a number of self-defense classes, had her trained in the use of firearms. She'd had little freedom until she went to college. Her memories of the kidnapping had faded over the years, but her distrust of strangers remained. He was surprised she had agreed to go out with him.

He fed quickly, then returned to his lair, more determined than ever to see the lovely Leia again.

Chapter Four

Leia smiled at her students as they burst into the classroom on Monday morning, laughing and giggling as only five-year-olds can. Twenty adorable children, eleven girls and nine boys, and she adored them all. She had always wanted an older sister. Of course, having an older brother was nice, and she loved Luke, but there were some things you could only share with another girl. She hoped to one day have lots of kids of her own.

After spending time with Rohan, Leia had decided to give her kids a lesson about Indians, especially the Lakota Nation. Before going to bed last night, she had scoured the Internet for facts about the Lakota people.

Naturally, in doing so, she had learned a lot more than she had time to teach. She was fascinated by what she had learned. She had never really wondered how Native Americans lived, but she had discovered that in the old days, the Lakota had lived in close-knit families, with men and women having different responsibilities.

Men did the hunting. They were responsible for protecting the village, as well as tribal ceremonies and rituals. They also taught the young men how to hunt and track and helped them prepare for their vision quests.

Women raised the children and taught them the Four Great Virtues of Life, which were bravery, fortitude, generosity and wisdom. Women also grew the crops and tanned the hides which were used for making clothing and lodges. They also cared for the sick.

Leia took what she'd learned and came up with a lesson her class could easily understand. And they loved it. She taught them how to say a few words in Lakota. *Pilamaya,* meant thank you. *Kola* meant friend, *Hau* meant hello, *Wakan* meant holy.

She felt like her lesson had been a success when she heard the kids using some of the words the next day during class, pleased when they wanted to learn more.

The rest of the week flew by. At home on Friday after work, Leia kicked off her shoes and dropped down on the sofa. She hadn't heard from Rohan. She tried not to be disappointed. It had only been one date, after all. It was obvious he wasn't interested in another one. Too bad, she thought, because she was surely interested in him.

She tried not to let it get her down, but she was depressed just the same. Other than the fathers of her students, who were off-limits, she didn't meet many single men. As for the few she'd gone out with in the last year, one date had been enough. Apparently that was how Rohan felt about her, she thought glumly. One and done.

Shuffling into the kitchen, she decided to indulge in a hot fudge sundae. If she gained a few pounds, what difference did it make?

She carried the ice cream into the living room. The rest of the day stretched before her. She could always clean her apartment, she thought, licking whip crème from her lips.

Or go to a movie. Or shopping. Sadly, none of those options appealed to her.

With nothing better to do, she switched on the TV, surfing through the channels looking for something to occupy her for an hour or two. She paused when she came to a Western. It was one she'd never seen, but that wasn't surprising since she preferred romantic comedies and there was nothing funny about the Old West, just lots of gunfights and Indian attacks.

Still, she found herself caught up in the story of a white girl who made friends with a Cheyenne boy when she was just a little girl. As the story unfolded, the two grew up and fell in love, and after facing many hardships, they married and had children of their own.

Leia sighed as she switched off the TV. The actor in the movie had reminded her of Rohan. What would it have been like if they'd met back in the 1800s when the only good Indian was a dead Indian? Would people have looked down their noses at her for being in love with an Indian? Would her own people have shunned her? Would she have cared?

With a shake of her head, she went into the kitchen and dropped her bowl into the dishwasher. She was about to call Janae and see if there was any chance she could get away long enough to go out to dinner or bowling when her cell phone rang. Closing her eyes, she sent a quick prayer to heaven, praying the caller was Rohan. Taking a deep breath, she said, "Hello?"

"Leia, how are you?"

His voice caressed her, making her heart soar. "I'm fine. How are you?"

"Lonesome. I know it's short notice, but any chance I could take you out later tonight?"

She clamped her lips together, cutting off the quick "Yes" that rose in her throat. She didn't want him to think she had just been sitting around waiting for his call. "Don't you have to dance tonight?"

"I took the night off, hoping you weren't busy."

"Oh." Butterflies of excitement fluttered in the pit of her stomach at the thought of seeing him again.

"What do you say?"

"All right. Where did you want to go?"

"Anywhere you'd like," he said in that soft, seductive voice. "Dining, dancing, the movies?"

"There's a new movie at the Roxy that I've been wanting to see."

"Should I pick you up? Or do we need to take separate cars again?"

She laughed softly.

"Pick you up at seven?"

"All right." Somewhat hesitantly, she gave him her address.

"Until then," he said.

She was smiling when the call ended. She would have preferred to go dancing, but it was dangerous to be in his arms. His voice, the feel of those strong arms around her, the way his gaze made her insides curl... he made her feel vulnerable. Needy.

She showered, washed and dried her hair, slipped into a pair of slacks and a silky shirt, applied a bit of make-up, and all the while her heart was pounding with anticipation.

When the doorbell rang, she took a deep breath, and looked through the peephole to make sure it was him. Not wanting him to think she was over-anxious to see him, she counted to ten before opening the door.

Rohan whistled softly when he saw her. She really was lovely. Her russet-colored hair fell in careless waves over her shoulders. Her beautiful green eyes betrayed everything she was feeling. The shirt she wore matched the color of her eyes. His gaze moved down her slender legs, imagining them wrapped around his waist. *Damn!*

"Are you ready?" he asked.

Nodding, Leia grabbed her handbag from the table beside the door. She was acutely conscious of him walking beside her as they made their way through the apartment courtyard to the street where a sleek, silver Dodge Challenger awaited them.

Leia's eyes widened. "Is this yours?"

"Of course."

He handed her in, his fingers sliding up her arm before he released her to go around to the driver's side.

A single touch, she thought, and her whole body tingled. She stared at his profile, his jaw square and clean-shaven. She longed to sift her fingers through his hair. Beautiful black hair any woman would envy. Tonight, he wore it tied back with a leather thong.

"So, what is this movie you wanted to see?" he asked, as he pulled away from the curb. "Leia?"

It took her a moment to gather her thoughts. Embarrassed, she admitted, "I forgot the title. It's supposed to be a comedy."

He smiled, aware of her scrutiny. He was used to women staring at him. It happened so often, he rarely paid much attention. But the look in Leia's eyes pleased him more than it should have. She was fascinated by him, and more than a little wary.

He parked the car in the theater lot, opened her door for her, took her hand as they walked to the box office.

"Would you care for something to eat?" he asked, his nose wrinkling against the pungent odors of buttered popcorn, sodas, hot dogs and mustard.

"No, thank you." How could she eat when her stomach was in knots? She noticed women turning to stare at him. A few recognized him. One teenage girl was bold enough to ask for his autograph. He obliged by signing his name on a napkin.

The girl smiled from ear to ear as she hurried to show it to her friends.

"It must make you feel good when people recognize you," Leia remarked.

"Well, only people who've recently seen the show recognize me," he said with a shrug.

"Still, it must be nice."

"I'll admit it's flattering. But you must have met a lot of real stars, considering both your parents are in the business."

"Oh, yes," she replied. "Mostly when I was younger and they took me to the studio in the summer." But never anyone as outrageously handsome as he was.

The theater was crowded but they found a pair of seats close to the center of a row. A moment later, the house lights went down and the trailers started.

Leia found it hard to concentrate on the screen. Rohan's presence was impossible to ignore. He was so blatantly male, so physically imposing. So darn gorgeous. She kept stealing looks at him, unable to believe he was beside her.

Her cheeks flamed with embarrassment when he caught her staring. His gaze locked with hers and something she couldn't define passed between them, something so strong it was almost tangible. Her breath caught in her throat as his hand cupped her nape, drawing her closer as he leaned toward her. Fear and excitement raced through her when his mouth covered hers.

Time stopped as the theater fell away and they were standing in a grassy field beneath cloudy skies, his arms around her, his tongue plundering her mouth, nibbling at the skin along the side of her neck. She moaned softly, her hands fisted in his shirt front as she sought to be closer. Her whole body was on fire, aching for his touch...

Abruptly, they were back in the theater, surrounded by hundreds of people.

Leia blinked and blinked again. What had just happened? Had she fallen asleep? It didn't seem likely but what other explanation could there be? It had to have been a dream. Feeling light-headed, she stared at the screen.

The movie was soon over. Leia felt wobbly when she stood. She smiled uncertainly at Rohan when he reached for her hand to steady her.

"Did you enjoy the movie?" he asked as they left the theater and walked toward the parking lot.

"What? Oh, the movie. Yes, of course. Did you?" She hoped he didn't want to talk about it, because she didn't remember anything after the first few scenes.

He shrugged in reply. "Would you like to go for a drink?"

"I don't think so. I feel..." She didn't know how she felt.

"A drink will do you good," he said, as he opened the passenger door and handed her inside.

He took her to a bar she'd never seen before, guided her to a secluded booth, and ordered two glasses of red wine.

"I think I might be coming down with something," Leia murmured. "I feel so light-headed."

"I'm sure it will pass," he said, his gaze searching hers.

When their drinks came, she practically inhaled hers. "I didn't realize I was so thirsty," she said, embarrassed.

"Here." He thrust his glass into her hand, his gaze holding hers. "Have mine."

She wanted to object. Instead, she drained it nearly as quickly as the first. "Thank you."

He nodded. "It's late. I should get you home. You'll feel better after a good night's sleep."

"Yes," she murmured. "Sleep."

She didn't remember the ride home but the next thing she knew, they were in her living room, though she had no recollection of unlocking the door or inviting him inside.

"Sweet dreams, Leia," he whispered. Taking her hand in his, he kissed her palm. And then he was gone.

It was too early to retire for the night. Feeling the need to move, Rohan left his car in front of her place and strolled down the street, his hands shoved into his pockets. He loved the night, the quiet, the darkness. He inhaled deeply, his nostrils filling with a plethora of scents from the fragrance of night-blooming flowers to the pungent odors rising from a nearby garbage can.

The streets were nearly deserted at this time of the night, the houses dark, the inhabitants sleeping soundly, unaware that death passed by.

He licked his lips, remembering the warm intoxication of the woman's blood, the sweetness of her kisses, the feel of her slender body pressed intimately against his arousal the night they went dancing. He had never felt guilty for stealing a drink or two from the other women he'd preyed on. Perhaps it was because he didn't think of Leia as prey. Perhaps that was why stealing her blood made him feel like a thief in the night.

"Leia," he whispered her name to the midnight wind, relishing the thought of seeing her again.

Filled with anticipation, he returned to his car and drove to his lair.

Tomorrow night, he thought. He would see her tomorrow night, and if he had his way, for many nights to come.

Desire rose hot and swift within him at the thought of holding her again. Tasting her again. Feeling the warmth of her blood chase away the cold that was ever a part of him.

Tomorrow.

Chapter Five

Leia slept until almost eleven a.m. Saturday morning, something she never did. For a moment, she lay there staring up at the ceiling. She remembered going to the movies with Rohan but her memories of the rest of the night were hazy. She recalled feeling a little light-headed when they left the theater. He had suggested they go out for a drink and then he had taken her home, though she had no recollection of the drive...

She pressed a hand to her brow. Maybe she was coming down with the flu, but she didn't feel sick. Just terribly thirsty.

Throwing back the covers, she shuffled into the kitchen for a glass of orange juice, followed by a cup of coffee. She scrambled some eggs for breakfast and by the time she finished eating, she felt like her old self. Maybe it had just been a twenty-four hour bug.

After breakfast, she busied herself with her usual Saturday tasks—changing the sheets on her bed, doing the laundry, dusting and mopping and all the other fun stuff she tried to do on a weekly basis.

She thought about Rohan while dusting the furniture. True, he was tall, dark and handsome, but there was something a little off about him, though she couldn't put her finger on what it was. As much as she enjoyed being in the company of such a gorgeous guy, she wasn't sure she wanted to see him again.

She convinced herself that, should he call for a date, she would plead a headache or say she was busy, or that she wasn't interested in seeing him again.

The thought had no sooner crossed her mind when her cell phone rang. Probably Janae, she mused, as she picked up the phone. But it wasn't Janae.

"Leia?"

That deep, whiskey-smooth voice that tied her insides in knots poured over her. "Rohan. Hi."

"Are you busy tonight?"

All thought of refusing fled her mind. "No."

"How about a late date?"

"How late?" she asked, a teasing note in her voice.

"After the show. Say, nine-thirty?"

"I don't know," she said, even though her heart was screaming, *Say, yes!* "It's kinda late." Why was she playing hard to get, she wondered, when she had the feeling they both knew she would say yes.

"But not too late?" he coaxed. "I'd really love to see you again."

Who could resist that sexy voice? Certainly not her. And just like that, she had a date to go dancing with the best dancer of all.

⚜ ⚜ ⚜

He picked her up at nine-thirty sharp. She practically swooned when she saw him looking absolutely breath-taking in a pair of black pants and a black leather jacket over a white shirt. His smile was devastating.

"You look beautiful," he said, as his gaze devoured her.

"Thank you," she murmured. "So do you. How did you get here so fast? I mean, if your last dance is at nine…"

"I was so anxious to see you again that I might have exceeded the speed limit a little."

"Yeah, right."

He shrugged. "Are you ready?"

With a nod, she grabbed her handbag and followed him out to his car. Ever the gentleman, he opened her door and waited for her to get settled before rounding the car and sliding behind the wheel.

He took her to The Velvet Rose, a nightclub she'd passed by a couple of times. It was a rather elegant place, the lighting muted, the music unintrusive. The décor was understated but obviously expensive. Fresh roses in crystal vases decorated every table, as well as the reception desk and each end of the bar. Small, black lacquer tables were scattered around a large dance floor. A number of high-backed booths lined the back wall.

Rohan held her chair for her before taking his own seat. "What would you like to drink?"

Leia bit down on her lower lip. "A Grasshopper," she decided at length. She usually ordered a Sea Breeze but maybe it was time to try something new.

Rohan gave the waitress Leia's order and asked for a glass of red wine for himself.

Leia grinned. "I guess you're not much of a drinker, either," she mused. "I figured you for a whiskey man."

"Once upon a time," he said.

"Oh?"

"I overdid it in my younger days," he explained with a shrug. "Now I stick to wine. Tell me about yourself."

"I told you, I'm a schoolteacher."

"There must be more to you than that."

"I'm pretty much a home-body. Teaching takes up all my weekdays. I don't go out much."

"Why not?"

"I broke up with a guy not long ago. I haven't been ready to plunge into the dating scene again."

One brow arched. "Oh? You're out with me."

She felt a flush stain her cheeks. "Well..."

"Go on."

"It's kind of a thrill, being seen with someone famous," she admitted, and felt her cheeks grow hotter. "I guess I'm a little star-struck."

His laugh made her stomach curl with pleasure. "I'm hardly a star."

"But you *are* famous."

"I suppose. So, if I was just some guy on a dating app, you would have said no?"

"Definitely. That's how I met Ben."

"Ah, the ex-lover."

"We weren't lovers," she said quickly. "How about you? What do you like to do when you're not dancing? Or hunting?"

"I enjoy being with a beautiful woman, like you," he said, his voice low and seductive. "Let's dance."

Rising, he took her hand in his and led her onto the dance floor. Since he danced for a living, it was no surprise that he was light on his feet. As before, she had no trouble at all following his lead. She felt small and feminine in his arms. She had never been so aware of a man before. Or so aware that she was a woman.

They danced and talked for hours. Leia found herself telling him how she had always envied her friends who had lots of brothers and sisters and how she had always wished she had a sister to share secrets with.

"I'm lucky to have Janae," Leia confided while sitting at their table. "She's like the sister I never had. I can tell her anything." She smothered a yawn as she glanced at her phone. "Merciful heavens, look at the time. It's almost one."

"The shank of the evening," Rohan murmured.

"What?"

"You're right, it's late. Come on, I'll take you home."

Leia nodded, although she hated to see the evening end. He was so easy to talk to.

At home, he walked her to the door. "Okay if I kiss you good night?"

She smiled up at him. Emboldened by the drinks she'd had, she whispered, "I was hoping you would."

Leia swayed against him when Rohan took her gently into his arms, her eyelids fluttering down as his mouth covered hers.

Lost in his thrall, she was oblivious to his tongue laving the tender skin beneath her ear, and the prick of his fangs against her throat.

Smothering his guilt, he took only a little, wiped the memory from her mind, and kissed her again. "Can I see you Monday night? Same time as this evening?"

"Yes," she murmured.

"Until then." He kissed her one more time and bid her good night.

Still caught up in the magic of his kisses, she opened the door, floated inside, and went up to bed.

Leia groaned as the ringing of her cell phone roused her from a wonderful dream. She answered on the second ring with a grumpy, "Hello."

"Are you still asleep?" Janae asked. "Good grief, girl, it's almost noon."

"Noon!" Leia bolted upright. "I missed church."

"I know. I was there. I thought I'd better call and see if you were still alive."

"Very funny." Yawning, she tucked the covers under her arms. "How was the service?"

"I don't know. I kept worrying about you. I haven't heard from you lately. Something tells me you're still seeing that gorgeous Indian."

Just thinking of him made Leia smile. "Guilty as charged."

"So, I guess he's not a serial killer or anything."

"Janae! What a thing to say!"

"Sorry, but I'm worried about you. I've never known you to fall so hard, so fast."

"I know," Leia said dreamily. "Isn't it wonderful?"

Janae snorted in a most unladylike way. "I don't know, is it?"

"I've never known anyone like him. And yet..."

"Go on."

"Like you said, there's something about him. I don't know what it is. He hasn't said or done anything the least bit suspicious. He's polite, he treats me like a lady... I don't know."

"My advice is to follow your instincts. My mother always said any man who seems too good to be true usually is."

"I'll be careful. All we've done is kiss." Leia grinned inwardly, thinking his kisses were dynamite.

"Well, all right, I've got to go. The twins are clamoring for lunch. Keep in touch, hear?"

"I will. Hug Mark and Mike for me."

Leia was still smiling when she said goodbye, but Janae's words kept echoing in her mind: *Any man who seems too good to be true probably is.*

Time would tell, she thought. Padding to the kitchen to fix a late breakfast, she thought it odd that she was always so hungry and thirsty the mornings after a date with Rohan.

After breakfast, Leia turned on her computer and typed in Shadow Dancer's name.

There wasn't much to find, other than he was a well-known Native American dancer who had won many awards and prizes. He had never been married. His age was listed as thirty, birthplace, South Dakota. Several photographs accompanied the info. The photos went back ten years. She couldn't help noticing he looked exactly the same at thirty as he had at twenty. Good genes, she mused.

She played a couple of games of Free Cell, read her email, and shut down her computer.

She spent an hour on the phone with her parents. Her mother was excited about being hired by Marvel Studios for their next superhero movie since it featured two of her favorite actors. Leia laughed when she heard her father in the background muttering that his wife was too old to be so star-struck over a couple of guys young enough to be her sons.

"You'll be sorry you said that, Brian," her mother warned.

Leia grinned. She loved the way her parents kidded each other. She said goodbye a few minutes later.

The evening stretched before her. She wished it was Monday so she could see Rohan, then chided herself for being so smitten with a man she hardly knew. Sitting at her desk, she planned her activities for the next week, then leaned back in her chair and fell asleep...

She was in an Indian village. Conical hide lodges stood along a fast-moving river. The sky above was a bright, clear blue. Men clad in breechclouts and moccasins wandered through the camp, talking and laughing. Teenage boys stood near the river, shooting arrows at a distant target. Children ran and played near the lodges, while their mothers looked on. She saw other women stirring large pots, or skinning game. The smell of smoke and roasting meat hung heavy in the air.

And then she saw Rohan. He, too, wore only a breechclout and moccasins. His hair, adorned with an eagle feather, shone blue-black in the bright light of the sun. He rode into the village on a paint horse, a deer carcass slung over the animal's withers. A quiver filled with arrows was slung over one shoulder. There was a knife in a sheath at his side. He looked wild and magnificent as he slid from the horse's back.

And then he looked at her.

Leia woke with a gasp. "Only a dream," she murmured. And yet she would have sworn he had really looked at her.

Seen her.

Chapter Six

In the bright light of a new day, Leia chided herself for being so upset over the silly dream she'd had the day before. And yet... it hadn't seemed like a dream at all. She had felt his gaze on her, a tangible thing, as real as the blankets that covered her. She told herself it was impossible, but she couldn't shake off the feeling that she had been there, in the village.

Rising, she pulled on her robe and padded into the kitchen. Maybe a cup of hot chocolate would settle her nerves. She added a double amount of cocoa and a half-dozen marshmallows, sat at the table, and sipped it slowly.

It didn't help.

It hadn't felt like a dream. She had heard the voices of the people around him, the laughter of the children, felt the warmth of the sun on her face, smelled cooking meat... She was going crazy, she thought. That was the only answer that made sense. Maybe it explained why her memories of the times they spent together were so hazy. Sometimes, after he kissed her good night, she felt like she was waking from a dream.

Like last night. She lifted a hand to her throat, though she had no idea why. She remembered his kiss, remembered his asking if he could see her this evening. As usual, it had never occurred to her to say no.

She was in danger of falling head-over-heels in love with him. she mused, as she got ready to go to work, yet she knew little about him. And she definitely needed to know more before things went any further. Much more.

"Sheesh!" she exclaimed, when she looked at the clock. It was Monday and she was going to be late for school.

⚜ ⚜ ⚜

Rohan showed up promptly at nine-thirty that night, looking gorgeous, as always. Tonight, he wore a dark blue shirt, black pants, and boots. His hair, long and as black as a raven's wing, was pulled back and tied with a leather thong, accentuating the masculine beauty of his face.

"Where would you like to go tonight?" he asked.

Leia shrugged. "I don't know. What would you like to do?"

His gaze moved over her, warm with appreciation. "Can't you guess?"

She felt her cheeks flush. She had no doubt about what *he'd* like to do.

"Have you had dinner?" he asked.

"Of course. Who eats dinner this late?"

He shrugged. "I know a few people who do."

"Are you one of them?"

"No, I had a bite earlier."

"I could use a drink, though," she said, grinning.

"Rough day at school?"

She laughed. "Not really. But bars and theaters are about the only things in town open this late."

He took her to Bad Bob's, a nightclub on the eastside that sold drinks, hamburgers, and pizza. They had live bands on Friday and Saturday nights, usually some up-and-coming country group. A juke box was available during the week.

After they were seated, Leia ordered a strawberry daiquiri. Rohan ordered his usual—a glass of red wine. As a rule, she wasn't much of a drinker, but she had decided to try a different cocktail each time they went out.

"So, how was your day?" he asked.

"Hectic. Summer vacation starts Friday and the kids are so excited, it's hard to get them to concentrate on their lessons."

"You enjoy teaching?"

"I love it. Someday, I hope to be teaching my own kids."

"Want a big family, do you?"

She nodded. "My brother is six years older than I am, so we didn't have a lot in common growing up. He's a stuntman now. I always wanted a sister, but…" She shrugged. "My Mom couldn't have any more kids after me. Do you have a big family?"

"No." A shadow passed behind his eyes. "My parents died quite a while ago."

"Do you have any brothers or sisters?"

"I had three brothers."

"I'm sorry. I didn't mean to stir up unhappy memories." She was glad when her drink arrived. Rohan seemed lost in the past, she thought, as she sipped her daquiri. She wondered what had happened to his family. They must have all died young, she thought.

A moment later, the jukebox came on.

"Shall we?" he asked.

She nodded, smiling at the thought of being in his arms again.

There were a few other couples on the dance floor, but she was hardly aware of them. There was only Rohan, his arms strong around her, his gaze caressing her, his eyes filled with secrets she yearned to know.

"How much longer will you be in town?" she asked.

"I'm not sure. The show is closing here on Friday." The thought of his leaving hurt more than it should have.

"Oh. I guess you'll be going with it when it moves on."

He drew her closer. "Will you miss me?" he asked, his voice rough with an emotion she didn't recognize.

"Very much."

"Will you go with me when I leave?"

She looked up at him, eyes wide with surprise. "I don't think so. We've only known each other a few days."

"Change your mind."

She wanted to. Oh, how she wanted to. But saying yes implied a commitment she wasn't ready to make, not until she knew him better. A lot better. "I can't."

"Afraid of me?"

Afraid? Was she? A shiver ran down her spine when she recalled her dream. Maybe she was afraid.

"Leia." Just her name, but there was a world of longing in it.

It was oh, so tempting. "Where are they going next?"

"Arizona."

"I've never been there."

"Bisbee is celebrating Old West Days. They're having a pow wow. Our dance troupe has been invited to be part of the entertainment. It's only for a few days."

"Sounds like fun."

"It would be more fun if you were with me."

The song ended and he led her back to their table. "What is it?" he asked. "You look troubled."

"I had a dream about you."

"Oh?"

Haltingly, she told him about it. "It seemed so real, it was kinda scary."

Shit! He knew exactly what she'd seen. How the hell had that happened? It should have been impossible. He had been thinking of his past, of her. She shouldn't have been able to read his thoughts. Yet she obviously had. He could understand it if they had exchanged blood. Doing so would open a two-way link between them, but she had never tasted him. And then he frowned. How many other times had she caught a glimpse of his past?

"Rohan?"

"Dreams can't hurt you."

"But I could hear voices, smell roasting meat, feel the sun. I've never had a dream like that before."

He shrugged. "I can't explain it." Another song came over the sound system. Hoping to distract her, he said, "Shall we?"

She melted into his arms, lost in the music, in his nearness.

Later, outside her door, he took her in his arms again. "Will you think about going to Arizona with me?"

"I guess so, but…"

He pressed a finger to her lips. "Just think about it. It's only for a few days."

"All right."

His gaze searched hers and then he claimed her lips with his in a long, searing kiss that made her forget everything but the feel of his arms around her, his mouth moving seductively over hers, evoking sensations she had never known before.

Rohan held her close, thinking he had never, in over three hundred years, known a woman like her. Had he thought less of her, he would have put it into her mind that she wanted to go with him, that she would do anything he asked. But, for some reason he didn't quite understand, he wanted the decision to be hers, and hers alone.

"See you tomorrow night?" he asked.

"I can't. I'm going to dinner at my friend, Janae's, house."

"I'll miss you, my sweet Leia," he murmured, and kissed her one more time.

She was smiling as she went inside and closed the door.

Chapter Seven

Tuesday was a busy day at school. Leia loved her students. Of course, she had loved all her previous classes, too, but there was something about these kids that made them extra special. She was going to miss them next year.

After school, she tidied up her classroom, sorted through some of the children's schoolwork, separated it according to their last names, and placed the various papers and artwork in colorful folders to give to the parents.

With a last look around the classroom, Leia locked the door and headed for the parking lot. She ran a few errands before she drove home, where she changed out of her dress and heels and into a pair of jeans and a sweater. She brushed her hair, stepped into a pair of sandals, and then drove to Janae's.

The boys ran to meet her, both talking at once as they gave her hugs. She babysat for Janae often enough that the kids knew her. They were adorable and Leia loved them dearly.

"How was your day?" Janae asked when the boys settled down.

"Busy and quiet," Leia said, shrugging. "We mostly played games and colored pictures. I can't believe summer vacation starts on Monday."

"Me, either. The year is sure going by fast. Trent is working late tonight, so it'll just be us and the boys."

Leia followed Janae into the kitchen and set the table while Janae finished up dinner preparations. After the boys had washed their hands, everyone sat down. Janae asked Mark to bless the food and then she served dinner. She had made spaghetti, which was a family favorite, along with garlic bread and a Ceasar salad. It was also Leia's favorite. They didn't get much chance to talk until later, after the boys had gone to their room to play.

"So, are you still dating that gorgeous dancer?" Janae asked, putting the last of the dirty dishes into the dishwasher.

"Yes. But not for much longer, I guess." Leia glanced out the window, a sudden pain in heart at the thought maybe never seeing him again. "He's leaving on Friday to go to Bisbee."

"Oh?" Wiping her hands, Janae sat at the table. Leia had offered to help with the dishes, but Janae had waved her off, insisting she was a guest.

"The show is going there for some pow wow."

"I guess you'll miss him," Janae remarked. "But I'm glad he's going."

"Another psychic warning?" Leia asked. She had meant for it to be a joke but after the dream she'd had, it came out more serious than she intended.

"Nothing new," Janae said. "Just the same feeling that he's hiding something."

"He asked me to go with him."

"What? You just met the guy."

"You can stop worrying. I didn't say I'd go."

"Well, that's a relief."

Huffing a sigh, Leia told Janae about the dream she'd had.

"That is weird on so many levels."

"What do you think it means?"

"I'm not sure. I've never heard of anything like that. I mean, to actually hear voices." Brow furrowed, Janae shook her head. " Are you sure you didn't just dream you heard them?"

"I didn't understand a word, of course, but I heard them as clearly as I hear you. I felt the heat of the sun on my face, caught the scent of roasting meat. I've never experienced anything like that in any other dream. And yet, it couldn't have been real."

"My advice to you is don't see this guy again. There are other sexy guys out there."

"Not like this one," Leia muttered.

For once, Janae didn't disagree.

At home, Leia had no sooner kicked off her shoes and plopped down on the sofa when her cell phone rang.

It was Rohan. She bit down on her lower lip, debating whether to answer or not. But the thought of hearing his voice again was too hard to resist. "Hello."

"Hi. Did you have a good time at your friend's house?"

"Oh, yeah. She's a great cook and I love her kids. What did you do tonight?"

"Thought about you."

"Come on, what did you really do?"

"Nothing much. Had a few drinks. Any chance we could get together?"

"Tonight? I don't think so. It's almost ten and I have to be up early in the morning."

"All right. Maybe tomorrow."

"Call me."

"Count on it. Good night, Princess."

" 'Night." As soon as she hung up, she was sorry she'd said no. It would have been nice to see him, if only for a few minutes, maybe get another good night kiss. He would be leaving town in a few days and she would probably never see him again.

With a shake of her head, she went to get ready for bed, wondering if it was possible to get addicted to another person. And what she was going to do when he was gone.

With nothing better to do, Rohan went hunting. Prey was always plentiful in the cities and towns where the show played. Women were easy to win and woo. Like Leia, many had an unusual fascination for the Old West. He preyed on some, occasionally made love to others, but none of them had ever held his interest the way Leia did. He wasn't sure why. There was an openness about her, an innocence that he found captivating. She thought him handsome. She dreamed about him. But she wasn't about to surrender her virtue for an hour or two of pleasure. He respected her for that. He had no doubt that she was a wonderful teacher. She loved her students and he had no doubt that they loved her in return.

She wanted a big family. That was something he could never give her. Where the hell had that thought come from? He enjoyed her company, her laughter. Not only was she easy to be with, but she was one of the few truly honest women he'd ever met. But marriage and family? Not likely.

He had given up all hope of any kind of normal future after he was turned. Those were dreams from another lifetime, a life stolen one dark night on a lonely hill in the Great Plains over three hundred years ago. A life forever lost to him. One he hadn't missed. Until now. Leia was a forever kind of woman. She had been wise to refuse to accompany him to Bisbee. He knew that now. But he would miss her like no other when he left her behind.

Leia found it hard to concentrate at school the next day. All she could think about was that the show was closing and Rohan would be gone. He had once said something about taking a long vacation, but he hadn't mentioned it since.

As soon as the last student left for home, she pulled out her cell phone and called the theater, thrilled when she snagged a ticket for that night, front row center. She would have bought tickets for Thursday and Friday, too, but they were sold out.

She went grocery shopping on her way home, then stopped at the dry cleaners to pick up her clothes. Her last stop was a Chinese takeout place to pick up an order of rice and sweet-and-sour pork for dinner.

At home, she put dinner in the fridge, hung up her clothes, changed out of her dress into jeans and a tee shirt, then sat down at the kitchen table to figure out what she wanted to do in class tomorrow. She didn't plan any lessons for the end of the week. Thursday would be hectic. Friday was pretty much a free-for-all, with parents coming at different times to pick up their kids. She usually baked three kinds of cookies, bought donuts, and picked up some cartons of milk on her way to school. After all, it was the last day. Party time.

With a sigh, she glanced out the window. It was a beautiful day. What was Rohan doing? She figured he slept late, since he danced at night and usually took her out afterward.

How did he spend his afternoons? His online biography stated he was single and she had never questioned it. Still, for all she knew, he could have a wife and six kids somewhere, waiting for him to come home. She brushed the thought aside. Surely, he couldn't see her so often if he was married. He never got any mysterious phone calls. Maybe she should ask.

It was after seven when her phone rang. As always, she felt a thrill when she saw his number. "Hi."

"How you doing, pretty Leia?"

"I'm good. How are you?"

"Getting ready for the show. Can I see you later?"

"Sure." She stifled a grin, thinking how surprised he'd be when he saw her in the audience. "What time?"

"Same as always?"

"Okay. See you then."

She was smiling when she ended the call, until she remembered he would be leaving soon.

Butterflies of anticipation took wing in Leia's stomach as she found her seat that night. Was he as sexy, his dancing as wonderful, as she remembered? Or had she built up the memory in her mind?

The lights dimmed, and the MC stepped up to the mic. Tonight, Rohan had three dance numbers. Judging from the descriptions in the program, each one was more intricate than the previous one. She watched the other dancers, thinking none of them were his equal.

Finally, the MC introduced him. The lights changed. The drumming began. And he stepped out on the stage. She knew the instant he saw her. He paused a brief moment then continued on. She wondered if he was dancing just for her and then laughed inwardly. No doubt every woman in the place was hoping the same thing.

He was magnificent, the epitome of masculine strength and perfection. His copper-hued skin glistened in the spotlight, his hair shone blue-black as it whipped around his head and shoulders. Each intricate step was a thing of beauty. The applause was thunderous.

His second dance was even more complex than the first. But it was the third dance—a Lakota war dance—that was her favorite. Watching him, it was easy to imagine him in the past, preparing to go to battle. It sent a chill down her spine.

She stood at the curtain call along with everyone else. Rohan winked at her when he took a bow.

When the curtain closed, she hurried outside to the stage door, her heart hammering with excitement.

Tonight, he was the first one out. Ignoring everyone else, he swept her into his arms. "Why didn't you tell me you were coming?"

"I wanted to surprise you."

"Well, you did." Wrapping his arm around her shoulders, he led her through the crowd to the parking lot.

"You were wonderful tonight," she said as they neared her car. "Even better than the first time I saw you."

"I was dancing for you." His smile warmed her heart.

When he took her in his arms, she melted against him, her face upturned for his kiss.

Muttering something in a language she didn't understand, he claimed her lips in a kiss that was both savage and sweet. It took the strength from her legs and she swayed against him, her body on fire for his touch.

Rohan swore under his breath. It would be so easy to take her, to make her his. He kissed her again, and yet again, his hands gliding restlessly up and down her back. She leaned into him, her fingers delving into his hair as she writhed against him.

A low growl rose in his throat when he heard footsteps coming their way. With an effort, he put her away from him. "I'd better take you home before I ravish you here in the parking lot," he muttered, thinking she had no idea how close he'd come to doing just that.

"I have my own car," she reminded him, her voice shaky.

"I don't like you driving home alone at this time of the night. I'll come back and get my car later."

She smiled up at him. "Macho man."

He grunted softly. "You have no idea."

Leia handed him her keys, waited while he opened the door for her. Settling in the passenger seat, she watched him stride around the front of the car to the driver's side. Lordy, he was gorgeous. He walked with the same lithe grace he displayed while dancing.

She watched him as he started the car, backed up, and pulled out of the parking lot. There was something about him tonight, she thought, something she had never noticed before. A kind of... of what? Danger? Wildness? Whatever it was, it excited her at the same time it frightened her.

She gasped when he looked at her. His eyes... were red! She blinked and the illusion was gone. Chiding herself for imagining things, she told herself it was just the reflection of the traffic light.

"Would you like to come in?" she asked, when he pulled into the apartment parking lot.

"Not tonight."

"Oh."

He didn't miss the disappointment in her voice. "I'll call you tomorrow."

"All right."

He walked her to her door, dropped her keys into her hand, and gave her a quick kiss good night. "Sweet dreams, Princess," he murmured.

Leia watched him walk away until the darkness swallowed him up.

Confused, her body still hot and tingling from his kisses, she went inside and locked the door behind her. Suddenly, she felt like crying though she wasn't sure why.

Rohan prowled the night like an angry tiger. He cursed himself for his lust. It had come on him all of a sudden, unexpectedly, and more than a little troubling. Had that couple not come along when they did, he would have made love to Leia there, in the parking lot, her back against the car, her legs around his waist.

Taken her like some horny teenager with his first woman. Taken her sweetness, her body, her blood, and very likely her life.

What the hell had happened to him? He had been on the verge of completely losing control. Why? Was it the admiration he'd seen in her eyes while he danced for her? He had felt her desire for him, knew she thought he was sexy as hell, but so what? Lots of women looked at him like that. Was it the wildness of the war dance that had somehow fired his lust? He had danced for her in a way he had never danced before, every movement sensual, suggestive. *Shit!* He'd be surprised if he didn't get complaints from the management. Until tonight, the show had been rated G.

A few minutes later, he came upon a woman walking home alone. The temptation to drink from her, to drink it all, was almost overpowering. Muttering an oath, he willed himself to his lair. At the moment, he was no fit company for man nor beast, and especially not for a vulnerable woman. *Dammit!* Did he dare see Leia again?

Chapter Eight

When in Los Angeles, Rohan made his lair in the top floor apartment of a hotel that had been built close to a hundred years ago. The clientele tended to be men down on their luck, the rent was cheap. But everything worked and over the years, he had made a lot of changes and accumulated an eclectic assortment of furniture. All four rooms were painted the same shade of pale gray. He had replaced the old brown carpet with a plush dark blue. The fireplace in the living room was red brick, the sofa dark-brown leather, the round coffee table an antique he'd picked up somewhere in Italy. A state-of-the-art TV hung on the wall across from the sofa. The kitchen was empty, as he had no need for appliances. The bedroom was large and held only a king-size bed and a five-drawer dresser, also an antique. He'd had the bathroom redone with all the latest fixtures. He hadn't bothered to ask the management for permission for the upgrades, and since he'd paid for all the renovations himself, he figured the owner would have no reason to object to the improvements.

His lair in California was the closest thing he had to a permanent home. He had no need to own a house or much of anything else. Since joining the Native dance troupe, he had spent nine months of every year traveling from state to state and city to city. He bought new garments as fashions changed and discarded the old ones. He had nothing to tie him down. The clothes in his closet and his car were the only things he owned.

Now, reclining on the sofa, he let his mind wander to the distant past, when his people roamed the Great Plains and there were few whites west of the Mississippi. Life had been good then, the summer days spent hunting the buffalo, exploring the Black Hills, fighting their enemies, the Crow and the Pawnee, stealing their horses and their women. It had been a good life, until he tracked the white man who had killed his best friend.

He had intended to kill the *vehoe* when he found him, but things hadn't gone quite the way he'd planned. The man had turned out to be a vampire. Rohan would never forget his shock when he'd plunged his knife into the *vehoe's* belly and the man had laughed in his face. Shock had turned to terror when the *vehoe's* eyes went red. But the worst was yet to come. The vampire grabbed him by the arm and sank his fangs deep into Rohan's throat. That was the last thing he remembered until the following night, when he woke in a cave. Pain had ripped through him. Certain he was dying, he had stumbled out of the cave, driven by an urge he didn't understand.

It had taken several agonizing nights before he realized what his body was crying for. And then he'd come upon an injured fur trapper. One minute he was staring at the blood leaking from the man's arm. The next, he was lapping it up and when that wasn't enough, he had buried his fangs in the man's throat and drained him dry.

Horrified by what he'd done, he had vowed never to do such a thing again. It was, of course, a vow he couldn't keep. With time, he had learned he didn't have to kill. Just as he had learned he could do some truly amazing things. He had discovered he could simply think himself wherever he wanted to go and he was there. He could move faster than the human eye could follow, jump great distances, climb a wall like a spider. He learned that he healed almost immediately, that he was incredibly strong. He also discovered he could call his prey to him, that he could mesmerize them with a look, compel them to do his bidding.

Of course, early on, he'd left the tribe, not trusting himself to be near those he cared for. Those had been long, lonely years, when he hid out by day and hunted by night.

Years had turned to decades.

Decades turned to centuries and he didn't change, didn't age, while the world and its people evolved. And he had evolved with them. He learned to move among humans, to control his hunger, how to blend in with humanity, how to handle cash and drive a car, use a cell phone.

He had thought himself content with his existence, until the night Leia came to the stage door and changed everything.

Chapter Nine

In the morning, Leia woke still wondering what had happened the night before. One minute everything had seemed fine and the next... She still didn't know what had gone wrong. But there was no time to worry about it now. Tomorrow was the last day of school, always a busy time as she cleaned her room and packed up everything she couldn't leave over the summer. She was going to miss her kids when school ended, she thought again as she showered and dressed and ate a quick breakfast. There had been a few classes she'd been glad to see the last of, but this wasn't one of them. The boys and girls had all been well-behaved, bright-eyed and eager to learn, bubbling over with questions.

She arrived in her classroom half an hour early to get ready for the day. But always, in the back of her mind, was Rohan.

After school, she met Janae for lunch at their favorite pizza place where they ordered a ham and pineapple pizza, hot wings, and soda.

"So, one more day and you're free," Janae said, with a grin. "Got any plans for the summer?"

"Not really. My mother's working on a new movie, and you know my dad, he's always working."

"How's Luke?"

"He's in Italy shooting a movie and having the time of his life."

"I'll never understand how Hollywood didn't get you, too."

"No talent," Leia said with a laugh.

"Are you still seeing Mr. Sexy?"

"I don't know."

Janae paused in the act of taking a bite of pizza. "How can you not know? You either are or you aren't."

"Well, things ended strangely last night. I thought we were going out, but we didn't." Leia shook her head. "He gave me a kiss in the parking lot that threatened to melt my bones and then, abruptly, he pulled away and drove me home. When we got there, I asked him to come in and he refused. He gave me a quick kiss and left."

"Maybe he had another date," Janae said, with a shrug. "Or had to hurry home to the little woman."

"Be serious." She refused to believe Rohan had a wife, children. But what if Janae was right?

"I am serious. He doesn't strike me as a one-woman man."

"Well, his biography says he's single," Leia said, but her voice lacked conviction.

"Maybe it's better for him, professionally, if women think he's available."

"Enough!" Leia exclaimed.

"I'm sorry, but I know that man is hiding something. And if it's not a wife, what could it be?"

"I don't know. Maybe I'll ask him the next time I see him. If there is a next time."

Leia fretted about Rohan the rest of the day and when she wasn't wondering if he was married, she wondered if she would see him later that night. Naturally, since she was waiting for one particular call, she got several. None of them from him.

She baked chocolate chip cookies—her kids' favorite—and a pan of chocolate fudge brownies.

She had about given up on hearing from Rohan when, at nine o'clock, he called. She let it ring several times before she picked up. "Hello."

"Hi. How are you?"

"Fine, thanks," she replied, her voice cool. "Are you married?"

"What?"

"I think you heard me."

"What brought that up?"

"It's a simple question. Yes or no?"

"Of course not. I wouldn't be dating you if I was. What's going on?"

She blew out a sigh. "I don't know. You acted so strange last night. And then Janae... never mind."

"What about Janae?"

"She's psychic, or thinks she is, and she's sure you're hiding something from me."

"Oh?" *Shit!* Her best friend was psychic. Just what he needed.

"Are you? Hiding something?"

Damn. How was he supposed to answer that? *Nothing serious. I'm just a vampire.*

"Are you?"

"Yes. But it isn't something we can talk about over the phone."

"I don't know what to say."

"Can I come over?" No answer. "Leia?"

"I guess so."

"I'll be there in five."

After ending the call, she sat there, staring at the floor. What could be so bad that he couldn't tell her over the phone?

Rohan stood outside Leia's front door, wondering what the hell to say. Maybe he should just go home and forget it. There was no easy way to say, "Hey, I'm a vampire."

Either she wouldn't believe him, or she'd freak out. He could always tell her, and then wipe the memory from her mind... *Dammit!* He'd never told anyone what he was, and he wouldn't be telling Leia if he didn't care about her so damn much. But he did, and she had a right to know the truth.

He was a powerful creature, yet he stood there like some tongue-tied teenager on his first date, not knowing what to say or how to say it. In over three hundred years, he had never revealed the truth of what he was to another living soul.

Muttering an oath, he rang the bell, listened to her footsteps as she walked toward the door, the click of the lock as she opened it. They stared at each other for several seconds before she stepped back and invited him in. Hearing the pounding of her heart, smelling the faint scent of fear dancing over her skin, he said, "Do you want me to leave?"

"N...no. Please, sit down. Can I get you something to drink?"

His gaze moved to her throat as he settled on the sofa. "No, thank you."

She took the chair across from him, her hands tightly folded in her lap. "What did you want to tell me?"

"I don't *want* to tell you," he said, "but you have a right to know before things go any further between us."

Oh, Lord, she thought. *He is married.*

"Leia, I'm not married."

She stared at him. How had he known what she was thinking? But then, why wouldn't he? Hadn't she already asked him that?

"There's no easy way to say this. Just promise me you won't freak out."

It must be worse than she thought. "I can't promise that when I don't know what it is."

Tired of living a lie, he took a deep breath and let it out in a heavy sigh. "Years ago I got into a fight with a man who killed my best friend. It was a battle to the death. I stabbed the murderer with a knife..." He paused at the look of revulsion on her face, wondering if she could handle the rest.

Leia pressed a hand to her heart. He'd been in a knife fight. He could have been killed. Obviously, he hadn't been. The other man, what had happened to him? Taking a deep breath, she said, "Don't stop now."

"The man should have died," Rohan said, his voice devoid of emotion. "Instead, he laughed at me. And then he grabbed my arm and sank his fangs into my neck."

Fangs? She stared at him for stretched seconds before asking, "Is this a joke? If it is, it's in very poor taste."

"I wish it was."

"But..."

"The man was a vampire," he said flatly. "And now I am, too."

Leia shook her head. "There's no such thing."

"I'm afraid there is."

"I don't believe you." It couldn't be true. There was no such thing as vampires. Everybody knew that. She heard Janae's voice in the back of her mind, telling her there was something off about Rohan. Lord, what if she'd been right all along?

"I can prove it, if you like."

Her voice shaky, she said, "All right. Go ahead."

Between one breath and the next, he let her see him as he really was. With his eyes blazing red and his fangs extended, he let his preternatural power wash over her.

Leia stared at him, shivering as the atmosphere in the room changed. She remembered the other night when she'd thought his eyes looked red. Good Lord, he really *was* a vampire. But that was impossible. Such things didn't exist. She had to be dreaming again. Speechless, frozen with fear and disbelief, she could only sit there, mute and helpless, wondering if she was about to die.

Retracting his fangs and suppressing his preternatural power, except for letting a little of it tamp down her fear to ease her panic, he said, quietly, "I'm not going to hurt you."

Leia wrapped her arms around her middle. She didn't know what to say, what to think, what to do. Vampires were myths, legends. Yet she had no doubt he was exactly what he'd said he was. A vampire. She shuddered. He had held her in his arms, kissed her, and she had reveled in it. She knew she should run screaming from the room, but she couldn't seem to move. Shocked didn't begin to cover what she was feeling. Surprisingly, she was no longer afraid, which seemed odd. Still, he had never hurt her, she thought, and then she frowned. It explained so much—why she'd never seen him eat, never seen him drink anything but wine... but vampires existed on blood.

Eyes wide, she lifted a hand to her neck. "Have you... Did you ever...?"

"Drink from you? Yes."

"Why don't I remember?"

"Because I wiped the memory from your mind."

Good Lord, what else had he done to her that she couldn't remember?

"Dammit, I never seduced you! I admit I took a little blood from time to time, but I never took advantage of you... that way."

She wanted to believe him, but how could she? Their whole relationship had been built on a lie. "Vampire." She swallowed the bubble of hysterical laughter that rose in her throat. She had been worried that he was married, but this was much, much worse.

"Leia."

"I think you should leave now."

"I don't suppose there's any chance of seeing you again?"

"No," she said tonelessly. "I don't think that would be a good idea."

Rohan nodded. "You're probably right." Rising, he took a step toward her, only to stop abruptly when she flinched. "I enjoyed the time we spent together," he said. "I wish... hell, it doesn't matter now."

Trapping her gaze with his, he spoke to her mind, easing her innate fear, assuring her that he had never hurt her, that there was no need to panic, no need to tell the world, or run into the night screaming for help. No one would believe her, anyway.

Leia sat there quietly for several minutes after Rohan left. Gradually, as her mind cleared a little, the meaning behind his words hit her with the force of a sledgehammer while a distant part of her mind wondered how she had stayed so calm until now.

Huddled in a corner of the sofa, she began to shake violently from head to foot. *It can't be true. It couldn't be true.* The words of denial played over and over again in her mind. *There's no such thing. There's no such thing.*

She tried to tell herself she had imagined the red glow in his eyes, the fangs, the strange power that had possessed her, that lingered still. She knew somehow that it had been that power that had kept her sitting quietly instead of going into hysterics while he spoke to her. The same power that held her immobile now.

She sat there a long time, her mind blank save for one word that repeated itself over and over again. *Vampire.* He'd been right about one thing, she mused. No one would ever believe her.

Later, lying sleepless in her bed, she remembered the nightmares she'd had of a dark, handsome vampire bending over the slender throat of some helpless woman clad in a flowing white nightgown. Had she known, on some deep, instinctive level, what he was even then?

She had the same dream that night, only this time, she was the woman in the nightgown.

Leia would have called in sick in the morning, but it was the last day of school. Feeling numb inside, she showered and dressed, combed her hair, brushed her teeth. She didn't feel like eating. She carried the cookies and brownies out to her car, went back for her keys and her handbag, stopped on the way to school to pick up some milk and donuts.

Maybe she was losing her mind, having hallucinations. Or maybe it had all been a horrible nightmare. Of course, she thought. A nightmare. That had to be it.

She nodded to some of the other teachers as she walked to her classroom, hoping none of them would stop by later. She wasn't in the mood for idle chit-chat. Didn't have the energy to pretend everything was all right.

At the end of the day, standing by the door telling the last of her students goodbye, she couldn't remember anything else she'd said or done.

She quickly gathered up her things and hurried out to the parking lot, grateful she didn't see anyone on the way. She didn't feel like going home. With no destination in mind, she slid behind the wheel and pulled onto the freeway.

Rohan was a vampire. She knew it. She accepted it. She loved a vampire, or thought she did. She tried not to think about him, about what he was, but it was hopeless. She loved everything about him, but it didn't matter now. She was angry because he hadn't told her the truth sooner, and angry because he'd told her at all. She'd been so happy when she didn't know.

How could it be true? And yet she knew it was. He had done something to her to make her accept it so calmly. Feeling a headache coming on, she stopped at a fast-food place for a cup of coffee. And then another.

It was near dark, her gas tank dangerously close to empty, when she finally turned around and headed for home. Like the freeway, her life stretched before her. It took her a moment to realize she was crying. Tears blurred her vision and she pulled off the freeway onto a side road as her tears came harder and faster.

She didn't see the low concrete wall until it was too late. And then she saw nothing at all.

Chapter Ten

Rohan had just finished his last dance of the night when he sensed Leia's panic. A thought carried him to her location. He felt a rush of fear when he saw her car. The front end had been destroyed. The air bag had failed to deploy but the seatbelt had kept her inside the car. She lay slumped against the steering wheel, bleeding profusely from her forehead and numerous minor cuts from broken glass on her face and arms.

From where he stood, he couldn't tell if she was injured anywhere else. *Dammit!* She could be bleeding internally.

When the door wouldn't open, he ripped it from the hinges. He checked her over quickly, his preternatural senses assuring him that the worst of her injuries was the deep gash across her forehead.

After unfastening her seatbelt, he took her in his arms and willed them to his lair. Moving with preternatural speed, he pulled back the blankets, laid her gently on the mattress, and licked the blood from her forehead. His saliva sealed the wound more effectively than sutures or bandages. When that was done, he carefully picked the tiny particles of glass from her arms and cheeks, then licked those cuts as well.

He peeled her out of her blood-stained clothing, eased one of his tee-shirts over her head, and drew the covers up to her chin.

Lastly, he bit into his wrist and held it to her lips. "Drink, Leia."

It was an order she couldn't refuse.

He watched the color slowly return to her cheeks, listened to the steady beat of her heart, and breathed a sigh of relief. She would be all right.

Leia woke in a strange bed in a strange room. Her head ached and she was sore all over. She sat up slowly, her gaze darting around the room. Where was she? How did she get here? She searched her mind, trying to remember what she'd done last night. It came back to her in bits and pieces—learning that, impossible as it was to believe, Rohan was a vampire. She should have been horrified but all she remembered feeling was a sense of sadness and disappointment. She had gone for a drive… She lifted a hand to her forehead and flinched.

She remembered now. She had crashed into a retaining wall. Where was her car? Someone had obviously rescued her, but why hadn't they taken her to a hospital?

She sat up slowly, only then realizing she was wearing a tee-shirt. A man's tee-shirt. An indrawn breath told her it was Rohan's.

Alarm skittered down her spine. She had never been afraid of him before. Even when he told her what he was, she hadn't feared for her life. He'd done something to her, she realized, exerted some sort of supernatural power over her that had muffled her shock and filled her with a kind of calm acceptance.

She glanced around, her stomach knotting with fear. She was in his house. Alone and helpless.

She searched for her cell phone but it was nowhere in sight.

Overcome with a growing sense of panic, she scrambled out of bed and ran to open the door. She paused in the hallway. Where was he? She glanced back at the window. It was daylight. If the legends were true, he was probably sleeping in his coffin.

She hurried down the short hallway, through the living room, to the front door. But when she tried to open it, nothing happened. She tugged on the handle, twisted it back and forth, but it refused to open. Moving quickly across the floor, she pulled back the heavy drapes and tried to open the window. But, it, too, remained stubbornly closed. Just as well, she thought. It was a long drop to the sidewalk below.

Shoulders slumped in defeat, she sank down on the leather sofa and buried her face in her hands, more frightened than she had ever been in her life.

Leia's fear roused him from the dark sleep. Since he'd given her his bed, he had taken his rest in one of the vacant apartments on a lower floor. Rising, he dressed quickly and transported himself to his lair on the top floor.

With some trepidation, he opened the door and stepped inside. He didn't approach the sofa but waited where he stood.

Leia's head jerked up when she heard the door open. She felt her heart skip a beat when she saw Rohan standing there.

"There's nothing to fear," he said, his voice quiet and soothing. "You were in an accident. Do you remember?"

She nodded slowly. "How did you find me?"

He closed the door and leaned back against it, his arms folded over his chest. "I sensed you were in trouble."

"That's impossible."

He shrugged one shoulder. "It's true, nonetheless. You were unconscious when I found you. Your head was bleeding."

She lifted her fingertips to her forehead, and frowned. "How did you stop the bleeding? There's no bandage." And no scab.

She wasn't going to like his answer, he thought. "I licked up the blood and sealed the gash with my saliva."

She stared at him, wide-eyed with disbelief.

"I did the same to the smaller cuts on your face and arms." He took a deep breath. "And then I gave you some of my blood."

His blood. She shuddered. *Vampire blood.* "Like a…like a transfusion?"

His gaze met hers. "Not exactly."

"I don't understand." She looked at him helplessly. This couldn't be real, she thought desperately. She was dreaming again.

"I bit my wrist and bid you drink."

Disbelief quickly turned to revulsion. "You made me *drink* it?"

He shrugged again. "I could have let you die."

All the color drained from her face.

Fearing she was about to faint, he said, "Hey, I made a bad joke, okay? I got to you in plenty of time. You were never in any danger of dying."

"You made me drink your blood." She stared at him, face pale, eyes wide with alarm. "Am I…?"

"No. I vowed hundreds of years ago that I would never turn anyone against their will."

"How noble of you." She blew out a sigh as sweet relief washed through her. "Where are my clothes?"

"I asked the night maid to wash them. They should be in the closet."

She was dreaming again, Leia thought. None of this could be real. "My car. Is it...?"

"It's not totaled but it's gonna need a lot of work. Why don't you get dressed? I'll take you out to breakfast, and then I'll drive you home."

Rising on shaky legs, Leia made her way into the bedroom. As he'd said, her clothes, freshly washed and pressed, were in the closet. Her shoes waited beside bed. She had to be dreaming, she thought again as she dressed. None of this could possibly be real.

She washed her face and hands, ran her fingers through her hair. She needed a comb, she thought, and a toothbrush. Odd, there was no mirror in the room. Or maybe not so odd. Wasn't not having a reflection another vampire myth?

She started when he knocked on the door. "You'll find a new toothbrush in the top drawer. Feel free to use my comb."

He was reading her mind again. It was most disconcerting. "Th...thank you."

She grinned in spite of herself. Who would have guessed that vampires brushed their fangs?

They took the elevator to the main floor. Rohan held the front door open for her, then led her around to the parking lot, where he unlocked the silver Challenger. So many surprises, she thought as she settled into the passenger seat. Vampires driving sports cars and brushing their fangs.

Who'd have guessed? Her stomach clenched as he started the engine. She was alone with him. No one knew where she was. With school out for the summer, no one but her parents and Janae would even miss her.

"Leia, please relax," Rohan said quietly. "Trust me, I am not going to hurt you."

She wanted to believe him, had no reason not to, except... he wasn't human.

He took her to a pancake house and ordered breakfast for her—a strawberry waffle, scrambled eggs, sausage, and a large glass of orange juice.

"I can't eat all that," she protested when the waitress went to turn in her order.

"You need it."

"Do you ever eat?"

"No."

"I guess I should thank you for saving my life."

His gaze moved over her in a feather-light caress. "I was happy to do it."

Her food came a short time later. To her surprise, she was famished and ate every bite.

The ride home was tense. And quiet. She found herself glancing at him again and again, trying to reconcile the sexy Native dancer with the vampire. How could he look so normal when he wasn't even human?

Rohan grinned inwardly as his mind brushed Leia's. He had been a vampire so long, he'd forgotten what it was like to be afraid, to worry about getting hurt or sick. He had few needs—a safe place to take his rest, a ready supply of prey, a woman now and then to ease his desire. He had been reasonably content with his life until he met Leia. Being with her, hearing her laughter, the pleasure he found in her company, made him realize how empty his life had been.

He didn't want to lose her. He could keep her, if he chose to. He could mesmerize her, make her believe she wanted to stay with him. He could compel her to love him, to do anything he wished. But it would be meaningless.

Too soon, they reached her apartment. He pulled to the curb and killed the engine.

"I had your car towed to a repair shop on Main Street. They said it would take a couple of weeks to repair it."

"You shouldn't have done that," she said. "I can't afford to fix it right now."

"It's taken care of."

"What?"

"It's my fault you were so upset." He raised a hand to silence the protest he saw rising in her eyes. "I know it was my fault. And so do you."

"I don't know what to say."

"Say you'll go out with me again."

"Rohan..."

"Just to a movie. Or maybe dancing. No strings attached. Just one more date, and then I won't bother you anymore."

"What's the point?"

"I'd just really like to see you again. Maybe nothing will come of it. And then again..." He shrugged. "You never know."

She should say no, she thought, But how could she? He had saved her life. The least she could do was go out with him. But why just one more date? If he didn't want to see her again after that, why not just end it now? Was he hoping it would lead to another date and then another? She had no clue as to his thinking, but she found herself saying, "Tomorrow night?" And then wondered if it was her decision, or his.

"Sounds good," he said. "Where would you like to go?"

A movie would be the safest choice. But if she was only going to see him one more time, she wanted to be in his arms. She felt her cheeks grow warm as she murmured, "Dancing."

"Pick you up at eight?"

A trickle of anticipation spiraled through her when she nodded. "Eight."

Rohan walked her to her door, and though he yearned to kiss her, he didn't. It pleased him to know she was disappointed, just as it had pleased him to know she wanted to be in his arms.

Perhaps all wasn't lost, after all.

Chapter Eleven

Leia had intended to go to church Sunday morning, but she had too much on her mind. She spent the afternoon trying to sort out her feelings for Rohan. It would be so easy to fall in love with him. So easy. He was everything she had ever wanted in a man—thoughtful, easy to be with. He treated her with respect, made her feel important, cherished, even. Of course, it didn't hurt that he was beyond gorgeous, or that his voice was like dark velvet, or that his touch made her insides melt and her toes curl, or that he was mesmerizing when he danced.

On the downside, he was a vampire.

If only she could forget that.

She still couldn't wrap her mind around it. No one believed in vampires anymore. Sure, in the old days, superstitious people had blamed the Undead for anything that couldn't be logically explained, whether it was a cow that suddenly went dry, or bad weather, or any number of other ills. Just as they had once believed in witches and magic. But even witches were easier to believe in. They, at least, were human.

Rohan didn't eat. He drank blood and wine. He could read her mind. That was the scariest thing of all. What else could he do? Was he somehow making her think she loved him? Maybe she shouldn't have agreed to go out with him. But surely one more date wouldn't hurt.

Needing someone to talk to, she called Janae and invited her to come over.

"I can't some right now," Janae said, sounding flustered. "Trent's parents dropped by unannounced to see the boys. I'll be over as soon as the in-laws go home."

"All right. See you then."

With time to kill, Leia padded into the bathroom and took a long, hot shower and washed her hair. When she got out, she wrapped a towel around her hair and another around her middle and then went to look in the mirror over the sink. There was no scar on her forehead, no marks or scratches on her face or her arms. No one looking at her would ever believe she'd recently been in a serious accident. Had his blood truly healed the scars? And if so, how miraculous was that?

After drying off, she pulled on a pair of comfy jeans and a sloppy sweatshirt, stepped into a pair of fluffy slippers, and then, in dire need of comfort food, she scuffed into the kitchen and whipped up a batch of dark chocolate brownies. She loved brownies, but she loved the batter most of all.

Janae arrived at a little after four. She smiled as soon as she walked in the door. "Do I smell brownies?"

"You do, indeed."

Janae followed her into the kitchen and sat at the table while Leia cut the still-warm brownies, added a generous scoop of vanilla ice cream, and set the plates on the table, then poured two cups of coffee.

"Haven't heard from you in a couple of days," Janae remarked.

"I know. Sorry."

Janae lifted an inquisitive brow. "Spending all your time with that sexy dancer?"

"Not exactly."

"What aren't you telling me?"

"I've just been busy, what with the end of school and everything."

"Uh-huh. What's going on?"

"I think I'm going to stop seeing Rohan," she said, even as a little voice in the back of her mind whispered, *Vampire*.

"Oh!" Janae looked at her over the rim of her coffee cup. "Can I hope you finally took my warning to heart?"

"In a way."

Janae frowned as she put her cup down and leaned forward. "What's going on?"

"I found out something about him that troubles me."

"I knew it!" Janae exclaimed. "He's married."

"No, nothing like that."

"Well, what then?"

"I don't want to talk about it."

"Wow, it must be something really horrible."

Leia took a bite of her brownie, wishing she could confide in her best friend. It would be so good to pour out her feelings, her doubts, but something made her hesitate.

"I didn't see your car in the lot," Janae remarked.

"No. I was in a minor accident. It's being repaired."

"An accident? What happened? Are you hurt?"

"No, no, I'm fine."

Janae sat back in her chair, her eyes narrowing. "It isn't like you to keep secrets, or be so evasive. I have a feeling whatever you aren't telling me is really bad."

"Please, just let it go."

Janae sighed dramatically. "All right, friend, if that's the way you want it. But if you change your mind…"

"I know. How are the boys?"

"A handful, as always. Good thing they're cute," Janae said, with a laugh. "I'm not looking forward to summer vacation. Thankfully, my Mom is going to take them for two weeks. I know I'll miss them like crazy, but I could use a break." She ate the last of her brownie, drained her coffee cup. "I'd better go. I promised Trent I wouldn't be gone long,"

Leia walked Janae to the door, then went back to clean up the kitchen. It was after six. Rohan would be here at eight. Should she call and tell him she'd changed her mind? Was she being a fool to trust him?

Only time would tell.

Rohan let out a low wolf whistle when Leia opened the door. She had always been beautiful but tonight she looked radiant in white heels, a white skirt and a sweater the same shade of green as her eyes. She wore her hair down with the sides pulled back.

Leia blushed furiously, pleased and embarrassed by his reaction, even though it was exactly the reaction she had hoped for.

"Are you ready to go?" he asked, thinking he'd much rather stay in and make love to her all night long.

Grabbing a small black purse, she nodded. Her heart was beating double-time as they left the apartment. Outside he held the car door for her.

"Where are we going?" she asked nervously.

"I thought we'd go to The Carriage House," he said. "Is that all right?"

She nodded, wondering why her throat felt so dry. Nothing to be afraid of. She repeated the words like a mantra. And all the while the word *vampire* whispered in the back of her mind.

Rohan swore under his breath. It irritated the hell out of him that she was afraid of him now. What did she think, that now that she knew what he was, he was going to drive to some deserted backroad and ravish her? His gaze slid over her luscious curves. Not that it wasn't an appealing idea.

They reached their destination a short time later. Rohan parked the car, held her door for her, and followed her inside.

The Carriage House was an expensive, uptown restaurant that catered to an elite crowd. It was a lovely place, all done up in blue and gold, the furnishings classic, the lighting dim, but not too dark.

A waiter seated them immediately. Leia asked for a 7-Up, Rohan ordered his usual. "Not drinking tonight?" he asked.

"I'm really not much of a drinker," Leia replied, with a shrug. She glanced around, thinking she was underdressed. Most of the women wore silk and sported costly jewelry. "I've never been here before. Have you?"

"Once or twice."

"Oh." She was surprised to find herself feeling jealous that he had probably brought other women here.

Leaning forward, he whispered, "None of them were as lovely as you, Princess."

"Please stop reading my mind. It makes me feel naked." She clapped a hand to her mouth when she realized what she'd said.

Rohan laughed softly. "Sorry. Force of habit. I'll try not to do it anymore."

"Thank you." She was glad when their drinks arrived.

For a time, they listened to the band. Their repertoire was mainly old love songs.

Putting his drink aside, Rohan held out his hand. "Shall we?"

She hesitated only a moment before she put her hand in his. Being a Sunday night, the crowd was light, mostly older, retired couples, Leia mused.

"How long have you been teaching kindergarten?" he asked.

"Four years. How long have you been dancing?"

"With you? Not nearly long enough."

Some of the tension drained out of her and she made a face at him. "You know that's not what I meant."

"I've been with the dance troupe about eleven years, I guess."

When Rohan drew her closer, Leia forgot everything else but the magic of being in his arms. The music seemed to spin a web around them, enclosing them in a world of their own. She was keenly aware of his arms holding her close. His scent surrounded her, an enticingly masculine scent that caused everything female within her to respond. She shivered when he brushed a kiss across her cheek.

When she looked up, his gaze moved to her lips, then back to her eyes, a silent question in his own. When she didn't object, he claimed her lips with his. It was a gentle kiss, yet she felt it in every fiber of her being. She closed her eyes, wondering what it would be like to lie naked in his arms, to hold him and caress him and be caressed in return. She knew, somehow, that he would be an incredible lover.

They stayed on the dance floor, bodies pressed intimately together, until the musicians took a break.

Her legs felt wobbly as he guided her back to her seat. If being so close to him made her feel like that, she could only imagine what making love to him would be like. *Oh, Lord,* she thought, *I hope he wasn't lying when he said he would stop reading my mind.*

They ordered another round of drinks while they waited for the band to return. Time and again, she felt his gaze on her face. What was he thinking? she wondered. This was supposed to be their last date. What would she say if he asked for another?

They danced for another hour and with every passing minute, her dread of telling him good night grew stronger. Maybe his being a vampire didn't matter, Leia thought desperately. Maybe nothing mattered but the way he made her feel.

Her thoughts were in turmoil as he drove her home.

"Well, here we are," he said when he pulled into the apartment complex.

She nodded, bit down on her lower lip as he came around to open her door. Taking her hand, he walked her up the porch stairs.

Lifting her hand, he kissed her palm. "If you change your mind, I'd love to see you again." He wasn't ready to let her go, and it took all his self-control to keep from messing with her mind, to make her want to see him again, even if she didn't.

"I'll think about it."

He nodded. "You know where to find me."

Unexpected tears welled in her eyes. He was going to tell her goodbye and she would never see him again. She reminded herself it was for the best. He was a vampire. She had to remember that above all else. They really had no future together.

Giving her hand a squeeze, he murmured, "Have a good life, Princess."

Pain pierced her heart as she watched him walk away. She clamped her lips together to keep from calling him back, even as her whole soul yearned toward him.

He paused at his car to turn and look back at her.

"Rohan," she whispered. *Read my mind.*

He was at her side in an instant, his arms going around her, holding her close as he murmured her name, and then he was kissing her again.

And in that moment, nothing else mattered.

Chapter Twelve

Still holding Leia in his arms, Rohan opened her apartment door. A thought closed it behind them. Inside, he sat on the sofa with her beside him. "Are you sure about this?" he asked. "Nothing's changed."

"I know, but I hate to see it end like this when there's still so much I don't know about you."

"So, it's just morbid curiosity about vampires?" he asked with a wry grin.

She stared at him, not knowing what to say. Sure, that was part of it, but not the important part.

"I don't want to lose you," he said, "but I'm afraid knowing more about me isn't the answer."

"Maybe you're right. But I've never felt this way about anyone else."

"The whole vampire thing isn't going to go away, Leia. It's part of me, a part I can't change. But staying with me will likely change you. Are you willing to take that chance?"

"I honestly don't know." Leia clasped her hands in her lap. "I know you told me about how you were bitten, but I have the feeling you gave me the *Reader's Digest* version of the story. Is there more to it?"

"I'm not sure you should to hear it. Or what you might think of me if you do."

"Either way, I need to know who you really are."

Overcome with a sense of dread, he said, "It happened a long time ago, back when the Lakota were still free to roam the Great Plains and the Black Hills, which are sacred to my people. Like I told you, a white man killed my best friend. I tracked the man for a couple of days before I found him. I intended to kill him. He made no move to stop me, which I thought was odd, but all the whites were a little strange.

"Filled with the need for revenge, I plunged my knife into his belly. But he didn't die. Instead, he laughed in my face, then jerked the blade free and tossed it aside. I stared at him, too shocked to move, when his eyes turned red, too stunned to react when he grabbed my arm and buried his fangs in my throat. Frozen with terror, I couldn't move, couldn't fight back. Gradually, the world went red and then black. That was the last thing I remembered until I woke in a cave the next night."

"What happened to the vampire?"

"I don't know. I never saw him again, but I vowed I'd kill him if I ever did."

"What was it like, being turned?"

"It was hell. I had no idea what had happened to me. Our People had stories of witches, but not vampires. When I woke that first night, I was in terrible pain, although I couldn't find any wounds on my body. I felt physically stronger than ever before, yet my insides felt like they were on fire. I was hungry, but I couldn't keep anything down, not food or water. I was sure I was drying. I didn't know where to go, or what to do."

"It must have been terrible. How did you survive?"

"I was afraid to go back to my People. It wasn't until I came upon an injured trapper that I realized what my body was craving." He glanced at Leia, who was looking at him with horror, as if she knew what was coming. "He was lying beside a stream. He'd taken a nasty fall. He was bleeding from a deep gash in his arm. One minute I was staring at the blood..." He paused, wondering if he should tell her the rest. The picture he was painting wasn't a pretty one.

She swallowed hard. "Go on."

"Are you sure?"

She wasn't, but she nodded anyway. She had to hear how it ended, although she was pretty sure she knew.

"I knelt beside him and licked the blood from the wound. The agony I'd endured for days eased with the first taste." He laughed softly but there was no humor in it. "I didn't even know I had fangs until I buried them in his throat. By the time my hunger was satisfied, he was dead. It took me a long time to discover what it meant to be a vampire, how to use the preternatural powers that were now mine. How to feed my hunger without killing those I preyed on, how to blend in with humanity. I could run like the wind, mask my presence from those around me, compel others to do my bidding, and a hundred other things mortals couldn't do.

"I'd been a vampire about three years when I met another one of my kind who told me that my sire—the vampire who had turned me—should have stayed with me and taught me how to survive. It was comforting to know there were others like me."

"How many others?"

"I have no idea. I only know every country has them, no matter what name they go by. Some are cold-blooded killers. Others are more discreet. But we all need blood to survive, no matter how we get it."

"So, how was it actually done? His making you a vampire, I mean."

"He drained me to the point of death, then gave me his blood in return. I died that night and when I woke the next night, I was a vampire."

He saw the revulsion in her eyes, knew he never should have told her the truth about his past.

Silence stretched between them, as deep and wide as eternity.

"You don't seem like a blood-thirsty killer," she remarked after a long moment. "If you hadn't told me what you are, I never would have guessed."

He shrugged.

"How old were you when it happened?"

"Almost thirty."

"How long have you been what you are?"

"A little more than three hundred years."

Three. *Hundred.* Years. Merciful heavens. "I know you aren't married now, but have you *ever* been married?"

"Once, centuries ago."

The tone of his voice told her he didn't want to talk about it. What had his wife been like, she wondered. Did they have children? But she couldn't ask those questions. Instead, she asked, "Do you like being a vampire?"

"I don't have any other choice."

"Is there no cure?"

"No. Only death."

Leia stared into the fireplace, her mind replaying everything he had told her. She knew it was true, yet it was difficult to comprehend. She knew that in the old days people had believed in witches and vampires and evil spirits. It was much easier to blame the unexplainable on the supernatural than believe your neighbor might be a monster. And yet, she had seen the truth with own eyes, felt his supernatural power wash over her. He could read her mind. He'd bitten her.

"Do you sleep in a coffin?"

"Not for centuries."

She grimaced. "Are you dead during the day?"

"Not exactly, though I generally rest until the sun goes down if the troupe isn't booked."

"Do you feel pain?"

"Oh, yeah. Sunlight on new vampire flesh is especially agonizing."

"How did you ever become a Native dancer?"

"I was in South Dakota when I went to a pow wow. There was a Native dance group performing that night. I bought a ticket, curious to see if things had changed much since I lived among the Lakota. The dances were much the same, though the costumes were a lot more elaborate. I went backstage when it was over and talked to the manager. When he found out I was a full-blood Lakota, he asked if I wanted to dance with his troupe. I'd been hunting the vampire who turned me for centuries without much success. I was bored, so I said yes."

"What do you do when they have matinees?"

"His troupe doesn't do many afternoon shows. The sun doesn't bother me much these days, and most of the performances are inside."

Leia folded her arms over her chest. What a strange life he had lived. If he wrote a book, no one would believe it.

"So," he said, "where do we go from here?"

"I don't know. I think I'm going to need a couple of days to process everything you've told me." Everything had happened so fast—meeting him, falling for him so quickly, and now learning that he wasn't quite human. It was a lot to take in.

He nodded. "Understandable. I'm leaving for Bisbee late tomorrow afternoon. The show opens on Friday night." He had intended to quit the troupe after the last show in L.A., but now, having something to occupy his time seemed like a hell of a good idea.

"Oh." She had known he was going, but she couldn't hide her disappointment. Or her relief.

There was really nothing to say after that.

Rising, Rohan bent down and brushed a kiss across the top of her head. "Think carefully about what's been said, Princess. Because if you decide you want to share your life with me, I'll go anywhere you want to go, do anything you want to do. But know this, once you're mine, I'll never let you go."

Chapter Thirteen

In the morning, Leia woke feeling tired, lost, and confused. As she replayed her conversation with Rohan from the night before, it all seemed like a fever dream. In the early light of a new day, talk of vampires seemed ludicrous.

Rolling onto her side, she gazed out the window. The sky was a bright, clear blue. Birds were singing in the trees. She heard the laughter of the teenage girls who lived in the next apartment, the faint sound of a piano coming from the apartment on the other side, the barking of a dog. All the normal sounds of life. Of summer.

But there was nothing normal about Rohan. He was a three-hundred-year-old vampire. It was inconceivable and yet it was true. What was she going to do? Did she want to spend her life with a vampire? A man who would never grow old? Was love a strong enough foundation to build a life on when they were so different? Would those differences eventually tear then apart? How would he feel about her when she was old and gray and he was still young and virile and as sexy as hell? Would he grow tired of her? All the myths said vampires couldn't reproduce. Did she want to be childless her whole life? Sure, they could adopt a baby, but she wanted to bear the child of the man she loved.

She knew he fed on people and that he'd eventually learned to feed without killing. Lordy, if he fed once a night... Good grief, it would amount to thousands of people! And how many had he killed before he learned it wasn't necessary?

Feeling a tension headache coming on, Leia forced herself to get out of bed. Pulling on her bathrobe, she headed into the kitchen for aspirin and coffee. She needed a distraction, she thought, and reaching for the phone, she called Janae. "Hey, girlfriend, what are you doing today?"

"I'm supposed to take the kids to the zoo. Do you want to come along?"

She didn't, not really, but she agreed to go anyway.

"We're leaving in an hour, maybe," Janae said. "Can you be ready?"

"Sure."

"Okay, I'll give you a honk when we're out front."

"I haven't been to the zoo in ages," Leia remarked as they bought their tickets and went through the turnstile.

"I bring the kids once or twice every summer," Janae said, "even though it wears me out."

Leia grinned at the boys. They were well-mannered, well-behaved kids, a little shy, which meant they didn't often run off and get into trouble.

"How are things with Mr. Sexy?" Janae asked.

Leia sighed. "Not so good. He left for Arizona this morning."

"Oh?" There was a wealth of unasked questions in that simple word.

"The dance troupe is performing at a pow wow there for a few days."

"Ah. Did he ask you to go with him?"

"He asked me to think about it, but I decided against it. We've come to a crossroads in our relationship."

"I see."

Leia shook her head. "No, you don't, and I can't explain it to you."

"Hey, this is me, your best friend. You can tell me anything."

"Not this, although I'm dying to tell someone."

They stopped in front of the giraffe exhibit, which housed close to a dozen of the critters of various sizes. Janae bought some lettuce and they lifted the boys up so they could feed the animals. Mike let out a startled wail when a long, black tongue plucked the lettuce from his hand, and then he laughed. "It tickles!"

Up and down the hills they went. "Lions, and tigers, and bears, oh my," Leia muttered as they stopped to rest in front of a lion's cage. Close up, the beasts looked huge. The female paced back and forth while the male slept on a rock at the top of the enclosure.

At noon, they stopped for lunch and were lucky enough to find a table in the shade.

"Leia, what you're not telling me is driving me crazy," Janae said, wiping ketchup from Mike's mouth.

"Maybe when we get home," Leia said. "Where there are no little ears to hear."

"I'll hold you to it, see if I don't."

"Oh, I have no doubt of that," Leia muttered.

It was near dark when they returned home. "I'll be over as soon as the kids go to bed," Janae said as she pulled up in front of Leia's apartment.

Leia nodded as she stepped out of the car, wishing she had never said anything. What if Janae believed her? What if she didn't?

Leia sighed when the doorbell rang. She had hoped Janae would forget about coming over, or that her husband would have made plans or the boys wouldn't go to bed. No such luck.

"All right," Janae said. Sweeping past Leia into the living room, she sat down on the sofa as if she intended to stay a while. "Let's hear it."

"I don't know where to start. It's so fantastically unbelievable." Leia paused, wondering how to begin.

"Well, what's the big secret?" Janae asked impatiently. "Is he from Planet Krypton or something?"

"Worse. He's a vampire."

"Uh-huh. Sure he is. And I'm Wonder Woman."

"It's true," Leia insisted, and wondered again what Rohan had done to her to keep her from freaking out when he'd told her. "I saw the proof with my own eyes."

"If you're making this up, I'll never forgive you," Janae declared. And then she grunted with satisfaction. "I told you from the start there was something off about him. And I was right." She shook her head. "I'm sorry, I just can't believe it."

"Janae..."

"Why don't we hear anything about it on the news? I haven't heard any reports of bodies drained of blood being found in the streets, or anywhere else."

Leia set out a sigh. She never should have said anything.

"So, where is he now?"

"I told you, he went to Arizona."

"Good riddance, vampire or not," Janae murmured.

"You can't tell anyone," Leia said, leaning forward. "Promise me."

"Don't worry. No one would believe me."

"Promise me."

"I promise I won't tell anyone."

"That includes Trent."

"Don't worry, he's the last person I'd tell. He'd never believe it."

"Just forget I told you, all right?"

"I'd be glad to." Janae shook her head. "Vampires, indeed."

Leia made a face at her." Stop looking at me like I'm insane."

"Right now, I'm not sure you aren't."

"It's not funny, girlfriend. I was this close to falling in love with him."

"Well, let's hope you've seen the last of him. That is what you're hoping, right?"

"Oh, right," Leia said, although she didn't mean it.

And from the doubt in Janae's eyes, her best friend didn't believe she meant it, either.

⚜ ⚜ ⚜

Rohan took a last bow and left the stage. They'd had a packed house for opening night, and he'd heard from one of the other dancers that every performance was sold out.

He went to his dressing room to change and then, not wanting to go out the stage door, he dissolved into mist and left the building. He materialized a few blocks away.

It had been decades since he'd been to Bisbee. Once the largest city between St. Louis and San Francisco, it had become a popular destination for tourists, thanks to its art galleries, vintage shops, and great places to drink and dine. Artifacts from Bisbee's mining history could be seen in museums, including the Bisbee Mining and Historical Museum. The city also offered Old Bisbee Ghost Tours. Thousands of dollars in gold, copper, and silver had been mined here in the old days.

The old days...when the Lakota and the Cheyenne had roamed wild and free and no one had ever heard of the *wasichu*, or George Custer and the Seventh Cavalry, or imagined a time when the buffalo would be gone and the People would be confined to reservations, their freedom lost, their way of life changed forever.

Dammit! Why was he thinking of the past? He swore again. Perhaps to keep from thinking about the present, and Leia.

Leia. He hadn't known her very long. How could he miss her so damn much?

As happened from time to time, he found himself thinking about the vampire who had turned him so many years ago. As he stalked the dark streets, he felt the old anger rise within him. How many others had his sire turned? How many other lives had he stolen?

Rohan swore softly. He didn't think about his sire very often these days, but being with Leia reminded him of all he'd lost—his humanity, the chance to marry and raise a family, perhaps father a son.

There were other things he had naturally missed in the beginning. He'd had to leave the village because, as a fledging, he'd had to sleep from sunrise to sunset. There was no way to explain that to his family or his friends. People were bound to wonder why he didn't eat, why he no longer participated in buffalo hunts, why he avoided the sunlight. Damn the man! If he ever got his hands on his sire...

Rohan blew out a heavy sigh. If he hadn't found his sire in the last three hundred years, it was unlikely he'd ever find him now.

"About time you got home, honey," Trent said, smiling. "What did you have to see Leia about tonight that was so important? You just spent the whole day with her."

Janae shrugged. "Oh, you know," she said, not meeting his eyes. "The usual things."

"No, I don't." He patted the seat beside him and when she joined him, he slid his arm around her shoulders. "Is she in some kind of trouble?"

"Not really," Janae said, shrugging. "She met this guy and they broke up and, well, you know, she's upset."

"Uh-huh." His gaze probed hers. "What aren't you telling me?"

"Nothing."

"Janae, I know when you're hiding something."

"I promised not to tell. Besides, you'd never believe it." She scooted out from under his arm and stood. "I'm going up to check on the boys," she said, and hurried out of the room. A promise was a promise, she thought, as she tucked Mark under the covers, but what if what Leia said was true? What if Rohan really was a vampire? Leia's life could be in danger.

Janae shook her head. The whole idea was ludicrous, and even it was true, she thought, dropping a kiss on Mike's forehead, there was nothing she could do about it. She was a suburban housewife, for goodness sakes, not a vampire hunter.

Chapter Fourteen

Leia moped through the apartment. It was summer, the weather was beautiful, and all she wanted to do was cry. Nothing held her interest—not reading, not rearranging the furniture, not going to the movies or working crossword puzzles or watching any of the mediocre shows on Netflix.

Somehow, one day turned into another and when she woke up Friday morning, she decided enough was enough. She was going to Bisbee to see Rohan dance again. She wasn't going to talk to him or let him know she was there. She just wanted to know if seeing him again would have the same impact on her as it had the first time.

An hour later, she had booked a flight, reserved a room in the Copper Queen hotel, and after a few inquiries, found out where Rohan's troupe was performing. She said a hurried prayer as she dialed the number of the box office, praying she'd be able to get a ticket. Luck was with her and she managed to get a ticket on the aisle in the last row.

She arrived at the hotel in Bisbee late in the afternoon and was immediately enchanted by the old world feel of the town. According to a Guide Book, Bisbee had been founded in the 1880s and had grown quickly, thanks to a thriving mining industry. The town had been well-preserved and the early 20th century atmosphere drew visitors from around the country and around the world, appealing to bird watchers, hikers, wine connoisseurs, and those who enjoyed exploring museums and historic sites.

In her room, she showered and washed her hair. Wrapped in a fluffy hotel towel, she unpacked and laid out her clothes for the evening—a pair of black slacks and a silky, turquoise-blue blouse. After dressing, she spent twenty minutes fussing with her make-up and another fifteen on her hair, assuring herself it had nothing to do with Rohan.

After leaving the hotel, she wandered around for a while before finding a place for dinner. By the time she finished eating, it was time to head to the venue.

Leia felt her heart skip a beat when she reached the theater and saw a life-sized cutout of Shadow Dancer outside the box office. Just looking at his image took her breath away. During his absence, she had convinced herself that he couldn't be as gorgeous and sexy, as desirable, as she remembered. But he was all that and more. In spades.

She picked up her ticket at the box office and hurried inside, her stomach churning with excitement and anxiety.

The show started promptly at eight. The lights, the music, the colorful costumes of the Native dancers were all as beautiful and impressive as the first time. It was truly amazing to watch the men as they executed the intricate steps of the Traditional Dance, the Fancy Dance, the Grass Dance. The bells tied to their ankles tinkled with every move. The women were lovely and graceful as they dipped and swayed to the Fancy Shawl Dance and the Jingle Dress Dance.

Leia held her breath as the MC introduced their star performer, Shadow Dancer of the Lakota Nation. He was the only performer who danced alone. She pressed her hand to her heart as he stepped out on the stage, as handsome and mesmerizing as she remembered, his movements fluid and powerful, his body twisting and turning, every step executed perfectly. She felt her heart skip a beat when he gazed out into the audience. Hoping he hadn't seen her, she hunkered down in her seat and bowed her head.

Rohan paused briefly between steps, his eyes searching the crowd. *She was here.* He felt her presence in every part of his being.

The crowd was on its feet when he finished. He acknowledged their applause with a nod and left the stage. When the applause continued, he went out again, his gaze drawn to the back of the theater. With a wave, he went into the wings.

A moment later, the MC came out to assure the still-applauding crowd that he would be back before the end of the show.

Leia sat up, hands clasped in her lap. He knew she was there, she was sure of it. She was tempted to leave before the show was over, but the thought of watching him dance again was irresistible.

The other dancers were wonderful, but none of them danced with the same power and authority as did Rohan, his body as fluid as silk. Not surprising, she supposed, since he had learned from his ancestors hundreds of years ago.

She hurried out of the theater as soon as he finished his last dance. Hopping into her rental car, she drove back to the hotel as fast as she could, parked in the lot, and ran up to her room as if pursued by demons.

She had scarcely had time to kick off her shoes when there was a knock at her door.

It was him. She knew it as well as she knew her name. Knew she had been lying to herself when she said she was coming just to watch him dance. He had captured her heart and soul and, right or wrong, she was his.

Her hand trembled as she opened the door. For stretched seconds, they gazed at each other without speaking.

And then she took a step back and he crossed the threshold.

The door seemed to close of its own accord as he drew her slowly into his arms, his eyes hot with desire as he lowered his head and covered her mouth with his. When he swung her into his arms, she rested her head against his shoulder, wondering why she had ever thought she could let him go.

Somewhere between the living room and the bedroom, their clothing disappeared. Naked, entwined in each other's arms, they fell on the bed. His gaze burned into hers as he caressed her, his hands masterful as he aroused her, his kisses hotter than the desire in his eyes. For a time, she lay there, caught up in his nearness, the magic of his touch, his kisses, the sheer beauty of the man.

"Touch me," he growled.

And she had no thought to refuse.

Feeling suddenly bold, she explored the hard lines of his body, her fingertips tracing the hard muscles in his arms, the width of his powerful shoulders, his hard, flat belly. She smiled when he groaned, knew a moment of panic when he rose over her, his long, black hair falling forward like a dark curtain. She gasped his name as he possessed her in one, swift thrust that fulfilled her every desire and made her his forever.

Leia woke slowly, surprised to find Rohan lying in bed beside her. For a moment, she admired the beauty of the man and then, as the events of the night before came crashing back, she felt herself blush from the top of her head to the soles of her feet. He had made love to her last night, and she had gloried in it. But now, in the bright light of a new day, she was filled with doubts. What had she done? There had been no words of love spoken last night, no mention of forever. Had he cast some sort of supernatural spell over her that had made her surrender her virtue like that? What had she been thinking? she wondered, and then snorted. She hadn't been thinking at all, that was the problem.

She rolled onto her side, letting her gaze move over him again. Long, thick, black hair. Skin the color of pale copper. Broad shoulders and chest. Six-pack abs. Long arms and legs corded with muscle. Clever hands that had played over her body until she melted like butter on a hot day. She traced his lips with the tip of her finger, gasped as he flipped her onto her back and rose over her.

For a moment, his dark eyes were fierce, and then he grinned at her. "Sorry, Princess. I'm used to waking up alone."

"No problem," she squeaked.

He rolled onto his side, carrying her with him, so that they lay face to face, bodies pressed intimately together. "I need to rest a little longer," he murmured, his fingertips caressing her cheek. "But as long as I'm awake, I could probably keep my eyes open long enough for a quickie."

"A quickie!" she exclaimed. "I don't think so." And so saying, she pushed him away, scrambled out of bed, ran into the bathroom, and locked the door. "A quickie!" She slammed her fist on the counter top. "I'm not some hooker he bought for the night." *No,* she thought with a guilty flush. *You gave it away for free.*

"Leia?" He rapped lightly on the door. "Leia, I'm sorry."

"Go away."

There was a moment of silence. And then the bathroom door opened.

Leia glared at him. "How did you do that? It was locked."

A slow smile spread over his face. "How do you think?"

"Some kind of vampire voodoo, I suppose."

"I'm full of tricks."

"Well, I'm not one of them!"

"Leia," he purred, drawing her into his arms. "I said I was sorry. I didn't mean to insult you. Or hurt your feelings."

"Well, you did." She had expected tenderness and he'd made jokes about 'a quickie.'

He put his forefinger under her chin and tilted her head up. "I really am sorry," he said. "Forgive me?"

How could she refuse when he was looking at her like that, his dark eyes filled with tenderness?

"Let me get some rest and then I'll take you out for dinner. How does that sound?"

"I was planning to fly home late this afternoon."

"And now?" His fingertips caressed her cheek, slid down her neck to settle in the hollow of her throat.

Her gaze slid away from his. "I don't know."

"Stay," he coaxed.

She looked up at him, her eyes filled with hurt and confusion.

He should have waited a while longer before he made love to her, he thought. But, dammit, she had been warm and willing and he'd been wanting her since the night they met. Still, that was no excuse for taking advantage of her in a weak moment, because she wasn't the kind of woman who gave her body without giving her heart and soul, as well.

Gripping her shoulders, he pulled her up against him. "I'm crazy about you, Leia. I care for you as I have never cared for any other woman. And I want you as I've wanted no other." His gaze burned into hers. "Are you still going home?"

"No."

"I'll be back at six," he said, and kissed her until she was weak and breathless. "Six," he said again, and vanished from her sight.

Afraid her legs wouldn't hold her any longer, Leia sank down on the edge of the bathtub, her arms folded over her breasts. When her breathing returned to normal, she took a long, hot shower. Then, wrapped in a hotel bathrobe, she went to the window and opened the drapes. Standing there, trying to decide what to have for breakfast, it occurred to her that if she stayed with Rohan, she would never have to worry about what to fix him for breakfast, or for any other meal, for that matter.

Staring into the distance, she wondered if staying with him was the right decision. He hadn't made any declarations of love last night, or spoken of a future together, although this morning he *had* said he cared for her. Perhaps vampires couldn't love the way mortals did. She shook her head. What was she thinking? They had only known each other for a few weeks. Surely it was too soon to talk of love. But not too soon to let him make love to her, she thought wryly. She wasn't even sure if what she felt for him was love, or merely infatuation for a gorgeous hunk of a man who had only to look at her to make her want him.

Still, she'd had no qualms, no doubts, about anything while in his arms last night. His sheer masculinity had been overpowering, his voice mesmerizing. But he was no ordinary man. She had to remember that. She shivered as she recalled something he had told her. *If you decide you want to share your life with me, I'll go anywhere you want to go, do anything you want to do. But know this, once you're mine, I'll never let you go.*

It had sounded so romantic when he'd said it, but thinking of it now, it seemed more like a threat. It reminded her of something else he had said, something about his not being able to change what he was, but that, if she stayed with him, it would change her. At the time, she hadn't thought to ask what those changes might be, but it would probably be wise to find out before she made any permanent commitment.

So much about him she didn't know. He had told her a little about his past, about how he'd been made a vampire. He had told her what it was like. She had seen some of his supernatural abilities in action, like disappearing from view and being able to read her mind, healing her injuries, drinking from her and making her forget. And yet, he was still a mystery. Was he the man he appeared to be, or was there another side to him, a side he hadn't let her see?

She stared down at the people on the sidewalk. Ordinary people leading ordinary lives, getting married, having children, worrying about braces for their kids and how to pay the mortgage and the rising price of groceries, with no idea that vampires were real. Or that there was one in their town even now. She watched a young family waiting at the corner to cross the street and wondered if Rohan had preyed on any of them.

With a shake of her head, she turned away from the window, stuffed her belongings into her suitcase, and called the airline to exchange her ticket for an earlier flight.

Chapter Fifteen

Rohan knew she was gone as soon as he walked into the hotel. Muttering under his breath, he went to the front desk.

"May I help you, sir?" the clerk asked.

"Any chance you have a message for me. Rohan Stillwater?"

"Let me check." He returned a moment later and handed Rohan an envelope. "Will there be anything else, sir?"

"No." Finding a quiet corner, Rohan opened the envelope and withdrew a sheet of hotel stationery.

Rohan ~
I have a lot to think about and home
is the best place to do that.
Leia

He read the note twice, then crumpled it in his hand. His steps were short and angry as he left the hotel. He was tempted to go after her and demand an explanation, even though he knew it was the wrong thing to do. He couldn't blame her for running away. She did have a lot to think about. Living with him would change her life in myriad ways, and although there would be challenges, they weren't insurmountable.

Still, he knew she had questions—a lot of them. He could understand that, too. His only fear was that the answers would drive her away for good.

For now, he would give her some space. When the pow wow was over, the troupe was headed for another one in six weeks, this one in Billings, Montana. Maybe this would be a good time to take that vacation he'd been promising himself, he mused, and then chuckled. He wasn't going anywhere for any length of time. And Leia was the reason why.

His steps slowed as he remembered the feel of her in his arms, the silk of her hair, the smooth satin of her skin, the way she had melted in his embrace. Something had spooked her, but no woman made love to a man so completely without caring deeply. He would give her a day or two to think things over and then he would go her. He knew she had questions, questions she hadn't asked before because she was afraid of the answers.

But she loved him, of that he had no doubt.

Even if she didn't know it yet.

Chapter Sixteen

For the next two days, Leia threw herself into cleaning the apartment. She washed the windows, scoured the sinks, the toilet, and the tub, cleaned the stove until it gleamed like new. She emptied the refrigerator and washed the inside. She dusted everything in sight—furniture, knickknacks, the blinds in the spare bedroom, the lamp shades and the light bulbs. She washed her bedspread and shampooed the carpets, watered the plants, cleaned the mirrors, washed the dishes on the top shelf that she rarely used.

Each night, she fell into bed, exhausted. And each night, she lay there, unable to sleep, longing to hear Rohan's voice, see his smile. Her body ached for his touch.

Maybe she'd been wrong to leave as abruptly as she had. Maybe she should have stayed and poured out her doubts, given him a chance to put her fears to rest. She was surprised he hadn't called by now. In truth, she had expected to hear from him the day she left. Had she hurt his pride? Made him angry? Disappointed him in some way?

It rained the morning of the third day. Glancing out the window, she decided that the dark clouds perfectly suited her mood. She was angry now, angry that he hadn't cared enough to call and make sure she'd made it safely home, disappointed that he hadn't come after her and begged her to stay. But then, why would he? She had said she would stay and then she'd run away like a little girl afraid of the dark.

Sighing, she pulled on her bathrobe and went into the kitchen. She hadn't eaten much of anything for the last two days and even though she wasn't hungry, she forced herself to sit down and eat a fried egg sandwich and drink a glass of orange juice. Oddly, eating spiked her appetite and she ate a bowl of cereal topped with a banana.

After doing the dishes, she wandered into the living room and sank down on the sofa. Could he read her thoughts when he was so far away? Did he know how much she missed him? Did he miss her? Clutching a throw pillow to her chest, she let the tears that she'd been holding back flow down her cheeks unchecked and felt better for it.

Rising, she wiped her eyes and blew her nose, then grabbed her cell phone and called Janae.

"Hey, girlfriend," Janae said enthusiastically. "I was just about to call you. My Mom's taken the kids for a few days and Trent's out of town, and I've got nothing to do."

"Well, I've got plenty to do," Leia said, "but I don't want to do it." She still had the outside of the windows and the screens to wash and the weeds in the window boxes to pull, but she couldn't do that in the rain. "So, what do you say? Lunch?"

"Sounds good.," Janae replied, a smile in her voice. "Where do you want to go?"

"Doesn't matter."

"I'll pick you up in an hour, okay?"

"Better make it two," Leia said. "I just had breakfast."

Janae laughed. "Okay, two hours. See you then."

Leia's mood brightened considerably as she ended the call and went to shower and dress. She wouldn't have to sit home alone and mope all day, after all.

⚜ ⚜ ⚜

Janae was as good as her word. Two hours later, Leia heard the quick *honk-honk* of her horn. Grabbing her keys and her handbag, she hurried out the door.

"I thought we'd go to Jimmy Jax," Janae said as Leia settled in the passenger seat. "Is that okay with you?"

"Sure."

"So, I haven't heard from you in a few days," Janae remarked. "What have you been doing?"

"Mostly cleaning house."

"Yuck."

A short time later, Janae pulled up in front of Jimmy Jax, which was only a short distance from Leia's apartment building.

It was early for lunch and the crowd was light. They found a booth near the front window, ordered burgers and fries and sodas when the waitress came by.

"Where did Trent go?" Leia asked.

"He didn't say. You know how hush-hush he is about his job."

"I don't think you've ever told me what he does."

"Well, he's never really told me, either. All I know is that he works for the government, although I don't know which branch, and he's on call at a moment's notice. And the pay is very, very good," she added brightly. "In fact, lunch is on me."

After their order arrived, Janae asked the inevitable question, "So, whatever happened to Rohan? You haven't mentioned him once."

"I guess we broke up."

"No kidding? That's the best news I've heard all day."

Leia made a face at her. "I miss him."

"Of course you do. The man was gorgeous, but you're better off without him."

"You don't know that."

"Yes, I do. There was a dark aura around you when you were seeing him. Now, it's gone."

Leia glanced heavenward, as if seeking divine help.

"I know you don't believe me, but it's true."

"You never said anything about a 'dark aura' before."

"I didn't want to scare you."

"Well, you don't have to worry anymore," Leia said, with sigh. "So put your crystal ball away."

"Very funny." Reaching for a French fry, Janae asked, "What are you doing tonight?"

"Nothing."

"How about a movie?"

"As long as it's not a happy-ever-after romance. I don't think I could handle that right now."

Janae laughed. "No worries. It's the latest Spiderman."

"Wait a minute! Doesn't the hero always get the girl?"

It was close to an hour later when Janae dropped Leia off at home. "Pick you up at 7:30?"

"Right. See you then." Leia watched Janae pull out of the driveway, then unlocked the door and stepped inside. She froze in the entryway, certain there was someone else in the apartment.

"Relax," said a familiar voice. "It's just me."

Her heart fluttered wildly when Rohan materialized next to the sofa. She started to ask how he'd gotten in, then bit back the question, knowing what the answer would be.

"How are you, Princess?" His deep voice washed through her like warm whiskey on a winter night.

"What are you doing here?"

"What do you think?"

Moving into the room, she dropped her handbag and keys on the hall table, her whole body yearning toward him.

He didn't move, merely watched her, his dark eyes unreadable.

Suddenly nervous, she sat on the edge of the sofa, her hands clasped in her lap. She could feel his gaze on her face when he came to stand in front of her.

"Why did you leave?" he asked quietly.

"I don't know."

He quirked a disbelieving brow at her. "Why, Leia?"

"If you must know, I was afraid."

"Of me? Why? Have I ever hurt you?"

"No, but…"

"You have questions," he said, his voice flat. "Ask them."

She took a deep breath, then blurted, "Do you hurt the people you…you feed on?"

"Is that what you think?"

"I don't know what to think," she retorted.

"No, I don't. I take what I need, wipe the memory from their minds, and send them blithely on their way. Just like I did with you." He shoved his hands into his back pockets. "I told you I killed people when I was first turned."

"But never since then?"

"I didn't say that. I've killed people in self-defense when it was my life or theirs."

"What other powers do you have besides the ones you told me about?"

"I'm strong. I'm fast. I heal quickly. I never get sick. If I drink from someone who's drunk or ill in any way, it doesn't affect me. My senses are incredibly sharp. I can smell you when you're a mile away. I can think myself wherever I want to go."

She blinked at him, mightily impressed, but a little frightened to think he possessed such inhuman powers. "Can you make me do things against my will? Tell me the truth," she said, when he hesitated to answer.

His dark eyes held hers, a silent promise in their depths. "I could, but I never have, and I never will."

"Have you ever turned anyone into a vampire?"

"No."

"Never? In over three hundred years?"

He shook his head. "It was forced on me against my will. Why would I ever do it to someone else?"

Why, indeed? she thought.

"Anything else you need to know?" he asked.

"I want to know where you got the name Rohan. You said you'd tell me when you got to know me better. I think you know me better now."

He chuckled. He did, indeed. "Rohan was the name of the first man I killed after being turned. I took it because I never wanted to forget how guilty I felt when I realized what I'd done. As for Stillwater, I picked it out of a phone book."

"Oh."

"I probably shouldn't have told you any of this." He knelt on one knee in front of her and took both of her hands in his. "Give us a chance, Leia. Put your fears away. I would never hurt you, or force you to do anything that makes you uncomfortable or unhappy. I love you, and I think you love me."

She trembled with anticipation as he slowly leaned toward her, closed her eyes as his lips found hers. His kiss was achingly sweet, filled with love and need and hope.

She felt bereft when he lifted his head.

His gaze searched hers. "Leia?"

"Heaven help me, I do love you." Unable to resist, she melted against him when he pulled her into his arms and fell back on the floor, drawing her down on top of him.

He rained kisses on her cheeks, the tip of her nose, her chin, before his mouth covered hers in a long, searing kiss that drove every doubt from her mind.

When she was breathless, he wrapped his arms around her and stood in a fluid motion, drawing her up with him.

"Do you want to go out for dinner?" he asked. "Or stay home and make out like randy teenagers?"

"I can't."

"What? Why not?"

"I'm supposed to go to the movies with Janae."

He blew out a sigh. "Okay if I wait here until you get home?"

"Aren't you going to ask me not to go?"

He shrugged. "I don't want to interfere in your life or keep you away from your friends."

Leia didn't know whether to be hurt or pleased. And then she grinned. "You could come with us."

"Is that a good idea?" he asked. "As I recall, she wasn't too keen on our dating."

"True," she said, and frowned.

"Change your mind?"

"I was just thinking of something she said at lunch today."

"Oh? What was that?"

"It's silly, but she said that when we were dating, I had a dark aura around me."

Well, damn, he thought. *Maybe Janae really did have some psychic ability.*

"You don't believe in that kind of thing, do you?" she asked.

Rohan grunted softly. "In this instance, I think I do."

"What do you think it means?" It worried her that Rohan didn't brush it aside as foolishness.

"It's probably because you're hanging around with a vampire, darlin'."

"You don't think it means something more ominous?"

"Like what?"

"Like something bad is going to happen to me?" she asked. And frowned. Where had *that* thought come from?

He smiled reassuringly. "I'm not going to let anything happen to you. Stop worrying. Go have a good time with Janae. I'll be here when you get back."

"I'm not really a Spiderman fan," Leia remarked as she fastened her seatbelt, "so this better be good. What's wrong?" she asked when Janae didn't reply.

"You're with him again, aren't you?"

Leia stared at her. "How can you possibly know that?"

"Dark aura," Janae said curtly. "Do you have a death wish, or what?"

"Let's not start all that *dark aura* stuff again," Leia said. And then, unable to help herself, she asked, "What do you think it means?"

"That he's dangerous. Maybe not to you, but then again…" Janae shrugged. "Just be careful."

"Are we going to the movies or not?"

With an aggrieved sigh, Janae pulled out of the parking lot onto the street.

"I asked him to come with us," Leia said, after a moment.

"Well, I'm glad he didn't." Janae paused. "Why didn't he?"

"He said he didn't want to interfere in my life or keep me from seeing my friends."

"Well, that was darn nice of him," Janae said, her voice thick with sarcasm. "Just promise me you'll be careful. You haven't slept with him, have you?"

Leia felt her cheeks heat as she struggled for an answer.

"You have, haven't you?"

"Just once."

Janae sighed as she pulled into the theater parking lot. "You'll never leave him now," she muttered darkly.

Later, on the way home, Leia wondered if either of them had paid any attention to the movie. She had felt Janae worrying about her the whole time, imagining the worst. Good thing Janae had blown her off when she'd told her the truth about Rohan. If Janae had believed her, she would probably come running over with a wooden stake in one hand and a bottle of holy water in the other as soon as they got home. Since neither of them had ever mentioned Rohan's being a vampire again, perhaps her psychic friend had forgotten about it. Either way, she certainly wasn't going to bring it up now.

"I'll call you soon," Janae said.

"Why don't the four of us go out to dinner when Trent gets home?" Leia suggested. "It will give the guys a chance to get to know each other, and you'll realize you're all wrong about Rohan."

"I'll ask him," Janae said. "In the meantime, you be careful, girlfriend."

"Yes, Mother. Good night."

Leia found her vampire reclining on the sofa when she entered her apartment. He'd kicked off his shoes and looked right at home.

"How was the movie?" he asked.

She shrugged. "Okay, I guess. Spiderman saved the day."

He sat up, beckoning for her to join him. When she did, he slipped his arm around her shoulders. "What's wrong?"

"It's Janae. She keeps warning me about you." She bit down on her lower lip. "A while back I told her something I shouldn't have."

Shit. He had a bad feeling about this. "Let me guess. You told her what I am?"

Leia nodded. "But she didn't believe me, and she hasn't mentioned it since. I think she forgot about it."

"Maybe." But he doubted it. Later tonight, after Leia had gone to bed, he would go to Janae's house and wipe that little bit of damning information from her mind while she slept. Erasing what he was from her memory would be safer for him. And for her. Fortunately he could manipulate her mind from outside the house, since she wasn't likely to invite him in.

And while he was at it, he would prevent Janae from seeing that damn, dark aura around Leia.

That would be better for all of them.

Chapter Seventeen

Leia woke early in the morning, her thoughts conflicted. She loved Rohan, or thought she did. When she was with him, she had no doubt of it, but when they were apart... When they were apart, she was troubled by the differences between them. Would those differences eventually drive a wedge between them, or bring them closer together? What if he wanted her to become a vampire? That was definitely a deal-breaker! She liked being human, thank you very much. No matter that he could do some amazing things or that he could live forever. It just wasn't natural. When they were together, he seemed normal, human, and yet there was no disguising that dark undercurrent that was as much a part of him as the color of his hair.

If only he had never told her the truth. Maybe ignorance really was bliss.

Sighing, she ate a quick breakfast, loaded the dishes into the dishwasher, and returned to her room to dress. The day stretched before her. The apartment was squeaky clean. The sky a beautiful, clear blue after the rain. She didn't really feel like washing the windows or doing anything else. What was Rohan doing? Silly question. Probably resting.

If they stayed together, she would likely spend most of her days alone. She told herself it wouldn't be too bad during the school year. And he could be awake during the day…

Before she could talk herself out of it, Leia stepped into her shoes, grabbed her keys and her handbag, and drove to Rohan's hotel. She parked on the street, hurried inside, and rang for the elevator as if she belonged there. Her stomach was in knots by the time the elevator reached the top floor.

Heart pounding like a freight train, she took a deep breath and knocked on the door. Several long minutes passed. Maybe he wasn't home. Feeling a rush of disappointment and a dash of relief—he might not be happy to have her drop in uninvited. She was about to leave when the door opened and Rohan stood there. Clad in nothing but a pair of black briefs, his hair falling over his bare shoulders, he was cover model gorgeous.

A slow smile spread over his face. "Well," he drawled, taking a step back, "this is a pleasant surprise. Come on in."

Suddenly uncertain, she stepped inside, knew a moment of doubt as she heard the door close behind her.

Arms crossed over his broad chest, he asked, "What brings you here?"

Leia shrugged. "I was bored."

"Well, then," he drawled, "I guess I'll have to find a way to entertain you."

She licked her lips as his heated gaze moved over her. She didn't need three guesses to know what he had in mind. Truth be told, it was on her mind, too.

He smiled as he pulled her gently into his arms. "We can just sit and talk, if you'd rather."

Sit and talk? Was he kidding? She could hardly think with him standing there practically naked. Mercy, the man had the body of a Greek god and her fingers were itching to explore every inch of it.

"Damn, woman, if you don't stop thinking like that, we're gonna do it on the floor, right here, right now."

She blushed from head to toe as he swung her into his arms and carried her into the bedroom. Dark drapes completely blocked the sun. A blessing, she thought, as he placed her on the mattress and caressed her out of her clothing and shucked his briefs.

"It's not too late to change your mind," he murmured, as he rained kisses over her cheeks, her eyelids, her lips, the hollow of her throat.

Smiling, she whispered, "Yes, it is," as she pushed him onto his back and straddled his hips.

It was an odd sensation, making love in the dark, and yet freeing somehow. She kissed and caressed him, boldly exploring, touching and tasting to her heart's content until, with a low growl, he rolled over, placing her beneath him. She was more than ready when he rose over her, his voice husky with desire as he whispered that he adored her.

Rohan sighed as Leia fell asleep in his arms. They had made love again before she fell asleep. While they lay spent in each other's arms, he had asked if he might taste her and she had said yes without a second thought. Her blood was indescribable. Warm and sweet, yes, and so much more.

His gaze moved over her. Even in the pitch blackness of his room, he could see her clearly, her glorious red hair spread like a silken flame across the pillowcase, her lips bruised from his kisses.

She had pulled a sheet over her nakedness, but he knew every curve and hollow, every delectable inch of her. He had made love to many women, but none had captivated him the way she did, or pleased him as much, or in so many ways. He had been delighted and surprised to find her at his door and even more astonished to discover the reason for her visit.

He smiled faintly as he ran his tongue along the length of her neck. Later, he would ask her for another taste. But for now, he was content to lie beside her as he drifted into oblivion.

Leia woke to darkness. Momentarily confused, she wondered where she was but then, feeling Rohan lying beside her, she grinned. She had acted like a trollop, she thought, and she didn't regret it at all.

Slipping out of bed, she padded into the bathroom, quietly closed the door, and stepped into the shower, hoping it wouldn't wake him. When she finished, she wrapped herself in a towel and tiptoed into the bedroom, feeling around for her clothes, which lay in a heap on the floor.

She couldn't find her bra and didn't want to turn on the lights, so she left it wherever it was. She dressed in the living room, found her handbag and her keys on the floor, and tiptoed out of the apartment.

The desk clerk gave her a knowing smile as she hurried outside, leaving Leia to wonder if lone women coming in and out of the hotel in the middle of the day was a usual occurrence. And then she frowned. Good grief, he probably thought she was a hooker!

She grinned all the way home.

Her cell phone rang as she pulled into her parking space. "Janae, hi. What's up?"

"You remember we talked about the four of us going out to dinner? Well, I asked Trent about it and he said sure, so, what's a good night for you two?"

"I don't know. I'll have to ask Rohan."

"How is that handsome hunk?"

Leia frowned. Handsome hunk? That didn't sound like Janae. "He's fine."

"Great. Well, let me know when he's free. Trent should be home for a few days."

"All right, I will." Disconnecting the call, Leia stared at her phone. No warning about dating Rohan? No mention of death or dark auras or disaster? What the heck was going on?

Rohan woke with the musky scent of their recent lovemaking still in the air. Leia had been a surprise in more ways than one, he mused. Warm and eager, she came alive in his arms, willing to give him everything he asked for. He'd never known a lover like her. Fire and silk, he thought, and although she blushed easily, she wasn't shy about letting him know what she wanted, what she liked. And what she didn't. How had he existed so long without her?

He grinned in the darkness. If he had his way, he would never be without her again.

Anticipation brought a smile to Leia's face as she hurried to answer the door that evening. "Hi," she said, breathlessly.

"Hi, yourself," he murmured as he pulled her into his embrace. "How was your day?"

"Wonderful."

He chuckled as her cheeks turned bright pink. "Can I hope I had something to do with it?"

"You know you did. Stop fishing for compliments." Taking his hand, she led him to the sofa and pulled him down beside her. "How do you feel about a double date with Janae and her husband?"

He shrugged. "I'm game if you are. But it might be wise to skip dinner."

"Right. How about a movie and maybe drinks after?"

"Whatever you want, love."

"When?"

"I think I'm free for the next couple of weeks," he said. The troupe was practicing for a new show, but he hadn't yet signed up for it. "So any night is fine with me."

"All right. I'll call her tomorrow. When I talked to her today, she didn't sound anything like herself," Leia remarked. "She didn't even warn me about how dangerous it was for me to date you."

He grunted softly.

Leia cocked her head to the side. "You wouldn't have anything to do with her sudden change of heart, would you?"

"Who, me?" he asked innocently.

"What did you do?" she asked, alarmed by the thought of Rohan messing with Janae's mind.

"I wiped all thoughts of danger, vampires, and dark auras from her mind."

Leia frowned. "I'm not sure I like that."

"It's for the best, believe me. I haven't lived this long by being careless. The fewer people who know what I am, the better."

Well, that made sense, she thought. And then frowned again. "If we stopped seeing each other, would you erase your memory from my mind, too?"

He didn't have to answer. The look in his eyes said it all.

She understood his reasons, but it saddened her just the same.

"That bothers you." It wasn't a question.

"Yes. Even if we part, I don't ever want to forget you."

"Then I promise I will not erase your memories of me completely, only the fact that I'm a vampire. Can you live with that?"

She thought it over a moment and then nodded. *Vampire.* It still seemed unreal. Impossible.

"Would you like to go out?" he asked.

"No. Let's stay in tonight."

"As you wish." His gaze moved over her. "What would you like to do?"

"Hear more about your past."

"Whatever for?"

"I want to know *everything* about you. When you dance, it's like you're far away in another time."

"You're very perceptive. Dancing always takes me back to the past. It reminds me of long summer nights on the Plains. I remember the scents of roasting meat and sage, listening to the Old Ones relate the ancient stories of our People. I remember the excitement of going to war, the thrill of my first coup, the pain and glory of the Sun Dance."

"I saw a depiction of that in a movie once."

He snorted. "You cannot capture the wonder of it on film. It was painful, yes, but spiritual in the deepest sense of the word."

"Did you have a vision?"

"Yes. It was from that vision that the shaman gave me my name."

She wanted to ask him what he saw, but knew, somehow, that he wouldn't tell her.

"What's it like for you, when you rest? Do you sleep? Do you dream?"

"It's difficult to explain. It's like falling into dark water. Vampires rarely dream."

"Are you really dead to the world?"

He laughed softly. "In a way. But I am also aware of what's going on around me, every noise that's out of place, every scent that shouldn't be there." He grinned at her. "It's very hard to sneak up on an old vampire. Easier on the young ones." He drew her closer. "Enough talk about the past," he said, tracing her bottom lip with his fingertips. "Let's talk about you. Your warmth, your sweetness. The way you make me forget what I am," he murmured. And then he grinned. "Although at this moment, all I can think about is tasting you." His gaze searched hers, seeking permission.

"Does blood taste the same to vampires as it does to mortals? I mean, I've tasted my blood and..." She shrugged. "It just tastes kind of salty and coppery."

"Your blood tastes like the finest wine," he said, his gaze moving to the pulse throbbing in the hollow of her throat. "Warm and sweet and intoxicating."

Leia felt her heart skip a beat. Who would have thought such a conversation would be arousing? But it was. She canted her head to the side, closed her eyes as he bit her ever so gently, sighed as he lifted her into his arms and carried her to bed.

Chapter Eighteen

As happened every time Leia spent time in Rohan's arms, she woke smiling, her whole body tingling with the memory of his touch, the soft caress of his voice whispering that he loved her more than life itself. She wished he had spent the night, but he'd left while she slept. Would he stay if she asked him to?

She lay there for a long time, thinking about what a remarkable man he was. How incredible, to have lived so long, to have experienced more than three hundred years of life. She couldn't imagine the things he had seen and done. He had obviously loved his previous life with the Lakota. She could tell he missed it even now, after so many years. How sad, to see everything you had known and loved be swept away. Had he lost many people he cared for over the centuries? Or had he never let anyone get close to him, knowing he would inevitably lose them in a few short years? How many women had he loved?

She slammed the door on that train of thought. He was a virile, handsome man. No doubt he had known hundreds of women. The knowledge was like acid in her soul. She told herself it was foolish to be jealous of women who were long dead. And then she frowned. Maybe they weren't all dead. Who knew what he'd been doing, who he'd been seeing, before they met? For all she knew, he might be seeing other women when he wasn't with her.

Once that little seed of doubt had been planted, it took root and try as she might, she couldn't dig it out.

Leia called Janae later that afternoon to let her know she'd talked to Rohan about double dating and he had agreed. "What do you think about a movie and drinks afterward?" Leia asked.

"Sounds good to me. How about tomorrow night? I'll ask Mrs. Johnson next door to sit with the boys."

Leia checked her phone. "The first evening show is at 6:30, or would you rather go later?"

"No, that's fine."

"Okay. We'll pick you up at six."

"Can't wait. See you then."

Leia smiled as she ended the call. She couldn't remember the last time she'd been out on a double date. Her last date had been over a year ago, when she'd broken up with the man she'd been seeing for almost that long. She'd thought Jeff was 'the one' until she discovered he had a rotten temper. Things had come to a head the night he'd slapped her because she didn't agree with something he'd said. She couldn't remember now what it had been.

Leia made a quick trip to her favorite shop where she bought a pair of gray knit slacks and a long-sleeved blue sweater with a square neck. She picked up a pair of gray heels, as well.

She ran a few errands, stopped at her favorite fast food place for some sweet-and-sour pork and fried rice for dinner, and headed home.

Rohan was waiting at her front door when she arrived.

"Hope you didn't have plans," he said as he unlocked the door and followed her inside.

She dropped the garment bag on the side table. "What do you think?"

"I think I'm the luckiest man alive."

"You're here awfully early tonight," Leia remarked, heading for the kitchen.

He shrugged one shoulder. "What can I say? I missed you." He wrinkled his nose when she lifted the Styrofoam cartons out of the sack. "I think I'll go in the other room while you eat."

"Sure you don't want to share it with me?" Leia asked, smothering a grin.

"No, thanks."

She laughed as she pulled a plate from the cupboard, poured a glass of milk, and sat at the table. She had never considered what it must be like for him, with his enhanced senses, to be around food he could no longer eat. How awful, to have to give up the food and drink you loved before you became a vampire, to exist on nothing but the blood of others and an occasional glass of red wine. She had withdrawal pains if she went more than a day or two without chocolate.

She ate quickly, threw the takeout boxes in the trash, rinsed her dishes and placed them in the dishwasher.

Rohan smiled when she joined him on the sofa. "How was your day?"

"Fine. I talked to Janae and we're all set for the movies tomorrow night. I bought a new outfit. Hope you like it."

"I'm sure I will, if you're inside it."

"How was *your* day?"

He snorted. "Same as any other."

"If I ask you something, will you tell me the truth?"

"I don't know. Depends on what it is."

She punched him in the arm.

Raising his hands in surrender, he said, "All right, all right, the truth. What do you want to know now?"

"Does my asking questions about your past bother you?"

"No, love. I told you before, you can ask me anything."

"Have you been with a lot of women?"

Well, damn, he should have seen that one coming. "Define a lot."

She huffed an impatient sigh.

"Yes, I've been with a lot of women. I may be a vampire, but I'm still a man with all of a man's needs."

It was the answer Leia had expected, but it hurt just the same. She knew it was foolish to be jealous of his past. After all, he'd lived hundreds of years before she was born, and he'd live hundreds more when she was gone.

Rohan muttered an oath as he put his arm around her shoulders. "Leia, don't think about it. The past is past. The future isn't guaranteed to anyone, not even me. There's just now."

She snuggled against him. He was right, of course. And then he was kissing her and nothing else mattered but his arms around her, his mouth hot on hers, his voice telling her he loved her. Would always love her.

Leia was a nervous wreck the next evening as she dressed for their double date with Janae and Trent. What if the men didn't get along? She didn't know Trent Frumusanu very well. He'd always been polite, if a little reserved, when she saw him but he was also very stern and at times, a little overbearing. He was also very strict with his boys, though he treated Janae like a queen.

"Stop worrying," Rohan said, coming up behind her. "It's just a movie with your best friend."

"I know, I know. How do I look?"

He whistled. "Like a million bucks, darlin'. Why don't we skip the movie and stay home and make love?"

"Is that all you ever think about?"

"You're thinking about it, too," he said with a wicked grin.

"I am not!" she exclaimed. Although she was now.

"Come on, it's time to go."

With a sigh, she took a last look in the mirror, grabbed her handbag, and followed him out of the apartment to his car.

"Nice ride," Trent remarked as he opened the back door of the Challenger for Janae.

Rohan nodded. "Thanks." He closed the passenger side door for Leia, then walked around the car and slid behind the wheel.

Leia knew a moment of relief as they pulled out of the parking lot. She'd been worried when Janae had made the introductions earlier, but nothing untoward had happened. The two men shook hands and exchanged a few pleasantries while Janae grabbed her coat. Now, she glanced at Rohan, wondering if she was imagining the tension she felt between the two men. She told herself it was just her imagination. There was no reason for any strain between Rohan and Trent, but she felt it just the same.

Rohan winked at her. "Stop worrying."

With a sigh, Leia settled back in her seat. It was only one night. Rohan parked the car and the four of them walked a short block to the theater. The men paid for the tickets. Trent bought popcorn and a Coke for Janae. Rohan bought a frozen lemonade for Leia.

They found four seats in the middle of the theater. Leia and Janae sat side by side, flanked by the men.

Rohan put his arm around Leia's shoulder and gave her a squeeze. "Relax, love."

She forced a smile. "I'm fine."

He chuckled. "What are you afraid of? That I'm going to bite your friends when the lights go down?"

Leia glared at him and then burst out laughing. A moment later, the house lights dimmed.

Leaning toward her, Rohan whispered, "I might bite you, though."

"So, where shall we go for drinks?" Trent asked as they returned to the car.

"Anywhere is fine with me," Janae said. "As long as they have a dance floor."

"The Velvet Room is nice," Leia said.

"Oh, yes," Janae said. "Let's go there."

"The Velvet Room it is," Rohan said as he pulled out of the parking lot.

During the drive to the nightclub, Janae and Leia talked about the movie. Rohan glanced at Trent in the rear-view mirror, wondering if his wife knew he was a vampire hunter.

Rohan grinned inwardly. He and Trent had recognized each other immediately. It was the cause of the tension Leia had sensed in the car earlier.

"I love this place," Janae gushed as they waited to be seated. "It's been ages since we've been dancing. Oh! Trent, you should see Rohan dance. He's fantastic. Too bad the show closed."

"Yeah, sorry I missed it."

The hostess showed them to their table a few minutes later. Trent ordered a beer, Janae and Leia opted for strawberry daiquiris, and Rohan asked for a glass of red wine.

As soon as the band broke into a new tune, Janae grabbed her husband's arm. "Come on, honey, this is my favorite song."

"So, what do you think of Trent?" Leia asked.

"He seems like a nice guy. A bit stiff."

"I can feel the tension humming between the two of you," she remarked.

He grunted softly.

"I'm not imagining it, am I?"

"No."

"So, what's the deal?"

"He's a hunter."

"A hunter?" Leia exclaimed, then clapped her hand over her mouth. "You mean, someone pays him to kill vampires?"

"Yeah."

Leia stared at him in disbelief. "How do you know?"

"I can sense what he is, just as he senses what I am."

"How is that even possible?"

"It's something vampires and hunters are born with. Frumusanu is an old Romanian name. His family has hunted vampires for centuries."

"Why didn't you tell me sooner? You let me put your life in danger. What if he…?"

"Calm down, darlin'."

"But… you said…"

"Leia, he's been hunting vampires for maybe five years. He's no threat to one as old as I am."

"Does Janae know what he does?"

Rohan shook his head. "Hunters are sworn to secrecy. The penalty for telling anyone what they do or who they're hunting is death. And that includes their family."

Leia shuddered. "That's terrible."

"What does Janae think he does?" Rohan asked.

"She told me he works for some secret government organization, but she doesn't know exactly what his job is. She thinks he hunts wanted men and brings them in for questioning."

"Interesting," Rohan remarked. "Come on, let's dance."

The rest of the evening passed pleasantly. Janae seemed totally oblivious to the tension at the table. After an hour and a half, Leia couldn't stand it anymore and pleaded a headache.

Trent and Janae decided to stay a while longer and take a taxi home.

"I'll call you tomorrow," Janae said. "Hope you feel better soon."

"I'm glad that's over," Leia remarked as they pulled into the apartment parking lot.

"What were you worried about?" Rohan asked as he parked the car and walked her to her door. "He wasn't about to jump me at the table."

"I know. But the tension between you and Trent was thick enough to cut with a knife. I'm surprised Janae didn't feel it, too."

Rohan shrugged. "I need to go," he said, drawing her into his arms. "See you tomorrow night?"

Leia nodded, her eyelids fluttering down as he kissed her.

"Sweet dreams, love," he murmured.

She watched him drive away before going inside. Sitting on the sofa, she replayed everything Rohan had said about Trent. And then she huffed a sigh at the strange turn of events. What were the odds that she would meet and fall in love with a vampire, or that her best friend would be married to a hunter?

Chapter Nineteen

"You've been awfully quiet," Janae remarked as she and Trent got ready for bed that night.

"Have I?"

"You hardly said a thing at the club. Seems like all you did was glare at Rohan. Do you two know each other, or something?"

"In a way."

Janae frowned. "In a way? What does that mean?"

"Has Leia said anything about him?"

"Well, sure."

"Well?" he asked impatiently."

"You know, just that she thinks he's sexy and she loves to watch him dance and, you know, girl stuff."

"I don't know," he muttered. "I'm a guy, in case you haven't noticed."

"Oh, I've noticed," she murmured, running her hands over his bare chest.

Trent caught both of her hands in one of his. "This is serious, Janae."

Pulling her hands from his, she crossed her arms over her chest. "What's going on?"

"You know I can't tell you. Let's just say the people I work for are interested in him."

Janae's eyes widened. "Good heavens, is he wanted for something? Is Leia in danger? You have to warn her!"

"Listen, don't say a word about this. It could cause a lot of trouble for me and for Leia. So, mum's the word. Got it?"

Janae nodded, her mind racing. Rohan was wanted by the government! Was he a foreign spy? A terrorist? A drug dealer? A serial killer? What if Leia really was in danger? How could she *not* warn her?

"Remember," Trent said, pulling on a pair of striped pajama bottoms. "Not a word. Promise me."

Janae nodded again. She had to trust that Trent knew what he was doing. The last thing she wanted to do was put her best friend's life in danger.

Later that night, when Janae was sound asleep, Trent went into his office and shut the door. Booting up his computer, he typed in his password and ID number, then pulled up the Vampire Data Base and searched for the name Rohan/Shadow Dancer, which led to a brief bio containing damned little information. His age was estimated to be three hundred, there was a short physical description, and that was it. No mention of the number of kills he'd made or close contacts in the vampire community. No mention of the vamp who had turned him. A lot of hunters had tried to find Rohan through the years. There was a long list of towns, cities, and countries where he'd been tracked. But no one had ever caught him or even come close.

Until now, Trent mused. Smiling, he shut down his computer and went back to bed.

Rohan strolled through the night, thinking Fate must be having a good laugh at his expense. Here he was, in love with a woman whose best friend's husband was a *bona fide* vampire hunter on the government payroll. He wondered idly what the good old USA was paying for heads these days. He didn't know why he was surprised to discover hunters still roamed the country. Maybe it was because it had been over fifty years since the last time he'd run across one. Somehow, he'd figured the Bureau would have found a more modern way to track vampires and destroy them. But apparently, the Von Helsing method was still the best.

Damn!

If it wasn't so serious, it would have been comical the way Trent's eyes had widened with surprise when they were introduced. The man had kept a wary eye on him all night, as if he expected Rohan to suddenly go berserk and attack everyone in the nightclub.

Rohan shook his head. Vampires hadn't survived this long by being stupid. As a rule, they were discreet in their kills, careful not to leave bodies drained of blood lying around in the open. It was rare that they preyed on the rich and famous, or killed those who would be missed, because instances like that tended to show up on the nightly news. Street girls, pimps, transients, druggies and drug dealers—if they came up missing, no one seemed to notice or give a damn.

He had never cared for feeding on the refuse of humanity, but then, he didn't kill his prey, either. He took enough to satisfy his thirst, erased the memory of what he'd done from the minds of his victims, and sent them merrily on their way, none the worse or the wiser.

Of course, not all vampires were discreet. There had been one, years ago, who had gone through a dozen young Hollywood starlets, leaving a trail of blood and bodies in his wake. There had been lurid photos of beautiful young women with their throats torn out. Headlines screamed **MONSTER ON THE LOOSE IN L.A.** As quickly as the killings had begun, they had ended. The culprit had never been found. Whoever the vampire had been, he had gained quite a reputation among the vampire community.

Rohan's thoughts turned to the vampire who had made him. In three hundred years, he'd never run across his sire. Of course, the world was a big place. Still, the number of vampires were relatively few. Was his sire still alive? Or had some hunter like Trent Frumusanu taken his head?

Rohan grunted softly as he started back to his lair. Likely, he would never know.

Chapter Twenty

Trent spent the next day in his home office, with the door locked. Logging into his work account, he pulled up the official *Government List of Known Vampires, Dead or Alive,* which was different from the database he'd searched last night.

He typed in **Shadow Dancer, aka Rohan,** then sat back while the search engine scrolled through page after page, only to mutter an oath when the words **NO INFORMATION FOUND** appeared on the screen.

Dammit! How was that possible? He widened his search to include countries other than the United States. And got the same results.

Well, he thought, that was a first. How had the bloodsucker managed to stay under the government radar all this time? Of course, he didn't know for sure how old Rohan was, although the Vampire Data Base had listed him as three hundred. Trent was inclined to agree. You could always tell the old ones. They had an aura of power about them that the young ones lacked.

He leaned back in his chair, his fingers tapping the arm. And then he pulled up a New Entry page and typed in both of Rohan's names, the fact that he currently resided in the USA, and added his physical description:

Height: 6'3"

Weight, approx. 230 lbs.
Ethnicity: Native American
Hair: Black (long)
Eyes: Dark Brown
Scars: None visible
Place of birth: Unknown
DOB: Unknown
Current residence: California
Notes: Dances with Native American Dance Group based in South Dakota.

Trent leaned back in his chair again, elbows bent, fingers steepled, while he wondered how upset Janae would be if he destroyed the vampire. It was the right thing to do, but his family had no idea what he did for a living, and he'd like to keep it that way, for his safety and theirs. Who knew if the vampire had any bloodsucking friends who might avenge him? One thing for sure, he needed to have a little talk with Rohan and find out what his intentions were toward Leia. And then he laughed. He sounded like a worried father, but he liked Leia, she was Janae's best friend, and he didn't want to see anything happen to her. The vampire might act like a gentleman around Leia and Janae, but underneath, he was a predator, a cold-blooded killer, just like all his kind, and not fit to live.

Trent grunted softly as he hit Enter. Sooner or later, he'd catch the vampire alone. He just hoped he'd survive the encounter when he did.

As luck would have it, Trent was driving past Leia's apartment late the next night when he saw Rohan pull out of the driveway. Grinning with satisfaction, he pulled in behind the vampire, curious to see where he was holed up.

Five minutes later, the bloodsucker turned onto a side street and pulled over to the curb.

Trent debated whether to stop, then parked behind the Challenger and got out of the car.

Rohan grunted softly, wondering what the hunter wanted. The man wasn't very bright, trailing a vampire down a dark street alone, late at night. Curious, he rolled down the window and watched the hunter's approach.

"We need to talk," Trent said, grateful that his voice didn't quiver as a hint of the vampire's power rolled over him.

"Yeah? Why?"

"Why not?" Trent countered.

"I've run across a lot of hunters," Rohan replied. "I never saw the need to make conversation with any of them."

"First time for everything," Trent jerked his thumb at the passenger seat. "Mind if I sit down?"

"Be my guest," he said, with a wry grin. "I haven't eaten yet."

Trent scowled at him, then went around the front of the car and opened the door. He settled into the passenger seat but left the door wide open.

"So, what do you want to talk about?" Rohan asked.

"Leia."

Rohan lifted one brow. "What about her?"

"I don't want to see her get hurt."

"Who do you think you are? Her father?"

"No. But she's a friend of ours. We're worried about her."

"She's perfectly safe with me. Not that I give a damn what you think."

"Why don't you just move on and leave her alone?"

"Why don't you mind your own business?"

Trent glared at him.

"Listen, hunter, I'm in love with Leia. I'm not going to hurt her, or turn her, if that's what you're worried about."

"Love?" Trent scoffed. "What do *you* know about love?"

"As much as any other man," Rohan retorted.

"But you're not a man, are you?"

A muscle twitched in Rohan's cheek. "You got any more to say?"

"If you hurt her, or anyone else in the city, I'll destroy you."

"Killed a lot of us, have you?" Rohan asked, a sneer in his voice.

Trent shrugged one shoulder. "A few."

Tired of this conversation, Rohan unleashed more of his power, letting it fill the car. He knew a sense of satisfaction when Frumusanu flinched.

"Listen to me, hunter, and listen good. Stay out of my life. I've killed a few hunters in my time, and it won't bother me in the least to kill one more. So get the hell out of my car, and mind your own damn business, or your wife might wake up one morning and find herself a widow. Do I make myself clear?"

"Crystal." Not wanting the vampire to think he was afraid of him, Trent waited a minute before he stepped out of the Challenger. It took every ounce of self-control he possessed not to slam the door.

Trent swallowed hard as the vampire pulled away from the curb. He stared at the Challenger's tail lights as they faded into the distance. *Dammit.* He hadn't been that scared—or that close to death—in a long time.

Chapter Twenty-One

"I had an interesting conversation with your friend's husband last night," Rohan remarked. He had taken Leia dancing earlier. Now, they were snuggled on the sofa in her apartment. She had kicked off her shoes, and so had he. Soft music played in the background.

"Really?" she asked curiously. "About what?"

He looked at her, one brow raised. "What do you think?"

"Oh. Oh! He's not planning to ... you know?"

"Take my head?"

She grimaced at the image. "Is he?"

"Not right now."

"What do you mean, not right now?" she asked, worried by the implied threat.

"He said he'd kill me if I hurt you or anyone else in the city. The usual vampire hunter warning."

"And what did you say?"

"I told him to stay out of my business or his wife will be a widow."

Leia bolted upright. "You didn't! You wouldn't!" In any conflict between the two men, she was certain Rohan would win. And just as certain that Trent's death would also be the death of her friendship with Janae.

"What did you want me to say?"

"Well... I don't know, but..." Leia bit down on her lower lip, her brow furrowed. What had she expected him to do? Run away like a whipped cur? He'd never do that, nor would she want him to.

Rohan put his arm around her again. "Don't worry about it, love. He's not going to do anything, and neither am I."

Relief washed over her. She didn't know what she'd do if Rohan made good on his threat. Still, he had a right to defend himself, if necessary.

He cupped her face in his hands and kissed her lightly. "Don't think about it," he murmured, kissing her again. "Whatever happens, happens. No use in worrying about it."

He ran his tongue along the side of her neck, sending a wave of heat spiraling through her.

In answer to his unasked question, Leia canted her head to the side, giving him access to her throat. She sighed, her eyelids fluttering down, as he bit her. Why did she find something that should have been disgusting so arousing?

A moment later, he sealed the tiny wounds, pulled her into his arms, and carried her to bed. He quickly shed his own clothing and then, his gaze burning into hers, he undressed her ever so slowly.

Lying beside him, with his hands and lips arousing her, pleasuring her in a hundred ways, Leia forgot everything else but the incredible man rising over her, carrying her to heights and depths she had never imagined.

Much later, when he rose to leave, she tugged on his hand. "Why don't you move in with me?"

"Are you sure about that?"

She giggled at the surprised look on his face. "I'm sure. I hate it when you go home after we make love. You want to, don't you?"

"Oh, yeah. I've almost asked you a couple of times, but..." He shrugged. "I didn't know how'd you'd feel about it."

"Why didn't you just read my mind?"

"I'm trying not to pry," he said, with a grin.

She smiled up at him as he slid back under the covers and took her in his arms again. What would he say, she wondered, if she asked him to marry her?

Leia frowned when she woke in the morning, surprised to find the room still dark, until she glanced at the windows. Sometime during the night, Rohan had used her spare blankets to block the sun's light.

"Looks like I'll be needing some black-out curtains," she murmured, wondering what other changes she might have to make to accommodate her new roommate.

She showered and dressed, then tiptoed out of the bedroom. There was a whole new feel to the apartment, she mused, though she couldn't explain the difference. Was it merely the presence of another person? Or that dark aura Janae had so often mentioned? It didn't matter, she decided, as she scrambled two eggs, then popped a couple pieces of bread into the toaster. Her life shouldn't change too much, she thought. After all, he slept half the day and didn't eat.

Smiling, she dished up her breakfast and sat at the table. Later today, she'd go shopping for curtains, and maybe a sexy new nightgown or two. Or three.

❖ ❖ ❖

Leia was looking at nightgowns when she saw Janae in the adjoining aisle. "Janae, hi!"

"Hi! If I'd known you were coming to the mall, we could have ridden together."

"It was kind of a spur of the moment decision," Leia said. "Wanna grab some lunch later?"

"Sure." Janae waggled her brows at the nightgown in Leia's hand. "Sexy."

Leia felt a blush climb into her cheeks. "I hope Rohan thinks so." She frowned as a shadow passed behind her friend's eyes. "Learn to live with it, girlfriend. He's moving in with me."

Janae blew out a long sigh. "Oh, Leia."

Leia frowned. Since Rohan had wiped Janae's memory of what he was, she hadn't expected her friend to still object to her dating him.

Janae came around the end of the rack. Lowering her voice, she said, "You need to dump him. Now."

"Why would I do that? I've never been happier."

Janae glanced around. The store was having a lingerie sale and there were women young and old alike pawing through bras and panties and nightgowns as if they were going out of style. "We can't talk about it here. Are you almost done?"

"I guess so." Curious now, Leia quickly paid for the three nightgowns she'd decided on. They took the escalator up to the food court, ordered Chinese food, and eventually found a table for two.

"So, what's going on?" Leia asked, setting her packages on an empty chair.

"I can't tell you anything except he isn't who you think he is, and you're in danger every minute you spend with him."

Leia sat back, stunned by what Janae had said. "What on earth are you talking about?"

"I wish I could tell you," Janae said earnestly. "But I promised Trent I wouldn't tell anyone. Not even you."

As soon as Janae mentioned Trent, Leia blew out a sigh of relief. She didn't know what Trent had told his wife, but she was pretty sure he hadn't told Janae that Rohan was a vampire.

Rohan was still at rest when Leia got home. She unwrapped the new blackout curtains and spread them over the back of the sofa. Maybe he would help her hang them later. She left the nightgowns in the bag so as not to ruin the surprise.

It was hours until sunset. Maybe he'd rise early. He had often done so in the past. What was it like to go to asleep and never dream? To just fall into oblivion? She shivered, thinking it would be scary to be awake and aware one minute and trapped in utter darkness the next. He'd mentioned he used to sleep in a coffin. Why did he stop? Thank goodness he had. That was just too creepy to even think about.

After grabbing a soda out of the fridge, Leia sank down on the sofa and switched on the TV. She had just found a movie she wanted to see when the station broke in with a news alert.

She was about to change the channel when the reporter said, "…completely drained of blood, the body was found in a culvert. The victim had no identification. If you have any information, please notify the police immediately. In other news..."

Leia sat back, chilled to the bone. A body. Drained of blood. Oh, Lord. She switched the TV off, not wanting to hear more.

Forty minutes later, she was still sitting there when Rohan, clad in black jeans and shirtless, entered the room. He stared at her face, listened to the erratic beat of her heart, and wondered what the hell had upset her. "Leia?" He repeated her name when she didn't respond. "What's happened?"

She looked up at him then, and quickly looked away.

What the hell? He let his mind brush hers and then he knew. Some vampire had left his kill where it could be found. *Dammit.* That was going to put Trent Frumusanu on his tail like a redbone hound on the scent of a coon, sure as hell and damnation. "Leia, I swear on my love for you, it wasn't me."

She didn't say anything, but the relief on her face was evident. "I didn't really think it was, but..." She looked away but not before he saw the guilt in her eyes. Not that he could blame her. As far as she knew, he was the only vampire in town. He'd thought so, too, but apparently that had changed.

He was about to ask if she wanted to talk about it when the doorbell rang. A vicious oath escaped his lips as he caught Frumusanu's scent. *Well, hell,* he thought irritably. *That didn't take long.* "I'll get it," Rohan said. "It's Janae's husband."

"I wonder what he wants," Leia remarked, and then bit down on her lower lip.

"What do you think?" Rohan muttered, as he unlocked the door.

Frumusanu didn't waste any time. As soon as the door opened, he said, "I need to talk to you."

Rohan stepped out onto the small porch and pulled the door closed behind him. "Save your breath. It wasn't me."

Trent snorted. "Why the hell should I believe you?"

"Because I said it. I'm not stupid enough to leave a fresh kill in the town where I live."

That took Frumusanu aback. Looking somewhat embarrassed, he shoved his hands into his pants' pockets. "I guess you'd have to be a damn fool to do so. Any idea who the bloodsucker might be?"

Rohan shook his head. "Until tonight, I thought I was the only one in town. I haven't sensed any others." Even as he spoke the words, he caught the faint scent of vampire on the wind. He swore under his breath.

It was a scent he'd never forgotten.

The scent of the vampire who had turned him over three hundred years ago.

Rohan stood on the porch for several minutes after Frumusanu took his leave and then, unable to resist, he descended the steps. Lifting his head, he turned in a slow circle, trying to locate the scent again. Had he been mistaken? More than likely, he decided. After all, it had been centuries. What were the chances he and his sire would wind up in the same town at the same time? He snorted softly. What were the chances they would have met the first time, he thought darkly. Fate? Bad luck? Or just being in the wrong place at the wrong time?

He walked to the sidewalk but if the scent had ever been there, it was gone.

And yet, in the back of his mind, he knew the SOB who'd turned him was out there, waiting.

❧ ❧ ❧

"Is everything all right?" Leia asked, when he returned to the living room.

Rohan shrugged. "Frumusanu naturally assumed that I was the killer," he said, a note of bitterness in his voice. "But then, why wouldn't he?" Hell, the thought had crossed Leia's mind, too. Not that he could blame her, but it cut, just the same.

"He believed you, didn't he? When you told him it wasn't you?"

"I guess so." He stood in front of her, hands fisted on his hips. "Do you?"

"I'm sorry," she said, a guilty flush staining her cheeks.

"Oh, hell," he muttered.

Leia frowned. The tone of his voice told her something else was bothering him.

Rohan dropped down onto the sofa beside her, one brow raised. What the hell? Was *she* reading *his* mind now? How did she know he was on edge?

She tilted her head to the side, an unspoken question in her eyes.

He huffed a sigh. "When I was outside talking to Frumusanu, I caught the scent of the vampire who made me." Leia stared at him, eyes wide with... what? He wasn't sure if it was disbelief or fear. Hell, maybe it was both.

"How could he find you after so long?" she asked tremulously.

"There's a strong blood tie between sire and fledgling. He'll always be able to find me, if he's looking. But..." Rohan clenched his hands into tight fists. "I don't think he's looking for me. I think it's just an unfortunate coincidence that he's here."

Later that night, after Leia had fallen asleep, Rohan willed himself to the place where the body had been found. The air still smelled of blood and fear and death.

And his sire's never-to-be-forgotten scent.

Chapter Twenty-Two

The vampire strolled the dark city streets. He had not been to this part of the world in over three hundred years, give or take a decade. Much had changed, but then, the world was always changing. Only he and his kind remained the same. These days, it took a lot to surprise him, but he had been truly astonished tonight. Earlier, while prowling the city, he had detected the near-forgotten scent of one he had turned centuries ago. He plucked the warrior's name from the deep recesses of his mind—Shadow Dancer, of the Lakota people.

Josiah remembered few of those he'd turned, but this one, ah, this one he had never forgotten. Perhaps because of the man's Indian blood. He had been the first Indian Josiah had ever turned. Perhaps it was because of the warrior's startled expression when he plunged his knife deep into Josiah's belly, and Josiah had laughed in his face because it had no lasting effect on him. Although Josiah had laughed, he hadn't been amused. The knife thrust had hurt like hell. In his anger, he had buried his fangs in the Lakota's throat. And instantly regretted it. The man had shown courage when he tried to avenge his friend's death, and courage was one of the few things Josiah still admired. Deciding the warrior shouldn't have to forfeit his own life for his bravado, Josiah had turned Shadow Dancer into a vampire, instead of draining him dry as he had intended. Turned him and left him without a backward glance.

Josiah grinned into the night. He had been a real SOB back then, with no regard for the lives he had carelessly taken or for those he'd thoughtlessly turned. Until this evening. To his surprise, he was curious to know how this particular fledgling had survived with no one to tell him what he'd become or how to survive on his own.

Perhaps he would track Shadow Dancer down one of these nights and see what the warrior had made of himself.

Chapter Twenty-Three

Rohan stared at the message on his phone. *The Troupe's been offered a gig in San Diego starting this Thursday night. I know this is short notice and you're on vacation, but do you think you could spare us a week or two? It's only three nights a week—Thursday, Friday, and Saturday. They're dark the other four nights. I wouldn't ask, but the theater manager is a friend of mine and he's in a jam. The act that was booked had to cancel at the last minute.*

Short notice, indeed, he thought, as he read the message a second time. This was Tuesday.

Rohan glanced at Leia, sleeping peacefully beside him. He hated to leave her, even for a couple of days, but he owed Jay Deer Killer a favor. Besides, he had few friends other than those he shared the stage with.

He agreed before he could change his mind. What the hell, he could take Leia with him if she wanted to go. Might be a good idea to get out of town for a couple of days anyway, he thought, what with his sire in the vicinity. Putting a few miles between them seemed like a smart thing to do.

He put it to Leia that evening. "The troupe has a two-week gig in San Diego, and they've asked me to meet them there. Do you want to come along?"

"I'd love to!"

"I was hoping you'd say that," he said, giving her hand a squeeze. "I'm only dancing three nights a week. Do you want to stay there for the run of the show, or just the days I'm dancing?"

"The whole two weeks," she said enthusiastically. "I love San Diego!" They were sitting side-by-side on the sofa in the living room. Reaching into the drawer of the side table next to the couch, Leia pulled out a small notebook and a pencil. "Let's see, I'll need a new bathing suit and maybe a new cover-up, and sandals. A new hat, of course. And sunglasses. How soon are we leaving?"

"Thursday."

"That doesn't give me much time!"

"Don't blame me. I just found out about it this morning." Grinning, he watched her double-check her list.

"I think I'm done after San Diego," Rohan remarked.

Leia looked up, her list forgotten. "Done? Do you mean you're quitting? For good? But..."

"But what?"

"I won't get to see you dance anymore."

"Darlin'," he said, taking her in his arms. "I'll dance for you any time you want."

She giggled as he took the notebook and pencil from her hand and laid them aside, then pulled her down on the floor and taught her some steps she had never learned before.

Wednesday was a busy day. While Rohan slept, Leia cleaned out the fridge, packed the clothes she planned to take, went shopping for the things on her list, and called Janae to tell her she'd be gone for two weeks.

"Two weeks!" Janae exclaimed. "Where are you going?"

"San Diego, with Rohan. His troupe is dancing down there."

"Oh, I love San Diego," Janae said, with a sigh. "We haven't been there since the boys were born. So, I guess things are working out between you and Rohan?"

"You could say that."

"There was another killing last night," Janae said, her voice almost a whisper. "Did you hear about it?"

"No." Leia felt her stomach clench at the news. Was it the vampire who had turned Rohan?

"You're lucky to be getting out of town," Janae remarked. "Hang on a sec. Mike, put the cat down. You're gonna get scratched. You don't want to take a couple of kids to San Diego with you, do you? Trent's been so busy lately, I've hardly seen him the last few days and the boys are driving me crazy."

"Sorry," Leia said. "Not this time. I'll call you when I get home."

"Okay. Have fun."

"You, too," Leia said, laughing as she heard Mark and Mike arguing over who the cat liked best. And then she sobered. If she stayed with Rohan, she would never hear the sound of her own children giggling or fighting, never tuck them into bed at night, or listen to their prayers.

⚜ ⚜ ⚜

They left for San Diego late Thursday morning. Because Rohan felt like driving, they took the Challenger. She had to admit, flying down the freeway was exciting.

"Aren't you afraid of getting a ticket?" she asked as the speedometer hovered near eighty.

He shrugged. "There isn't much traffic. I'll slow down if it gets heavy."

It was a beautiful day, the sky a bright blue, the air clear for a change. Soft rock came over the radio. "Does it ever bother you that you can't have children?"

Rohan slid a glance in Leia's direction. "What brought that up?"

She shrugged. "I was talking to Janae yesterday, and I heard her boys fighting, and ... " Her voice trailed off.

"And it reminded you that if you stayed with me, you'd never have kids."

She nodded.

"It bothered me when I was first turned," he said. "But I had other things to worry about at the time, things like surviving and finding a safe place to rest during the day, and how to avoid detection by hunters. There were a lot more vampires back then, and a lot more hunters."

"Sounds scary."

Rohan made a dismissive gesture. "I had some hairy moments in the beginning." But she wasn't thinking about vampires or hunters. She was imagining a future without children. He had told her he loved her, she had admitted she loved him, but they hadn't made any commitments to each other. Everything had happened so quickly between them, perhaps too quickly, at least for her. He knew what he wanted. After three hundred years, he had been everywhere he wanted to go, seen everything of interest, done everything he wanted to do, and finally found a woman he adored. But Leia was still young, with her whole life ahead of her.

He slid another glance in her direction. Perhaps she wasn't ready to settle down with someone like him, a man who owned nothing but a car, tended to sleep most days until the sun went down, couldn't share a meal with her, or give her children. Perhaps he'd been a fool to think loving him would be enough for her, or for any woman who wanted a normal life with a normal man. What right did he have to ask her to give all that up?

Leia felt Rohan watching her. She didn't have to be a mind reader to know what he was thinking. She was pretty sure she was thinking the same things herself. Maybe they needed to slow down a little, wait until the newness wore off their relationship to see if what she felt for him was strong enough to last.

Leia bit down on her lower lip as she felt an invisible gulf open between them. He was reading her mind, she thought bleakly. He knew she was again having second thoughts about their relationship. Maybe she should have stayed home. It was hard to think when he was so near, when she ached to be in his arms. She loved him desperately, she thought, but was she *in* love with him? In love enough to give up her dreams of a home and children? To live with a man who could never share her whole life, as she could never share his? He had told her once that she would have to make changes if she stayed with him. At the time, she had wondered what he meant. Now she knew.

Rohan was watching her, his face impassive. "I can take you back, if that's what you want."

She turned away so he couldn't see the tears in her eyes.

"Leia?"

She shook her head.

"If you change your mind, just say the word."

⚜ ⚜ ⚜

As usual, Rohan had reservations in the best room in the best hotel in town. Once they were settled in, he said, "I have to go rehearse with the troupe for an hour or two. Will you be all right?"

She wondered if he really had to rehearse or if he just wanted to get away from her for a while. "Don't worry about me," she said brightly. "I'll be all right."

"I won't be needing the car," he said, handing her the keys to the Dodge.

"Thank you." Warmth engulfed her as his fingers brushed hers. "I do love you, you know."

"I know." He drew her into his arms. "I wouldn't go if I didn't have to." He brushed a kiss across her lips. "I'll be back as soon as I can." He kissed her again, and then he was gone.

Leia blew out a sigh, wondering if she would ever get used to his just disappearing like the wind. Wondering if falling in love was always so complicated. She'd had little experience with men. After graduating from high school, she had been so busy working, studying, and attending college she hadn't had much time for a social life. The few men she had dated seemed shallow and she hadn't gone out with any of them more than once or twice, except for Jeff. And even that hadn't lasted.

Staring at the keys in her hand, she thought finding time to go see her folks sounded like a prime idea. Maybe she would do just that when she returned home. Although her parents didn't live that far away, it was too far to just run over and say hello.

Since she wasn't in the mood to go anywhere or do anything, Leia kicked off her shoes and turned on the TV. She was half-way through the first episode of a new series on Netflix when her stomach growled. Hitting pause, she called room service and ordered a cheeseburger, fries, and a chocolate malt for lunch.

After lunch, she started to watch TV again, and then frowned. Why was she sitting in a hotel room when she could be down at the pool, or shopping, or just driving around enjoying the fresh air?

She switched off the TV, grabbed the keys and her handbag, and left the hotel, trying to decide what to do first.

Rohan met up with the other dancers at the theater. After exchanging greetings and the usual teasing banter, Jay Deer Killer said, "Glad you could join us."

"Happy to do it, but next time, it'll cost you extra."

"Uh-huh. Listen, I know you usually perform two solo numbers, but you are the main attraction…"

Rohan grinned as Angela Gray Horse said, in a teasing voice, "Teacher's pet," which made the rest of the company laugh.

"As I was saying," Deer Killer went on, "I'd like you to do a third solo after intermission."

"Anything in particular?" Rohan asked.

"Whatever you like."

"Maybe a strip tease," Angela suggested, waggling her eyebrows.

Rohan grinned at her. Angela was young and single and sexy as hell. They'd had a brief, torrid affair that had flared like a 4th of July firecracker and lasted about as long since neither of them had been looking for any kind of lasting commitment.

"Shoot, he's almost naked now," Charlie Lone Eagle muttered with a grin. "If that breechclout was any smaller, we'd be raided."

Rohan laughed along with the rest of the company.

"All right, people, enough chit-chat," Jay Deer Killer said good-naturedly. "Let's get to work."

Two hours later, Rohan headed back to the hotel. He found Leia asleep on the sofa. An empty candy wrapper sat on the table beside the couch. The TV was on. For a moment, he simply stood there staring down at her, wondering where their relationship was going. She was having second thoughts again. What would he do if she decided to leave him? Beg her not to go? Mesmerize her so she would believe she wanted to stay with him even if she didn't? Or just let her walk out of his life?

Bending down, he brushed a kiss across her cheek.

Her eyelids fluttered open, a soft smile playing across her lips as she pulled his head down and kissed him.

Lifting her into his arms, he carried her to bed and stretched out beside her. Only half awake, Leia clung to him. She sighed when he caressed her, closed her eyes as he undressed her, then shucked his own clothes and gathered her into his arms.

"Leia?"

"Make love to me," she murmured, her voice husky. "I don't want to think about anything else."

He wasn't sure she knew what she was asking, wasn't even sure if she knew he was really there, or if she thought she was dreaming, but he didn't care. She might decide to leave him tomorrow, but for now, she was his.

Rohan had snagged a front row center seat for Leia. She sat there now, glancing around, listening to a couple of Native singers chant softly before the show started. There was something about the music that spoke to her, though she couldn't say what it was. She didn't understand the words, had no idea if the chanting even meant anything, and yet it called to something deep within her.

She felt a thrill of anticipation as Jay Deer Killer took the mic to announce the first dance. She had seen the show often enough to know that some of the dances and the costumes were new.

She held her breath as Shadow Dancer took the stage. The lights dimmed, the drumming began, soft and low at first, becoming louder and faster as his steps grew quicker, more intense, more intricate. His skin glistened in the light. Muscles flexing, rippling, his long, black hair whipping around his face and shoulders, he was all man. A warrior from another time. She could imagine him riding a painted pony across the Plains, his handsome face streaked with war paint, an eagle feather fluttering in his hair, a lance in his hand as he swept her off her feet and carried her away.

When he finished, the applause was deafening. Leia smiled when he winked at her.

Rohan exited the stage but lingered out of sight, all his senses alert as he peered through a narrow opening in the curtains, searching the faces in the crowd.

His sire sat in the second row, right behind Leia. Though Rohan hadn't seen the man in hundreds of years, he still recognized the face of the vampire who had made him.

A muffled oath escaped his lips. What the hell was his sire doing here?

The next dancer had just taken the stage when Leia heard Rohan's voice in her head. *Leia, take my car and go home.*

Home? To L.A?

Yes!

What? Why? Are you all right?

Dammit, just do as I say. Go home and lock all the doors and windows. I'll explain when I get there. Now, go!

Heart pounding, she stood and made her way to the aisle.

From his place behind the curtain, Rohan watched his sire to make sure he didn't follow Leia out of the theater.

Chapter Twenty-Four

Leia drove like a maniac, fleeing from the nameless fear aroused by the urgency in Rohan's voice. She made it home in record time. She parked the car, locked it up, and ran into her apartment. She set the dead bolt and the safety chain, checked all the doors and windows, drew all the curtains, then stood in the middle of the living room, her whole body quaking like a leaf in a high wind. If she hadn't heard Rohan's voice in her mind before, she would have thought she had imagined it.

What was going on? Why had he wanted her out of there? Did he expect something terrible to happen?

Too nervous to sit still, she paced the floor. The show should be over by now. She pulled her cell phone from her handbag and willed it to ring. What was keeping him? With his vampire powers, he should be here by now. Unless... She shook her head. He was a vampire, he had nothing to fear.

Nothing but a hunter.

She went into the kitchen for a cup of hot chocolate, but left it on the counter, untouched.

Where could he be?

Rohan and the rest of the troupe took a final bow to thunderous applause. In his dressing room, he changed into his street clothes, opened his senses one more time to make sure Leia had made it safely home and headed for the stage door, eager to get to her place and see for himself that she was all right.

"Hey, Rohan!"

He turned at the sound of Jay Deer Killer's voice.

"We had such a great show tonight, we're all going out for a drink to celebrate. Why don't you come, along?"

"Not tonight," he said.

"Come on," Angela Gray Horse coaxed. "Just one drink."

"I think all the applause he got tonight has gone to his head," Charlie Lone Eagle mused. "Too good for us now, I guess."

"Next time," Rohan said. "I've got a beautiful woman waiting for me at home."

Outside, he took a deep breath, drawing in the scent of cool, fresh air. He was about to give Leia a call to let her know he was on his way home when, too late, he sensed his sire's presence. He swore under his breath as he felt his sire's ancient, preternatural power wrap around him, binding him more tightly than any rope. *Dammit to hell!*

He swore again as his sire materialized in front of him. Wearing an expensive suit, his shirt collar open, he was taller than Rohan remembered, broad-shouldered, slim-hipped. He looked to have been in his early twenties when he was turned.

"All right, you've had your fun," Rohan hissed. "Now let me go."

"Just thought I'd check in with one of my fledglings, see how you were doing."

Rohan snorted. "Right."

"I must admit, you put on quite a show. Women in the audience were practically drooling. I overheard several of them wondering what kind of lover you were."

"Jealous?"

His sire threw back his head and laughed. "Hardly. Although I wouldn't say no to that pretty little filly sitting in front of me. She's quite taken with you. And you with her." A sly grin spread over his face. "Your scent is all over her."

"What do you want from me?"

"Nothing. I was just bored. You know how it is. Every hundred years or so you feel the urge to do something crazy."

Rohan grunted. "So you came to California to kill a few people and leave their bodies lying around? Good way to stir up the populace. Spread a little fear."

His sire frowned. "You think that was me?"

"It's not me, and as far as I know, you're the only other bloodsucker in town."

"Apparently not," his sire said, with a negligent shrug.

"You sound pretty sure."

"I should be. The culprit is one of mine. And quite fearless she is."

"She?" Rohan swore. Female vampires were rare and tended to be more vicious and more deadly than the males. That was true of a lot of species, he mused.

"I turned her in Wyoming maybe fifty years ago. She's Lakota, like you. Her name was Zikana, but she changed it to Magdalena. She followed me to California. I'm not sure why, though I have a pretty good idea."

"Why should I give a damn who she is or what she's doing?"

"No reason."

"Did you leave her to fend for herself the way you left me?" Rohan asked, his voice laced with venom. "Did she wake up not knowing what the hell had happened to her?

Or how to ease those first excruciating hunger pangs? Did you tell her she didn't have to kill to satisfy her thirst?"

"Stop whining. You turned out all right."

"No thanks to you. One of these nights I'll catch you in a weak moment and..."

"And what? Destroy me? I give you leave to try anytime. That pretty little mortal will make a nice distraction after I rip your heart out."

"Dammit! Are you gonna release me?"

"I don't know. I have a feeling it would be better for my health if I just killed you now."

Rohan glared at him. There was no way to hide anything from his sire, and no way to break his sire's hold on him, either. "Why did you turn me instead of killing me?"

His sire rocked back on his heels. "I was hiding out in the Black Hills when I crossed paths with a warrior. When he attacked me, I broke his neck. I had intended to feed on him, of course, and then you came along. Well, you know how it is. Fresh blood is so much more palatable than the blood of the dead. I was close to draining you dry when I found myself admiring your courage. To my surprise, I decided you shouldn't have to forfeit your life for trying to avenge your comrade. Or perhaps I was feeling maudlin in my old age. Who knows? It was a long time ago."

"So you turned me," Rohan said, his voice edged with bitterness.

"Would you rather be dead?"

In all the years he'd been a vampire, Rohan had never asked himself that question.

"Well?" his sire asked again. "Would you? Rather be dead?"

Rohan shook his head.

"Three hundred years is a long time to carry a grudge."

"Dammit!" Rohan snarled. "Turn me loose!"

"Say please."

"Go to hell."

"I'd like to meet your woman. Too bad you sent her home." A faint twitch of the vampire's hand freed Rohan from his thrall.

Rohan flexed his arms and shoulders. "What the hell's your name, anyway?"

"Guess I never got around to telling you, did I? It's Josiah, smart ass. I made peace with what I am centuries ago. I suggest you do the same."

Before Rohan could respond, his sire vanished from his sight.

Unable to sit still, Leia wandered from room to room, her mind racing. What had happened at the theater? Why had Rohan ordered her to go home? Was he in danger? Was she? If so, from whom? She had tried calling his cell phone several times, but it went to voice mail.

One hour turned into two. She was about to go out of her mind when Rohan materialized in the room.

Weak with relief, she sank down on the sofa. "What's going on? Why did you send me home? Where have you been? Why didn't you call me?"

He blew out a sigh that seemed to come from the very depths of his soul. "My sire was at the show tonight."

She stared at him, eyes wide. The vampire who turned him had been there? The very thought sent an icy shiver down her spine. "What...what did he want?"

Rohan sat in the chair across from the sofa, his long legs stretched out in front of him. "He said he'd come to see how

I was doing. He's also looking for the vampire who killed those people in the city. Apparently, she's one of his."

"She?"

"Yeah."

Strange, Leis mused, she had never considered that there might be female vampires. She couldn't imagine living such a life.

"One good thing came of it," Rohan muttered. "After three hundred years, I finally know his name."

"Oh?"

'Yeah. It's Josiah."

"Is he the reason you sent me home?"

Rohan nodded. "I don't want you anywhere near him, although I guess there's no way to prevent it. He's got your scent."

She shuddered at the thought.

"As long as you're in your own home, he can't hurt you."

"Why not? What's to stop him?"

"The threshold. Vampires can't enter a residence without the owner's permission."

"Now you tell me," she muttered.

"It works in reverse, too," he said. "Anytime you want me to leave, all you have to do is revoke your invitation."

"As simple as that? I don't believe it."

He nodded. "I don't know why it works, but it does, every time."

"Am I in danger from your sire?" She didn't really want to hear the answer but she had to know.

"I don't know." He wondered if he should tell her that Josiah thought she was pretty and decided against it, figuring it would just worry her more.

"Does this mean I can't go back to San Diego with you?"

Rohan dragged a hand across his jaw. He could protect her from people and most other vampires, but after tonight, he wasn't sure he could beat Josiah in a fight. Vampires grew stronger with age, and while he had no idea how old Josiah was, he knew his sire had been around for a hell of a long time.

"Well?"

He shrugged one shoulder. "I guess it's up to you." He grunted softly when Leia smothered a yawn behind her hand. "It's late," he said. "You should get some sleep. I need to go out for a few minutes."

He needed to hunt, she thought, as she made her way into her bedroom. And wondered if she would ever get used to that part of his life.

Rohan drifted through the night like a shadow, all his senses alert. It was unsettling, knowing that his sire could be anywhere. He had sworn to kill Josiah. Now, having seen him again, having felt Josiah's power first hand, he wasn't sure he was strong enough to accomplish it, but should the opportunity arise, Rohan intended to take it.

He slowed as he approached a nightclub. He hadn't fed much in the last few days. Slipping into the bar, he took the empty stool next to a middle-aged woman who sat alone. There were only three other people in the place—a man slumped over the bar, and a couple sitting at a back table, with their backs toward him. When the woman beside him turned and smiled at him, he captured her gaze with his, leaned closer, and quickly drank from her. A moment later, he released her from his spell and left the club. He would need all his strength while Josiah was in the area. To that end, he intended to feed and feed well as long as his sire was a threat.

With his presence cloaked, Josiah followed his fledgling to a relatively modern apartment building on a quiet street lined with trees. He frowned as Rohan went inside. This was hardly the kind of place a vampire would choose for his lair, therefore, it must be where the woman resided.

The woman. Leia. He smiled as he thought of her. She was young and lovely. There was no doubt that his fledgling had the hots for her. Who could blame him? But was Rohan interested in more than her blood and the carnal delights of her curvy little body? Did he care for her as a woman, a mate? And if so, how deeply? Love was rare among his kind. Loving a human woman ultimately led to heartache, whether it came from watching them grow old and wither away, or leaving them before that happened. In the past, he had loved many and married several times, until he couldn't face another loss. Since then, he had taken lovers, always careful to leave them when he felt himself beginning to care.

With a sigh, he continued on down the street, wondering how long it would take his fledgling to learn that it was better never to love at all.

Chapter Twenty-Five

Smothering a yawn, Leia stood in the kitchen, waiting for the coffee maker to produce her morning cup. She had tossed and turned all last night, troubled by the appearance of Rohan's sire and wondering what it meant for their future—if they had one.

Rohan was resting in her bed. Although he hadn't said so, she knew he was afraid to leave her alone in her apartment. The fact that he was worried spiked her own fears.

He was supposed to dance tonight, and Saturday. The theater was dark the rest of the week. She had hoped to be there for every performance the rest of this week and the next, but now she wasn't so sure. She wasn't sure about anything, she thought glumly as she carried her coffee mug to the table and sat down. When this gig was over, she needed to do some serious thinking about her future and whether she still wanted Rohan to be part of it. Rohan couldn't father a child, but lots of couples couldn't have children, and they could always adopt. And lots of men who weren't vampires slept days and worked nights.

She could handle that, too. Then there was the age thing. Rohan looked thirty and would always look thirty. It wasn't a problem now, but, eventually, she would age and he wouldn't. How would she feel when she looked forty, fifty, sixty, and he still looked thirty? How would *he* feel when she began to look like his mother instead of his lover?

The words he had spoken soon after they met suddenly rang out in her mind. *The whole vampire thing isn't going to go away, Leia. It's part of me, a part I can't change.* He had also said if they stayed together, she would have to make changes. She had wondered several times since then what he'd meant and now, suddenly, she wondered if one of those changes referred to making her what he was. That would certainly change her! Funny, she had never considered that option. And she refused to think about it now. Surely no one ever willingly chose to be a vampire. It was a life against nature, unnatural, abnormal. Abhorrent.

But what if becoming a vampire was the only way for their relationship to survive? Was she willing to sacrifice her humanity to spend her life with him? That was the $64,000 question, she thought, chewing on her thumbnail. She just wished she knew the right answer.

Waking from the dark sleep, Rohan was instantly aware of where he was. He knew the sun had just set. Leia had finished cleaning up after dinner and was standing at the front room window, deep in thought about what had happened last night, but more concerned about what the future held for the two of them. Sadly, that was something she had to figure out for herself.

He rose effortlessly, showered and dressed. Showtime was eight o'clock. He had two hours to get to San Diego and get ready for his first number. After running a comb through his hair, he left the bedroom.

Leia looked over her shoulder when he entered the room. She had known he was awake. She'd heard the shower come on. Their gazes met, his impassive, hers troubled.

Rohan swore inwardly. He was about to read her mind to determine what she was thinking when she closed the distance between them. Eyes bright with unshed tears, she clasped her hands behind his neck.

"I don't want to leave you," she whispered brokenly. "Please tell me there's a way for us to be together."

He wrapped his arm around her waist and stroked her hair with free hand. "This is a decision you'll have to live with," he said. "And only you can make it." He brushed a kiss across the top of her head. "I didn't mean to involve you in my life," he said, gazing into the distance. "I thought I could love you for a little while and then leave, but..." He shrugged one shoulder. "I've never been in love like this before, darlin', and never again."

Love shouldn't be this hard, she thought. Other couples met, fell in love, married, and if they were lucky, they lived happily-ever-after.

"But we're not like other couples, are we?" he asked quietly.

Leia sighed as his hand stroked up and down her back, sending little shivers of delight dancing in the pit of her stomach.

"I know you're afraid you'll have to become what I am, but you don't. I will love you and care for you as long as you live."

She looked up at him, her eyes filled with doubt. "Is that how you want to spend your future? Looking after a decrepit old woman?"

He laughed softly. "I won't let that happen."

"Oh? Have you discovered the Fountain of Youth?"

"In a way. My blood can slow the aging process. You will be young and beautiful for a long, long time. Other women will envy you and wonder what your secret is."

"I don't believe you. That's not possible."

"I'll prove it to you, my love, when you get older. Right now, I have to get to the theater. Are you coming with me?"

She bit down on her lower lip, then nodded.

⚜ ⚜ ⚜

They didn't have time to drive that night so Rohan transported them to the venue. Not wanting to leave her alone, he took her into his dressing room while he changed into his breechclout, tied an eagle feather in his hair, and pulled on a pair of exquisitely-beaded moccasins.

Leia watched with fascination as he painted his chest and face. It was just a bit of red and black paint, yet it transformed him from Rohan to the warrior, Shadow Dancer. Tall and muscular, his skin the color of old copper, his hair as black as midnight, he looked gorgeous and dangerous.

"Are you doing a new dance tonight?" she asked. "I've never seen you wear moccasins."

"Gotta give the crowd something new every once in a while," he said, with a wink. "In the old days, I would have kidnapped you and carried you away to my lodge and made you my woman."

"Would you?"

He nodded. "You would cook for me and bear me strong sons, and every night you would share my blankets and tell me you loved me."

"I do most of that now," she said with a grin. And knew she wanted to do it every night for as long as she lived.

"Leia." Just her name, but there was a wealth of emotion behind it.

The five-minute bell sounded just then.

"You'd better go get your seat." He kissed her cheek. "I'll be dancing just for you tonight."

Feeling her heart glow with love, Leia hurried out of the dressing room and into the theater. As usual, they had a packed house. The other dances all ran together in her mind and then he took the stage, looking magnificent and proud. She had grabbed a program and she quickly scanned it when she didn't recognize the dance. It was one he hadn't done before. The Eagle Dance. The description said that this dance was a prayer to *Wakan Tanka*, the Great Spirit of the Lakota. In it, the dancer asked for a blessing on the People as he imitated the soaring flight of the eagle, which was a symbol of the Great Spirit. From time to time, he blew on a whistle to imitate the eagle's piercing cry.

It was the most beautiful, powerful dance she had ever seen. For some reason, it brought tears to her eyes.

"Quite amazing, isn't he?"

Annoyed, Leia turned toward the man sitting behind her, intending to ask him to be quiet. She gasped when she recognized the man as the one she had seen the night before.

The vampire who had turned Rohan.

She pressed a hand to her heart. Why was he here again?

Rohan sensed his sire's presence before he saw him. What the hell? Fear and anger rose within him when he saw Josiah leaning forward, talking to Leia. It was all he could do to keep from leaping off the stage.

Another few steps and the dance ended. He took a bow and hurried into the wings. He peered through a narrow gap in the curtains, ready to spring into action, if necessary, but when he looked, Josiah was gone. Relief washed through him when he saw Leia. What the hell was his sire up to with his little game of cat and mouse? Was he just amusing himself at Rohan's expense, or seriously plotting to steal Leia away from him?

Magdalena stood in the shadows at the back of the theater. She had been following Josiah for days. When she was human, he had vowed that he loved her, promised they would be together forever. After he'd turned her, he taught her the basics of what it was to be a vampire and then left her a week later without so much as a word of farewell. What she intended to do about it, she had no idea. But once she'd seen the Lakota warrior known as Shadow Dancer, she forgot everything else. What was a vampire doing dancing with a bunch of humans? He was magnificent. Never had she seen a man move with such masculine grace, such self-assurance. He was the very epitome of what a Lakota warrior should be. What would he say if she introduced herself to him? They were, after all, related by blood.

Leia waited in Rohan's dressing room while he changed, then followed him down the narrow hall to the stage door. Dozens of admirers—all female—were waiting for him. She fell back as they gathered around him, calling his name, thrusting souvenir programs at him to sign, elbowing each other out of the way as they tried to get closer to him, eager to touch him, to get a photo of him or with him, to tell him how wonderful he was.

She grinned inwardly, thinking how jealous they would be if they knew Shadow Dancer was hers.

She glanced at the dark-haired woman standing a little apart from the others. She was pretty, exotic, with copper-hued skin and black eyes. Was she Indian? Leia frowned when the woman glared at her. Odd, Leia thought, and then forgot all about the woman when Rohan glanced her way and shrugged, as if to say, *What can I do?*

Eventually, the crowd drifted away, all but the dark-haired woman who had looked so menacingly at Leia.

Disconcerted, Leia moved to Rohan's side. "Why is she looking at me like that?" she asked. "I've never seen her before."

"She's a vampire." Rohan inhaled sharply, then wrapped his arm around Leia's shoulders as he recognized the scent of the vampire who had done the killings in L.A. She didn't look like a savage killer, he thought, as the woman approached them. She was petite and pretty. And dangerous as hell. "What do you want?" he asked brusquely.

"To speak with you. Alone."

"There's nothing you can say to me that can't be said in front of my woman."

"Then I will tell you another time," she hissed, and was gone before he could say anything else.

"What was that all about?" Leia asked.

"I don't know, but I sense something familiar about her."

"Oh?" A sharp stab of jealousy speared through her. Was the woman a former lover he had somehow forgotten?

"Come on," he said. "Let's go home."

In a matter of moments, they were standing in her living room. "What do you think she wanted to tell you?" Leia asked as she kicked off her shoes and settled on the sofa.

Rohan shrugged. "Beats the hell out of me."

Leia picked up a sofa pillow and hugged it to her chest. "Can she follow us?"

With a shrug, he dropped down beside her. "Probably. But don't worry. She can't come in without an invitation, remember?" No sooner had he spoken than he sensed the other vampire's presence, knew she was standing in front of the apartment.

"It's late," he said. "I need to go out for a few minutes. Why don't you get ready for bed?" He brushed a kiss across her lips. "You can warm up my side while I'm gone."

She smiled up at him. "Don't be long."

"I won't." He kissed her again and vanished.

"I wish I could do that," Leia muttered as she headed for the bathroom. "Think of all the money I'd save on gas if I could just will myself wherever I wanted to go." And then she sobered. He wasn't going out for a good time, he was going out to hunt. Would she ever get used to that?

The woman smiled when she saw him, as if she'd been certain he would come.

"All right, I'm here," he said impatiently. "What do you want?"

She smiled, flashing white teeth. "I thought we should meet."

"Yeah? Why?"

"We are related, in a manner of speaking."

Rohan frowned. "Is that right? Funny, I don't remember having a sister."

"We carry the same blood," she replied, a note of bitterness in her voice.

Rohan stared at her. And then he opened his senses and knew what she meant. Josiah had turned them both. "You followed him here. Why?"

"I want to destroy him."

"I'm afraid you'll have to get in line," Rohan retorted. "Why do *you* want him dead?"

"My reasons are my own," she said. And then she frowned. "Why do *you* want him dead?"

He lifted one brow in amusement. "Why should I tell you?"

She shrugged.

"So, you're Magdalena."

"Did he tell you about me?"

"Just that he'd turned you. If you want him dead, why are you leaving bodies around town?"

"Why shouldn't I? Isn't that what vampires are supposed to do?"

"Not the smart ones."

She sucked in a breath, and let it out in a long, slow sigh. "Sometimes I can't help myself. I get so angry at how he treated me. Maybe when I've destroyed him, the urge to kill will pass."

Rohan grunted. He knew the feeling. "So why do you want him dead?"

"Because he lied to me! He told me he loved me. That when he turned me, we would be together forever. And then he left without a word and I vowed to destroy him."

"Can't say as I blame you."

"Why do you want him dead?"

Rohan shook his head. "I'm not sure my reason is as good as yours. My advice to you is go home. He's your sire. You'll never be strong enough to defeat him." Josiah was his sire, too, Rohan thought. What made him so sure he could destroy him and Magdalena couldn't?

"We would be strong enough together," she argued.

Rohan grinned at her. "You would have made a hell of a warrior."

"What makes you think I didn't?"

He looked at her with new-found respect. It wasn't unheard of for Lakota women to be warriors. In battle, they were as bold and brave as the men, sometimes more so.

"Will you help me?" she asked.

"Let me think it over for a day or two. I'll let you know."

"Do you love the woman with the flame-colored hair?"

" 'Fraid so."

"I will see you again," she said, and disappeared into the darkness.

She was a strange one, Rohan mused, as he went in search of prey. He fed quickly on the first lone female he saw, then willed himself back to Leia's apartment. He had thought to find her asleep, but she was sitting up in bed.

Her eyes were filled with suspicion when she looked at him. "You went to see that vampire woman, didn't you?"

Rohan swore inwardly. How the hell had she known? Woman's intuition? "She was waiting for me outside." He held up his hand, staying the next accusation. "She wants Josiah dead."

"Why?"

"She's madder than hell because he made some promises he didn't keep. I guess you could say it's a lover's spat."

"And she came to you for help?"

Rohan shrugged. "We're related, in a way. Josiah made her, too. If she was a man, I guess we'd be blood brothers."

"What are you going to do?"

"I don't know."

"She's very pretty, isn't she?" Leia asked.

"Yes, she is."

"You have a lot in common. She's a vampire. And she's Indian, like you, isn't she?"

Rohan blew out a sigh. He didn't want to have this conversation. Siting on the edge of the bed, he took one of Leia's hands in his. "Yes, she's pretty and a vampire and Lakota. And it doesn't mean anything. I don't have any feelings for her, darlin'. It's you I love and nothing will change that." He paused and took a deep breath. "Are you sure it's me you're worried about, or are you having second thoughts again? You need to make a decision, Leia. I know it's hard. I know there are a lot of differences between us, and that some of them scare you and some of them worry you, but if you love me enough, we can overcome them together. I love you and I always will, no matter what you decide."

Lifting her hand, he turned it over and kissed her palm. She shivered as ripples of pleasure spiraled through her.

"Think about what I said," he murmured. "Call me when you've made up your mind."

"You're leaving me?"

"I want you to be clear-headed while you think about it." He grinned ruefully. "I'm afraid you can't think objectively while I'm sharing your bed."

Leia glared at him. "Of all the conceited..." She gasped as he pulled her up against him and kissed her, his tongue dueling with hers in a long, slow mating dance that threatened to melt her very bones with its heat. She clung to him, desperate for more, for anything to quench the sudden fire burning through her.

"It's not conceit," he whispered against her ear. "It's part of what I am. And that's why you need to be alone to make your decision."

Leia gazed up at him, her body still throbbing with need, even as she admitted he was right, because at that moment, she would have said anything, done anything, he wanted.

Rohan brushed a kiss across her lips. "I'll be waiting for your call," he said quietly.

Silent tears trickled down her cheeks as she watched him walk away.

Rohan muttered every foul word he'd ever known as he prowled the night. It seemed he was always leaving Leia or thinking about leaving her for her own good. Perhaps this time, he should just leave the country for forty or fifty years. She might miss him for a while, but she'd get over it. In time, she'd fall in love with some decent young man, marry, have a couple of kids, and live happily ever after.

He growled low in his throat as his fangs pricked his tongue. Who was he kidding? He'd probably rip the heart out of any man who dared lay a hand on her. Another good reason to leave the country. With a wry grin, he admitted there were times when he wasn't as civilized as he liked to think.

With a muffled oath, he transported himself to the cold comfort of his lair. Leia had a lot of thinking to do. But then, so did he.

Chapter Twenty-Six

"Leia!" Janae exclaimed. "I'm so glad you called! I was beginning to think you'd dropped off the face of the earth."

"I wish I had."

"Oh-oh. Trouble in paradise?"

"You could say that."

"Well, mama's here to listen."

Leia sighed. How could she tell Janae what the trouble was when she couldn't tell her the real problem?

"Leia? You still there?"

"I'm trying to decide whether I want to stay with Rohan or not."

"Well, you know how I feel about it. But what's your problem this time?"

"It's complicated. We get along really well. He's a wonderful lover. He's kind and considerate and protective."

"And that's your problem?" she asked dryly. "He's nice?"

"No. It's just that there are some huge differences between us and I'm not sure we can resolve them."

"Like what?"

Leia ran her fingers through her hair. "Like I said, it's complicated." If only Rohan hadn't wiped the memory of what he was from Janae's mind, this would be so much easier, she thought. "Let's just say I found out something about him that bothers me. A lot."

"So you know?"

"Know what?"

"About his record," Janae said, then muttered an oath. "Oh, crap! It's very hush-hush. I'm not supposed to say anything about it. Trent will kill me if he finds out."

Leia frowned, thoroughly confused. Had Rohan told Janae that Trent was a vampire hunter? But surely she must know. And if she didn't, what did she think her husband did for a living? And what did she think Rohan was wanted for? What kind of record did she mean? A police record? Did Janae think Rohan was wanted by the law?

"Promise me you won't tell Trent I told you."

"I promise," Leia said, her mind racing.

"So, that's the problem, then? His being in trouble with the government?"

"Yes, that's it."

"Did Rohan tell you what he's wanted for? Trent wouldn't say."

"Neither can I. You understand?"

"I guess so." Janae sighed heavily. "These kids are driving me crazy. Hold on a minute. Mark! Get out of the cookie jar. Right now! Go play in the backyard and take Mike with you. Okay, I'm back. So, what are you going to do?"

"I wish I knew."

"Well, I'm here if you need moral support or a shoulder to cry on. Maybe we can get together for lunch one of these days when Trent gets home. He's off on business again."

Who was he hunting now? Leia wondered, as she ended the call. Rohan? His sire? The vampire, Magdalena? How many vampires were there in the world? In the city? How many had she met without even knowing it?

If Rohan had been a petty thief or a small-time crook, it might make her decision easier, she mused with a rueful grin. She could probably live with that. Not that being a bank robber or an embezzler or whatever was all right, but at least he'd just be a man in trouble. Thinking Rohan could be wanted by the law was ludicrous. He could read minds, manipulate or erase memories, shield his presence. Even if he *was* some kind of felon, the police would never know it. And yet, what if it was true? A vampire con man. She didn't know whether to laugh or cry.

Feeling a headache coming on, Leia fell back on the sofa and closed her eyes, afraid that no matter what decision she made, it would only end in misery and regret.

It was late afternoon when Leia woke. For a moment, she lay there, remembering the days and nights she had spent with Rohan. Impulsively, she grabbed a notebook and pencil from the drawer in the end table and made a list of pros and cons of staying with Rohan. When she was done, she had a long list on the pro side and only two things on the other side—*vampire* and, in smaller letters, *possible felon*.

She smiled as she tossed the notebook and pencil on the coffee table and reached for her phone.

Fighting off the dark sleep, Rohan reached for his cell phone and uttered a groggy "Hello?"

"Can you come over?"

Wide awake now, he sat up. "Leia. Is something wrong?"

"No. We need to talk."

That didn't sound good. "I'll be there in five minutes."

※ ※ ※

He was as good as his word. Five minutes later. he appeared in her living room. Leia felt her heart skip a beat when she saw him. Tall, dark, and gorgeous in a white shirt that complimented his dark hair and skin, and a pair of black jeans that emphasized his long, muscular legs.

"I'm here," he said, fighting the urge to read her mind. "What do you want to talk about?"

"You."

"What do you want to know now?" he asked warily.

"Janae thinks you're wanted by the law. You aren't, are you?"

"Don't be ridiculous. The police don't even know I exist. Anything else?" He frowned when she didn't answer. "Leia?"

"Is there still an us?" she asked, her voice so quiet only a vampire could have heard it.

Feeling a flicker of hope, he shoved his hands into his back pockets to keep from reaching for her. "I guess that's up to you."

She took a deep breath. "Do you still want me?"

"Silly girl, you know I do." He took a step toward her, and then another. "Are you sure this time?"

"Very."

He drew her into his arms. "So, if I asked you to marry me, what would you say?"

"I'd say, when?"

"Whenever you want." His gaze burned into hers. "What changed your mind?"

"I made a list of your good points and your bad."

His brows shot up in surprise. "And you still want to marry me?"

"I could only think of one objection," she said, with a shrug. "You can probably guess what it was."

"Yes," he said dryly. "I'm pretty sure I can."

She smiled up at him, her eyes shining with happiness. "In some ways, it's also a plus."

"Really?"

She nodded. "Like when I call you, you can get here in no time at all. We can talk mind-to-mind. I know I can count on you if I get into trouble."

He grinned at her. "Are those the only reasons?"

"Well, you love me."

"Indeed."

"And I love you."

"That's what I wanted to hear," he said. And then he kissed her.

Liquid heat spiraled through her and she leaned into him, wanting to be closer, closer, wanting to touch him and taste him, to wrap him in her love and never let him go.

Lifting his head, he asked, "What kind of wedding do you want?"

"Just a small one." She had never wanted a big wedding with all the fuss and frills, had never liked being the center of attention. "Just my family, Janae, and a couple of friends from school." She bit down on her lower lip. "Can we get married in a church?"

"If that's what you want."

"You don't have a problem with that?"

"Should I?" he asked, amused by the question.

"Well, in the movies, vampires are repelled by crosses and holy water and that kind of thing. I'd hate to see the groom go up in flames."

"It makes for good story-telling," he said, with a laugh. "But there's not much truth to it. The only thing that repels me is silver."

"Oh?"

"It weakens me and burns my skin if it touches me. So, how long will it take to plan the wedding?"

"I'm not sure. I've never done it before. We'll need to reserve a church and order a cake. And tell my folks, of course. And I'll need a dress." That was the one thing she had always dreamed of—walking down the aisle in a beautiful white wedding gown.

"Buy one that's easy to get out of," he said, with a wink.

"And you'll need a tux. Oh. I'm sure my parents will want to meet you before the big day."

"I was afraid of that."

"Is that a problem?"

"Only if your father is a hunter on the side."

"I love you, Rohan."

The words, softly spoken, went right to his heart. "And I love you. Do we need to talk about anything else?"

"I don't think so. Why?"

"Because I'm dying to take you to bed."

"We can't have that now, can we?" she replied, with a saucy grin.

"Hang on tight," he said as he swung her into his arms and headed for the bedroom. "I don't have much time, you know. I'm due at the theater at seven-thirty."

Chapter Twenty-Seven

Leia woke slowly, her body still warm and tingling from Rohan's caresses. They had made love again when he got home from the theater last night. She smiled at the memory. Last night, every nerve and cell in her body had come alive at his touch as never before. She wondered if he'd been holding back a little the other times they had made love, wondered if he felt differently about her now that she had agreed to marry him.

Raising up on her elbow, she let her gaze move over him. His long, black hair covered the pillowcase like a splash of ebony ink. She admired his muscular arms and legs, his broad shoulders and chest, his flat belly ridged with muscle. Not wanting to wake him, she clenched her hands to keep from running her fingers over all that tempting, copper-hued flesh.

She continued to admire him as she thought of the things she needed to do in the next few days—find a church, order a cake and flowers, call her parents and arrange for them to meet Rohan. She was sure Janae would agree to be her matron of honor, and her friend, Rosemary, would agree to be a bridesmaid. She couldn't wait to go shopping for a dress. Couldn't wait to be Rohan's wife.

She eased out from under the covers so as not to wake him, giggled when his hand curled around her arm.

"Where do you think you're going?" he asked, his voice whisky-rough as he drew her down on top of him.

"I think I'm staying right here," she said, stifling a laugh.

And it was a long time before she made it out of the bedroom.

⚜ ⚜ ⚜

After a late breakfast, Leia called her parents. Her mother answered the phone. "Leia! It's so good to hear from you. How are you, hon?"

"I'm fine, Mom. Guess what? I'm getting married."

"Married? Goodness, I didn't even know you were dating anyone."

"You'll love him."

"Well, what's his name? What does he do? Where did you meet?"

"Slow down, Mom," Leia said. "His name is Rohan. He's Lakota. And he dances for a living."

"Dances?" her mother asked dubiously. "Like on *Dancing With the Stars*?"

"No," Leia said, laughing. "He's a professional Native American dancer. That's how I met him. He performs under the name Shadow Dancer."

"I think I've heard of him," her mother said. "Yes. Yes, I have. I saw an ad for that show in the newspaper just the other day. I've been trying to convince your Dad to take me to see it, but he's dragging his feet. You know how he is. If it doesn't have guns or monster trucks, he's not interested. So, you're getting married. When's the big day?"

"Hopefully in two or three weeks, if I can get all my ducks in a row. I'll let you know."

"Why the rush? You're not…"

"No, Mom, I'm not pregnant. Just anxious. I don't like big weddings, you know, so it's just going to be a small affair, with our family, Janae, and maybe a few friends from school. I don't suppose there's any way Luke could make it home," she said, with a sigh. "So, what's a good day for us to come by so you and Dad can meet Rohan?"

"What about this Thursday, for dinner?"

Leia frowned. Dinner really wasn't a good idea. "How about this?" Leia said. "Why don't you and Dad come to the show Thursday night? That way you can meet Rohan and see him perform. We can go out for drinks afterward. I know it's a long drive…"

"That's a wonderful idea!" her mother exclaimed. "Your dad and I can make a day of it. A nice drive. Dinner by the ocean. The chance to meet our future son-in-law. Your Dad can't say no to all that."

"All right, it's a date then. I'll arrange for tickets. Say hi to Dad for me."

"Will do. Love you, honey."

"Love you, too, Mom. Show starts at eight. Get there a little early." Meeting after the show had been a stroke of genius, Leia mused as she ended the call. She wouldn't have to explain why Rohan didn't eat.

Leia spent the next half hour calling churches in the area and finally found one that was available on a Sunday night in two weeks.

Her next call was to Janae. She hesitated a moment before she clicked on Janae's name, certain Janae wouldn't approve.

"Hey, girlfriend," Janae said cheerfully. "What's new and exciting?"

"Plenty. Are you sitting down?"

"Yeah, why?" Janae asked. "Are you going to shock me?"

"I'm getting married."

Silence.

"Did you hear what I said?"

"I guess it's too much to hope that you've fallen madly in love with someone else."

"Janae…" Leia shook her head, disappointed but not surprised by her friend's reaction.

"I'm sorry. Congratulations."

"I know you don't approve of him, but please be happy for me. And please say you'll be my matron of honor."

"You know I will. And if you're happy, I'm happy. What should I wear?"

"Anything you want. It's going to be a small, informal affair, just my family, you, and maybe a few of my friends from school, if they're available."

"I'll have to buy a new dress," Janae said cheerfully. "Any particular color I should look for?"

"Anything but white," Leia said, with a chuckle.

Janae blew out a sigh, hoping against hope that Leia wasn't making a terrible mistake.

"Hey, why are you looking so glum?" Trent asked, coming into the kitchen. "Did you lose your best friend?"

"I hope not."

"What's that supposed to mean?"

"It's Leia. She's marrying Rohan."

Trent grunted, but said nothing. So, Leia was marrying the vampire. Never rains but it pours, he thought, because he'd recently become aware that there were two other vampires in the city. As if one wasn't enough. If any more showed up, he was going to have to call Headquarters for reinforcements. He wasn't worried about Rohan. He knew where to find that bloodsucker. As for the other two, he had no doubts he would find them, too, sooner or later. The older one might be a problem, but he'd worry about that killer when the time came. The Company didn't pay him the big bucks because he couldn't do the job.

Leia had just finished the dinner dishes when Rohan sauntered into the kitchen. "Good evening, bride."

"Oh, I like the sound of that."

"So do I." He pulled her into his arms and teased her lips with his. "What would you like to do tonight?"

"I don't know. Is there anything you want to do? Besides that?"

He huffed an exaggerated sigh. "Not even married yet and she's already tired of me."

Leia punched him playfully on the arm. "Hardly. I called my mom today."

"And how did she react to your news?"

"She was very excited. They're going to meet us at the theater Thursday night. You can get tickets, can't you?"

"Sure." Tugging on her hand, he led her into the living room, sat on the sofa, and pulled her onto his lap. "What did you tell her about me?"

"That you were a wonderful dancer and a sexy vampire."

He lifted one brow. "Very funny. Now, what did you really tell her?"

"Just that you dance professionally. She's eager to see you," Leia said, and then frowned. "They won't be able to tell you're a vampire, will they?"

"Of course not. I've never met anyone who could tell. Except for a few hunters, of course."

"I asked Janae to be my matron of honor. Is that going to be a problem?"

"Not if Trent behaves himself."

"I still can't believe she doesn't know what he does. Oh! I found a church. We're getting married two weeks from now. Is that okay with you?"

He nodded.

"Oh!" Leia stared at him, wide-eyed. "I almost forgot! We need to make an appointment to get a marriage license! I'll do that in the morning."

Rohan nodded and then he leered at her. "What do you say we go practice for the honeymoon?"

Leia sighed dramatically as she wrapped her arms around his neck. "Sex, sex, sex, that's all men want."

Rohan laughed out loud. "And it's all you think about."

"It is not!"

"Darlin', you can't lie to me. I can read your thoughts, remember?"

"All right, I confess. It crosses my mind briefly from time-to-time."

"Uh-huh. Well, if you're not in the mood…"

"Oh, shut up and take me to bed, you fool."

She let out a gasp as, between one breath and the next, he transported them into the bedroom and onto the bed. Somewhere along the way, their clothing had disappeared. "You never fail to amaze me," she muttered as he took her in his arms.

"You ain't seen nothing yet," he said, waggling his eyebrows.

"Show me," she whispered. "Show me everything."

Pleasure unfurled deep within her as he rained kisses on her brow, her cheeks, her lips, along the side of her neck. She frowned when, abruptly, he bolted upright. "What's wrong?"

"Magdalena is outside."

"What does *she* want?"

"Nothing good, I'm sure." He was out of bed and pulling on his pants as he spoke. "Stay here. I'll be right back."

Before she could protest, he was gone.

"What the hell are you doing here?" Rohan growled.

"Sorry to interrupt you, but I haven't heard from you. You said you'd get in touch with me in a day or two."

"I've had other things on my mind."

"Yes," Magdalena said, with a sneer. "I can smell that other *thing* all over you."

"Don't push me."

"I may not be able to destroy Josiah, but a human female would be no trouble at all."

Rohan bared his fangs as his power surrounded her. "You're on dangerous ground, Magdalena. You'd better think twice before you push me too far."

Magdalena stared at him defiantly, but not before he saw the fear in her eyes.

"Don't come here again," he warned. "You won't like what happens if you do." With a last warning glance, he disappeared from her sight.

"Well, what did she want?" Leia asked.

"Same thing she wanted before. She wants me to help her destroy Josiah." Rohan stepped out of his trousers and slid into bed beside her. "Seems he promised they'd be together forever after he turned her. But forever only lasted a year."

"What's that old saying? 'Hell hath no fury like a woman scorned'?"

"I've always found it to be true," he remarked.

"Oh?"

"Just kidding," Rohan said, with a laugh. "Pull in your claws."

"She worries me," Leia said, snuggling against his broad chest.

"I won't let anything happen to you, love," he murmured, sifting his fingers through the thick fall of her hair. And hoped it was a promise he could keep.

Chapter Twenty-Eight

In the morning, Leia found herself humming "Here Comes the Bride". Last night, she had called her mom to let her know she was going out to look at wedding dresses this morning, did she want to come along?

"Silly question," her mom had said, with a laugh. And they agreed to meet at noon.

Life had never been better, Leia decided as she smoothed her hand over her hair. Rohan loved her. In two weeks, they would be married. Last night, he had promised to buy her a house anywhere in the world she wanted to live. He had also told her she didn't have to work unless she wanted to.

She had mulled that over for an hour or so. In the end, she decided she enjoyed teaching too much to give it up. Besides, it would keep her busy during the day while Rohan rested. As for where she wanted to live, she had no idea. She was perfectly happy in her apartment. Still, it might be nice to have a home of her own, with a yard full of flowers and maybe a pool.

She frowned when there was a knock at the door. Her mother wasn't due for another half an hour. "Who is it?"

"Trent."

What on earth did he want? Leia wondered as she unlocked and opened the door.

His gaze swept the room behind her. "Mind if I come in?" he asked.

Leia bit down on her lower lip, all too aware of the vampire sleeping in her bedroom. Had Trent come hoping to destroy Rohan while he was at rest?

"It'll just take a minute."

"Let's sit out on the porch," Leia suggested. "It's such a nice day."

Trent sent her a knowing look but didn't object.

Stepping outside, Leia closed the door behind her. There were two chairs on her tiny porch. She gestured for him to take one while she took the other. "What can I do for you?"

"Janae tells me you're marrying that Indian dancer."

Leia nodded. "I hope you'll come to the wedding."

"Do you know who he is?"

"I believe so."

"Do you know *what* he is?"

"Trent, who I marry is really none of your business."

"I'm afraid it is."

"Oh? And why is that?"

"The man's a vampire. Are you going to tell me you didn't know?"

"Of course I know," she said, her temper rising. "And it's still none of your business."

"Dammit, Leia..." He paused to take a deep breath. "He's a bloodsucker. You must know you can't have any kind of normal life with him."

"I know that," she said, her patience wearing thin.

"It'll be a short marriage," he warned. "There's a hefty price on his head and I intend to collect it when the time is right."

Leia stared at him, too shocked to speak. She had known he was a hunter, but he was also a friend. Or so she'd thought. Foolishly, perhaps, she had expected him to leave Rohan alone. "He isn't hurting you or anyone else. He doesn't kill those he...he feeds on. Why can't you just leave him alone?"

"The man's evil. I know you can't see it, but it's true. He's killed before and he'll kill again."

"I wonder what Janae would say if she knew *you* were a killer."

Her barb hit home. Trent reeled back in his chair. "I'm not a killer, not like him. I'm a government employee doing my job."

"If you're so proud of it, why haven't you told your wife and kids?"

"I can't."

She had momentarily forgotten that there was a stiff penalty if a hunter revealed what he was to anyone, including his family, and the penalty was death. "Maybe you can't, but I can."

"Is that a threat?" he asked.

Leia shrugged. She would never knowingly put Janae's life in danger.

Trent stood abruptly, his face dark with anger and frustration. For a moment, he glared at her, and then he left without another word.

Leia's mother arrived a few minutes later. "Are you ready, honey?" she asked, enfolding Leia in a hug. "You have no idea how I've looked forward to this."

"Me, too."

"I remember dress shopping with my mom," Cynthia remarked as they left the apartment. "It's one of my fondest memories. Do you want to drive, since you know where we're going?"

"Sure!" Leia said, as if she would pass up the chance to drive her mom's Porsche.

It took only a few minutes to reach the bridal shop. Leia paused, wide-eyed, just inside the door. She had never seen so many wedding dresses. How was she ever going to pick just one? They came in all styles and colors—from modest and white to daring and black and every style and shade of the rainbow in between. She supposed she wasn't technically entitled to wear white, but she didn't care. She was only going to be a bride once and she wanted a long, white gown and veil.

"What kind of dress did you have in mind?" her mother asked.

"Something long and sort of sexy," Leia replied as she walked toward the nearest rack. She perused gowns made of silk and satin and lace. Gowns with long sleeves or short or off the shoulder. So many choices. How was she ever going to decide? She grinned as she recalled Rohan telling her to pick something easy to get out of.

Her mother made it fun, reminiscing about when she bought her own gown and how she had finally flipped a coin to decide between the two she liked the best.

Leia tried on a dozen or so before she found the one. It was long, with a flared skirt, and long sleeves made of delicate lace. The same lace edged the neckline. She found a matching shoulder-length veil. Unlike a lot of bridal shops, this one carried many of their dresses in the most popular sizes. Fortunately, Leia's size was one of them, which meant she could take the gown with her. If she'd had to wait for them to order one, it might have taken months. She also found a pair of shoes she liked.

When Leia stepped out of the dressing room, tears welled in her mother's eyes. "What do you think, Mom?"

"It's beautiful," her mother murmured, with a sniffle. "You look just like a fairy princess."

To Leia's surprise, her mother insisted on paying for everything and then suggested they stop for a late lunch and hot fudge sundaes on the way home.

"Thanks for going with me," Leia said as she pulled up in front of her apartment and put the car in Park. "Do you want to come in for a while?"

"Not this time. I promised your dad I'd be home in time to fix his dinner."

"You spoil him, Mom," Leia teased.

"I know, but it's too late to stop now. Lord help me, I love that man."

Leaning over, Leia kissed her mom's cheek. "See you soon."

After getting out of the car, Leia reached into the back seat to retrieve the garment bag holding her gown and veil and the shoe box.

She waved as her mother pulled out of the parking lot.

Rohan was waiting for her on the sofa when she stepped into the apartment.

"You're up early," she said, hanging her dress in the hall closet and placing the shoe box on the shelf.

"What did Trent want?"

Leia blinked at him. "How did you know he was here?"

"I can smell him. What did he want?"

"He warned me you were dangerous, a killer, and tried to talk me out of marrying you."

A muscle twitched in his jaw. "Did he succeed?"

With a sigh, Leia closed the distance between them and sat on his lap. "What do you think?"

"I think I'm a fool for asking."

"I think you're right." She worried her lower lip between her teeth. "He said he was going to kill you when the time was right."

"Don't worry about it. He's not much of a threat to me, love. I'm pretty powerful, if I do say so myself. I know he's dedicated to his work. He's fairly good at it. And he enjoys it."

"But?"

"Old vampires don't have much to fear where most hunters are concerned. If you live as long as I have, it's not easy to sneak up on us."

Leia shuddered. How could anyone *enjoy* killing? "How does he...you know?"

"Vampires are pretty hard to kill," he said. "A wooden stake through the heart will do the trick. Fire. Beheading. They all work."

Leia grimaced, sorry she'd asked as grisly images flashed through her mind.

"Don't think about it," Rohan said. "I've lived this long, and now that I have you, I intend to live a lot longer." He kissed the tip of her nose. "And now I need to go out."

She forced a smile. Hunting was a part of him, not a part she particularly liked, but it went with the territory. She frowned as a new thought crossed her mind. When he drank from her, it was an amazingly erotic sensation unlike anything else. Did the women he fed on experience that same pleasure?

"You think of the darnedest things," Rohan muttered.

She felt a faint flush warm her cheeks. But she had to know. "Do they?"

"As a rule, no."

"As a rule? What does that mean?"

"It's up to me whether they do or they don't."

"And how do you decide?"

"Sometimes, if the woman is lonely, or sad, or grieving, I let a little of my power surround her. But it's not the same pleasure you feel. For them, it's more comforting than sensual."

Leia considered that a moment, then asked, "Do you drink from men, too?"

"Rarely." He kissed her again. "I really need to go. I won't be long."

She grinned when he went out the front door instead of just vanishing from her sight.

His bride-to-be asked the damnedest questions, Rohan mused as he prowled the shadowy darkness. One of the reasons he loved Leia was because she was like no other woman he had ever known. And after three hundred years, that was saying something. He loved the sweetness of her blood, the silk of her hair, the way she gave herself to him completely, nothing held back, the way she looked at him, kissed him, held him. The way she accepted him for what he was. God bless the girl. With Leia, he felt loved. Almost human again.

He fed on the first single woman he found, then strolled back toward Leia's apartment. He could have transported himself there in seconds but sometimes he enjoyed wandering through the night, feeling the velvet darkness close in around him, seeing things mortals never saw, hearing sounds they could not hear. The wind whispered her secrets in his ear, the moon's light revealed the beauty of the world around him.

Rohan's preternatural senses warned him he wasn't alone moments before his sire materialized beside him. "What do you want now?"

"I'm curious," Josiah said. "How did you get the woman to love you?"

"You want advice about love, call the lonely hearts editor."

Josiah snorted. "I've had dozens of lovers."

"Like Magdalena? Did you promise them forever, too, and then split?"

"She grew boring after a while. Always asking if I loved her, always wanting a bigger house, another dress, another trip. There was no pleasing her." Josiah shook his head. And then he grinned. "Who knows? Perhaps vampire love isn't meant to last more than a week or two."

"It's gonna last a hell of a lot longer than that if I have anything to say about it. And now, if you'll excuse me, I have a lovely woman waiting for me." Rohan didn't give his sire a chance to comment, simply willed himself to Leia's apartment.

She let out a little cry of surprise when he swung her up into his arms and carried her to bed. There was no time for talk. Their clothing disappeared in an instant. He took her swiftly, masterfully, needing to feel her arms around him, to hear her cry out that she loved him, would always love him.

Exhausted, she fell asleep in his arms. He stayed awake far into the night, just holding her close, listening to the soft, even beating of her heart, and knew, deep inside, that he would never let death take her away from him.

Chapter Twenty-Nine

In the morning, Leia spent several minutes admiring her future husband's physique while he slept. It was becoming a habit, she mused, but she never tired of looking at him. He slept on his back, one arm thrown across his chest, the other at his side. Sometimes she imagined him dancing around a campfire with other warriors in the middle of a Lakota village, or hunting buffalo on the Great Plains, And sometimes she imagined herself lying naked beside him on a pile of buffalo robes in a hide lodge. But none of her daydreams were as wonderful as the real thing.

Smiling, she kissed him lightly on the cheek, then slid out of bed. Grabbing her robe, she headed into the kitchen, only to come to an abrupt halt in the doorway. Dozens of colorful bouquets in sparkling crystal vases were lined up along the counter and on top of the refrigerator. A delicate vase holding a single red rose stood in the middle of the kitchen table. A white envelope and a small, black velvet box stood beside the vase.

With trembling hands, she opened the envelope and withdrew a small card.

Leia,
I hope the ring is to your liking. If not, we can go shopping later and you can pick one you like. I will love you for eternity.
Rohan

Leia took a deep breath before she lifted the lid on the velvet box. Inside, nestled in a bed of dark blue velvet, she found the most beautiful engagement ring she had ever seen.

"It must have cost a fortune," she murmured as she lifted it out of the box, turning it this way and that, dazzled by the way the diamonds sparkled in the light. Blinking back her tears, she tucked the ring back into the box and closed the lid. It was all she could do not to run into the bedroom and throw herself in Rohan's arms, but she hated to rouse him so early. If only she could make time move just a little faster!

Not wanting to disturb his rest, she tiptoed into the bedroom, grabbed her underwear, jeans, and a sweater, and dressed in the living room. Scooping up her handbag and her cell phone, she left the apartment.

In the car, she called her favorite hair dresser to see if she had any openings. Luck was with her. Barbara had had a cancellation and could see her in thirty minutes. Next, she called around until she found a place to have her nails done. Anything to make the day go faster, she thought, as she turned on the engine, backed out of her parking space and headed downtown.

Later, with her hair and nails done, she went to a matinee.

It was five o'clock when she returned home. She smiled as she picked up the little black velvet box and again admired the ring Rohan had chosen for her. He had exquisite taste, she mused, and couldn't wait to tell him so. Box in hand, she was about to head into the bedroom to wake him when he appeared in the kitchen clad in his usual black briefs and nothing more.

"Rohan!" she exclaimed, throwing her arms around his neck. "I love it!"

He hugged her tight. "Do you?"

"Yes!"

"Then why aren't you wearing it?"

"I wanted you to slip it on my finger."

Pleased, he lifted the engagement ring from the box, took her hand in his, and slid the diamond on her finger.

"It fits perfectly," she said, turning her hand from side to side. "But it must have cost a fortune."

"It isn't polite to ask the price. But if you think it's too much, I'll take it back."

Seeing the crestfallen expression on her face, he grinned at her. "I'm kidding, love. It's yours."

She kissed him then, thinking she had never been happier, or loved him more. She shivered as he ran his tongue along the side of her neck.

"A taste?" he whispered.

She didn't answer, just brushed her hair out of the way, sighing with pleasure as he carried her to bed. His bite was sometimes tender, sometimes quick, and sometimes, like now, arousing.

They were in the middle of making love when Rohan's cell phone rang. He ignored it and it stopped. Then it rang again. Muttering an oath, he snagged it from the bedside table. "What do you want?" He listened a moment, murmured, "I'll meet you there," and ended the call.

Leia watched his face, wondering who had been on the phone and why he looked so grim.

"What's wrong?" she asked as he dropped the phone on the bed.

"Magdalena's dead."

Leia blinked at him. It was hard to think clearly when all she wanted was for him to finish what he had started. And then she chided herself for thinking of her own pleasure when a woman was dead. "What happened?"

"A hunter found her."

"Do you think it was Trent?"

Rohan shrugged. "What difference does it make? She's just as dead." He stood and reached for his jeans. It was likely Trent, he mused. As far as he knew, Frumusanu was the only hunter in town.

"Where are you going?"

"That was Josiah on the phone. He wants my help."

"Now?" she asked, and hated the whine in her voice.

"He's my sire," Rohan replied, an edge in his voice. "When he calls, I have to go."

"What does he want you to do?"

"He didn't say, but if I had to guess, I'd say he wants me to dispose of what's left."

Leia clapped her hand over her mouth. Horrific images flashed across her mind as she recalled the gruesome ways to destroy a vampire.

Rohan pulled on his boots and a shirt, bent down, and kissed her lightly. "I won't be long," he promised, and was gone.

Magdalena's corpse lay face up in a shallow depression in a vacant lot, shielded from view by a six-foot hedge. A thick wooden stake had been driven deep into her heart, anchoring her to the earth. Her body had been partially burned. Dark-red blood stained the dirt around her.

Josiah stood next to the body, his expression implacable. He glanced over his shoulder as Rohan materialized beside him. "Bad way to go," he remarked tonelessly.

Rohan snorted. "Is there a good way for our kind?"

"I guess not."

"So, what am I doing here? It doesn't take two of us to dig a hole."

"I'm not familiar with this town. Do you know of any place where we can bury her so she won't be disturbed?"

Rohan stared at his sire, surprised by the barely suppressed emotion in his voice. "I thought you were bored with her. Sounds like you still care."

Josiah glared at him. "She didn't deserve to be dumped in a vacant lot like a dead cat."

"There's an old cemetery about thirty miles east of here. It hasn't been used in decades, maybe longer. I don't think any of the people buried there would mind a little company."

Josiah wrapped the body in a blanket. Rohan took hold of his shoulder and transported them to the cemetery. From the look of it, no one had been there in years. The headstones were broken, the graves sunken or covered with weeds.

Rohan led the way to the oldest grave. With his preternatural strength it took only moments to uncover the casket which was, surprisingly, still intact. Taking a deep breath, he lifted the lid, and grimaced at the remains.

Almost reverently, Josiah lowered Magdalena's body into the coffin.

Rohan closed the lid. "Did you know she wanted me to help her kill you?"

Josiah chuckled. "She was a feisty thing."

"Is that why you destroyed her?"

"What the hell are you talking about? I didn't do it. If I had, the body would never have been found."

Rohan hadn't yet refilled the grave. Now, he lifted the lid again, took a deep breath, and swore.

"What is it?" Josiah asked.

"I know who killed her."

Leia was sitting up in bed when Rohan appeared in the room. She looked at him anxiously, a dozen questions in her eyes.

"We buried her in an old cemetery," he said, removing his boots and socks, his shirt. "As you suspected, Trent killed her."

Leia stared at him. She didn't really know Magdalena yet she felt a wave of pity for the other woman. Josiah and Magdalena had been lovers. She wondered if Josiah would avenge her murder. "Is Trent in danger?"

"Probably. Josiah seemed upset by her death." Which surprised the hell out of him, Rohan mused. He wouldn't have credited his sire with any tender emotions. He shook his head as he stepped out of his jeans and slid into bed beside Leia. "There's no way I'm getting into the middle of any war between Frumusanu and Josiah."

"Think about Janae. She might get hurt. And what about her kids? They haven't done anything wrong."

Rohan cursed softly. Entanglements with humans were always complicated.

"At least warn him that Josiah might be coming after him."

"Fine. What's his number?" Rolling out of bed, Rohan pulled his phone from his pants' pocket and punched in the numbers Leia gave him. The phone rang twice and then Trent picked up. "Who is this?"

"Rohan."

There was a brief pause. "What the hell do you want?"

"You killed a woman tonight. Her ex-lover found the body. He's not too happy about it. I'd advise you to take your wife and kids and get out of town for a while."

"How do you know about him?"

"He's my sire, and one of the oldest vampires I know. He's pretty pissed off."

Another pause, longer this time. "Thanks for the warning," Trent said, and ended the call.

"It's been a hell of a night," Rohan muttered. Placing his phone on the bedside table, he slid back under the covers.

Leia nodded, disappointed that he hadn't taken her in his arms. But she couldn't really blame him, not after all that had happened.

"Now," he said, reaching for her. "Where did we leave off?"

Chapter Thirty

Leia pulled the covers over her head in an effort to shut out the persistent knocking on the front door, but it didn't go away.

Slipping out of bed, she pulled on her robe, shuffled into the living room and opened the door. "Janae! What are you doing here? It's not even six a.m."

"I just had to talk to someone."

Leia blinked, only then noticing how pale Janae's face was, the tears trickling down her cheeks. "Come on in. What's happened?"

Janae collapsed on the sofa and buried her face in her hands. "It's Trent," she sobbed. "He's a..." Shudders wracked her body.

"A what?" Leia asked, fearing she already knew the answer.

"A bounty hunter. He works for some international government alliance that hunts felons and turns them in for the reward, like some Old West lawman. Dead or alive," she exclaimed with a shiver. "I asked if he'd killed anyone and he refused to answer. You know that means yes. How am I supposed to live with that?"

"It's no different than being married to a cop," Leia said, hoping to calm her friend down. "They hunt bad guys and sometimes they're forced to shoot them. It doesn't make them bad people."

Fresh tears dripped down Janae's cheeks. "It gets worse. One of the bad guys is after him and is threatening me and the boys. Trent told me to take the kids and get out of town for a while." Janae shook her head violently, as if she could shake the threat away. "I still can't believe it! What are we going to do? I'm scared to death." She dashed the tears from her eyes. "What do *you* think I should do?"

"I agree with Trent. I think you should pack up the boys and leave town just as soon as you can. Maybe go stay with your parents in Oregon for a while."

"Maybe you're right. The boys would like that. I'm sorry I bothered you so early," Janae said, rising. "I'm probably overreacting, just like Trent said. But no one's ever threatened my life before." She sucked in a deep breath.. "Well, I'd better get going. I have a lot of packing to do."

"Keep in touch," Leia said, walking Janae to the door. "And try not to worry."

Janae forced a smile, then hurried down the porch stairs to the parking lot.

Leia stared after her, praying that her friend and the boys would be all right, that Josiah wouldn't kill Trent. Maybe Rohan could do something to protect the family. Yawning, she shuffled back to bed and crawled under the covers.

"Everything all right?" Rohan murmured.

"Go back to sleep," she said, snuggling against his side. "We can talk about it later."

He muttered something indistinguishable before the dark sleep carried him away.

Leia spent the morning torn between worrying about Janae and fighting off a bad case of nerves as she thought about introducing her parents to Rohan at the show that night. Sitting at the kitchen table, drinking one cup of coffee after another, she told herself Janae would be fine. She could stay with her mom and dad in Oregon until it was safe to come home again. As for her own parents, she could think of no reason why they wouldn't approve of Rohan.

She forced herself to eat a couple slices of buttered toast and then, needing something else to think about, she dressed and went to the store. There was a certain odd sort of peace in pushing her basket up and down the aisles, checking brands and prices, making choices that weren't life or death. She wondered what Rohan's last meal had been before he was turned, before blood became the only item on his diet. Did he ever yearn for anything else?

Standing in the check-out lane, she thought about her favorite foods. What if she could only eat one of them for the rest of her life? How long would it take before she couldn't stand the thought of eating one more slice of pizza or another plate of pasta?

She shook her head as she paid for her groceries and headed for her car, amused by her bizarre thoughts.

At home, Leia put her groceries away, then called Janae. She frowned when there was no answer. Had they left town already? Even if they had, it wouldn't keep Janae from answering her phone. She waited a few minutes, then tried again, with the same results.

Worried now, Leia got into her car and drove to Janae's house. Even before she knocked on the door, she knew there was no one home. Truly worried now, she drove back to her apartment, wondering if she should wake Rohan. Perhaps, with his supernatural senses, he could determine if Janae and the boys were all right.

Trent was waiting for her when she reached her apartment. She didn't invite him in.

"I just came by to tell you that I sent Janae and the boys to stay with her parents," he said. "She left late last night."

"Why isn't she answering her phone?"

"I bought her a new one and told her not to contact anyone but me. I don't know how powerful this vampire is but I don't want him to be able to find her." He shrugged. "Better to err on the side of caution and all that."

"What about you?"

"I'm staying in a hotel for a while." He shuffled from one foot to the other. "Anyway, I told Janae I'd let you know she's okay."

"Is she? Really?"

"No. But I can't tell her the truth or she'd really freak out." Trent laughed, but there was no humor in it. "She's talking about a divorce, said she doesn't want to be married to a man who hunts other men for a living. Imagine how she'd feel if she knew I was hunting vampires." He stared into the distance. "My father was a hunter, and his father before him. He warned me not to get married. I guess I should have listened." His eyes narrowed. "Are you still determined to marry that bloodsucker?"

Leia nodded.

Trent blew out a sigh. "I know I can't talk you out of it, so I won't even try. Just be careful."

"You, too."

Trent went down the stairs to his car and opened the door. He stared at her over the hood, then said, "Be careful.

Rohan's not the only vampire in town." With that final warning, he slid behind the wheel.

Leia felt a wave of pity for Trent as she watched him drive away. It occurred to her that hunters and vampires both had to hide what they were in order to survive. She shook the thought away. There was nothing she could do for Janae and Trent except pray that they would be able to work things out between them, that their family would be safe.

She had worries of her own, she thought, as she went into the kitchen and poured herself a glass of milk. Introducing her parents to Rohan. Last minute wedding details... She sighed. The wedding wouldn't be the same without her best friend, who was also supposed to be her matron of honor, but that wasn't possible now.

Needing a distraction, she carried the glass into the living room and picked up the novel she'd been reading. Settling on the sofa, she opened the book, hoping to lose herself in a good mystery for an hour or two.

Leia glanced in the bathroom mirror, smiling as Rohan came up behind her, slipped his arms around her waist, and nuzzled her neck. "So, tomorrow night's the big event, huh?"

She turned in his arms, closed her eyes as he lowered his head to kiss her.

"What if they don't like me?" he asked, still holding her close.

"I guess we'll have to call off the wedding."

"No chance, darlin'. I'll be on my best behavior, I promise."

"See that you are," She ran her fingertips down his bare chest. "Rohan?"

"Hmm?"

"What's going to happen to Janae?"

"What do you mean?"

"Trent told her a felon is out to kill him and sent her to stay with her parents for a while. Is she really in danger from Josiah?"

"I don't know, but it's probably a good thing Trent sent her away. As for Trent?" Rohan shook his head. "I think his days are numbered."

"Can't you do something? I mean, you can't just let Josiah kill him."

"Do you think Trent would hesitate to take Josiah's head—or mine—if he had the chance?"

Leia stared at him, too stunned by his answer to reply. And yet, she knew without a doubt that Trent wouldn't hesitate to kill either man. That was what hunters did—destroy vampires. But to do nothing to help Trent seemed so cold-blooded.

She sighed. There was nothing she could do about Janae at the moment. And right now, her major worry was introducing Rohan to her parents. Maybe she was worrying too much. After all, either her parents would like him or they wouldn't, she thought with a sigh.

Tomorrow night would tell the tale.

Rohan slid an admiring glance at Leia as they drove to the theater. She looked as pretty as a spring day in a dark pink sweater and a white skirt. She had been unusually quiet since they left her place. He didn't have to read her mind to know she was stressing out about introducing him to her parents and still worrying about her friend's safety.

It was twenty minutes to show time when he pulled into the theater parking lot.

"They're here," Leia said, pointing at her dad's car, a pale blue Subaru.

"Here are the tickets," Rohan said, passing her a white envelope. "I'll have to meet them after the show. I don't have time now."

"All right." Leaning over, she kissed his cheek. "Break a leg."

"I never understood why that meant good luck," he muttered, with a grin.

"Me, either." She kissed him again, then opened the door and exited the car. It would have been faster for him to transport them to the theater, but how then to explain the lack of a car to her parents? Smiling, she watched him park near the stage entrance and hurry inside.

Her parents were waiting for her in the lobby.

"Leia!"

"Hi, Dad," she said as he hugged her. "I'm so glad you could come."

"Can't wait to meet the man who seems to have stolen my daughter's heart."

"Me, either," agreed her mother, elbowing her husband aside so she could get a hug.

"I found a church!" Leia said, her voice laced with excitement. "I'll text you the details. Let's go sit down, shall we? Unless you'd rather get something to drink?"

"Later," her father said.

Leia led the way into the theater. As always, Rohan had secured front row center seats.

"How did you meet this guy?" her father asked when they were seated.

"At one of his shows. I was so mesmerized by his performance that I went to the stage door to get his autograph." She laughed. "Something I haven't done since I was a teenager."

"He must really be something," her mother remarked, "to have won your heart so quickly."

"You'll love him," Leia replied, and prayed that, if they didn't love him, they would at least like him. "I haven't heard from Luke in months. Have you?"

"He called last week," her father said. "He's in Spain working on some Marvel movie."

"And he's in love with a stunt woman," her mother added with a grin.

Leia's brows went up. "Really? What's her name?"

"Diana something. It sounds serious."

Before Leia could ask any more questions, the lights dimmed and Jay Deer Killer welcomed the audience to the show. He came on before each dancer to announce the name of the performer, and give a brief explanation of the dance.

Leia's heart began to pound in anticipation as Rohan's first number was announced. She sat forward, watching as intently as she had the first time she had seen him perform. As always, she was enthralled by his sinuous movements, the way he stamped his feet, the power and beauty of each intricate step.

Leaning closer, her mother whispered, "He really is marvelous, isn't he?"

Leia nodded, her gaze fixed on Rohan. He made love the way he danced, she mused with a secret smile.

The applause was thunderous when he took his bow. The other dancers seemed tame compared to Rohan. Not that they weren't terrific dancers in their own right, Leia thought. But Rohan put his whole heart and soul into every performance. She grinned inwardly, thinking the extra *zing* in his dancing was probably due to his being a vampire.

Her mother let out a sigh when the show ended. "I do believe I could watch that man dance all night."

"Stop drooling, Cynthia," her father admonished with a wry grin. "It's unbecoming in a woman your age."

"Hah! I saw the way you were looking at that Cheyenne girl. Talk about the pot calling the kettle black."

"Yeah, well…" Brian Winchester cleared his throat. "Let's go meet Mr. Wonderful."

As expected, there was a large crowd at the stage door. Leia and her parents stayed back.

"Liable to get trampled in the rush," her father muttered dryly.

Leia had eyes only for Rohan as he patiently signed programs and posed for dozens of selfies with young girls, teenagers, and grown women of all ages. Every now and then, he looked in her direction and shrugged. She grinned at him, knowing this was his least favorite part of the night. Once, she had asked him why he didn't like it and he'd replied that it was hard, being surrounded by so many beating hearts.

Finally, the last admirer drifted away and Rohan strode toward her. "Mom, Dad, this is Rohan. Rohan, this is my mother, Cynthia and my father, Brian."

"Pleased to meet you," Rohan said, shaking Winchester's hand.

"You were wonderful!" Cynthia gushed. "I've never seen anything so colorful and inspiring. I've seen Indians… or do you prefer Native American?"

"Indian is fine."

"As I was saying, I've seen Indians dance in movies, but this... Well, words fail me."

"I'm glad you enjoyed the show. Leia said something about going out for drinks."

"Sounds like a prime idea to me," Brian said. "We'll follow you."

Rohan opened the car door for Leia, then rounded the car and slid behind the wheel. "Your parents seem like nice people."

"Oh, they are. You wouldn't think my mother would be the type to be star-struck," Leia said. "I mean, she rubs elbows with famous movie stars all the time."

"Well, I'm glad she enjoyed the show."

"She'll be talking about it for weeks."

Ten minutes later, they pulled into the nightclub parking lot. Her parents pulled into the slot beside them.

Cynthia took Leia's arm as they walked toward the entrance. "He's even more handsome than you said," her mother whispered. "He's like Redford and Newman and Harrison Ford all rolled into one."

"He's sexier than all three," Leia said, laughing.

Inside, a hostess led them to a table. Five minutes later, a waiter came to take their order.

"How long are you staying in town, Mr. Winchester?" Rohan asked.

"We're leaving in the morning. And since you're almost family, you might as well call me Brian."

"In the morning?" Leia asked. "I thought you had some time off?"

"I did," her father said, "but I got a call late last night. One of the security guards at the studio took sick and I'm taking his place for a few days."

"But we'll have to get together again real soon," Cynthia said, smiling at Rohan.

"Well, you made a hit with my Mom," Leia remarked later that night, at home.

Rohan shrugged.

"I think my Dad likes you, too."

"He seems like a solid guy." *And suspicious as hell*, Rohan thought.

"I can't wait for you to meet my brother." Leia kicked off her heels and ran her fingers through her hair. "I haven't seen him in months." Smiling at Rohan, she said, "You were wonderful tonight."

"Thanks, love. I danced my heart out just for you." He groaned dramatically. "I could use a back rub."

She quirked a brow at him. "Is this your sneaky way of getting me into bed?"

"Did anyone ever tell you that you've got a suspicious mind?"

She made a face at him. "If all you want is a back rub, stretch out on the sofa."

"The bed's more comfortable," he said with a wicked grin.

With a long-suffering sigh, she took his hand and led him into the bedroom. "Can you undress yourself, or do you need help?"

Stifling a laugh, Rohan said, "Help is always welcome."

With a shake of her head, she removed his shirt, his belt, unfastened his trousers. "Shoes," she said, pointing at his feet.

Obligingly, he toed off his boots, his fingers threading through her hair as he stepped out of his pants and sat on the edge of the bed.

Leia removed his socks and tossed them aside. "Lay down." He stretched out on his back on the mattress. Lord, he was gorgeous, she thought, every fiber of her being eager to touch him, to hold him and never let him go.

He smiled a knowing smile when his eyes met hers.

Leia fisted her hands on her hips, her brows raised. "I thought you wanted a *back* rub?"

"Well, my front could use a massage, too."

"You're incorrigible," she muttered as she stepped out of her skirt, peeled off her sweater and removed her underwear. "This is going to cost you," she warned as she stretched out beside him.

"Name your price," he said, his voice whiskey-rough with desire. "Everything I have is yours."

Chapter Thirty-One

"What did you think of our future son-in-law?" Brian asked as they got ready for bed that night.

"He seems very nice. He's quite charming, and it's obvious that he's crazy about Leia. Did you see her engagement ring? I'll bet it cost more than our first house."

"Yeah."

"What's wrong?" Cynthia asked, laying her hair brush aside. "Didn't you like him?"

"He's hiding something."

"What do you mean?"

"I'm not sure, but I can feel it. There's something just a little off about him." When Cynthia looked skeptical, he said, "I was a cop for over twenty-five years, Cyn. I know when someone is hiding something. I'm going to make a few calls tomorrow, ask Chet Wilkins at the Hollywood Station to do a background check on him."

"I hope you're wrong," Cynthia said. "If he's got nothing to hide and Leia finds out what you're doing, she'll never forgive you."

He snorted. "If it turns out he's a serial killer, I think she'll thank me."

"And if he isn't?"

Brian shrugged. "Better safe than sorry, my old sergeant used to say. Doesn't it strike you as odd that she's never mentioned him before and now, all of a sudden, they're getting married?" He shook his head. "I hope I'm wrong, but it won't hurt to do a little digging into his past."

Chapter Thirty-Two

Rohan left Leia's apartment and went for a walk shortly after she'd fallen asleep. He had a lot on his mind. His biggest concern was for Trent's safety, with Josiah a close second, and Leia's father a distant third.

He supposed he could let Trent and Josiah fight it out. That would be one less hunter to worry about, because if it came to a fight, Trent didn't stand a chance. Vampires grew stronger as they aged and Josiah had the strength of hundreds of years. Trent might have a slight advantage if he could catch Josiah at rest, but even then, it would be negligible. Even at rest, vampires could sense when they were in danger.

As for Leia's father... He shook his head. He had to give the man points for being suspicious as hell about him. Not many humans sensed that he was different, but Brian Winchester knew something was off. Rohan wondered briefly if any of Winchester's kin had been hunters in days gone by. Not that it mattered. If Leia's father got too nosey or too suspicious, Rohan would simply erase the doubts from his mind.

He had just dined on a lovely young female when Josiah materialized beside him. "I was hoping you'd left town," Rohan muttered as his sire fell into step beside him.

"You're never going to forgive me for turning you, are you?" Josiah remarked, seeming surprised.

"Probably not."

"Has your life as a vampire been so bad? Would you rather have spent the last three hundred years rotting in a grave"

"That's not the point," Rohan said curtly.

"What is?"

"I guess mainly I'm angry because it wasn't a life I'd chose."

"And if I'd given you a choice, what would you have said?"

Rohan frowned. What *would* he have said?

In a move too fast for even Rohan to follow, Josiah sank his fangs into Rohan's throat. Speaking to Rohan's mind, he said, *I'm giving you a choice now, vampire. Life or death?*

It's not the same thing, Rohan retorted.

Yes, it is. What will it be? Life or death?

"Life," Rohan said, his voice heavily laced with anger. "As you knew it would be."

Lifting his head, Josiah licked his lips. "You would have made the same decision if I'd asked you back then."

"How can you know that?"

"Because you're a survivor, like me."

Rohan snorted.

And Josiah laughed. "It's true, whether you like it or not. So, your friend, Trent, sent his family away," he said with disdain. "As if I couldn't find them."

"Leave them alone," Rohan snapped. "I don't care what you do to Frumusanu, but his wife and kids are off limits. She's Leia's best friend."

"Human entanglements are never a good idea," Josiah remarked with a shrug. "And what I do is none of your business." Slapping Rohan on the back, he said, "Thanks for the drink," and vanished from sight.

Rohan stood there for a moment, thinking about what Josiah had said. His sire was right, he thought. Given the choice all those hundreds of years ago, he would have chosen life. And it would have been the right choice, he mused. Had he chosen death, he would never have met Leia. Whistling softly, he willed himself home.

The days flew by. Leia spent most of her time getting ready for the wedding. She ordered a small cake, worrying and wondering how they'd explain why the groom didn't eat any. She also picked up a bottle of wine and some champagne. She ordered flowers for herself, her bridesmaid, her mother, and the church altar, boutonnieres for her father, Rohan, and Trent.

She went to the theater with Rohan Friday night. She never tired of watching him dance. She noticed the applause was always longer and louder for him. He never said much about performing. She guessed he must enjoy it or he'd quit. She tried to imagine what it would be like to be admired by hundreds, maybe thousands, of people.

On Saturday, she checked in with her friends from school to make sure they were ready. She had called Rosemary earlier and asked her to be her matron of honor, since Janae couldn't be there.

Sunday morning she got up early and went to church, feeling guilty because she hadn't gone for such a long time. She almost laughed out loud when the minister announced the topic of his sermon was accepting those among us who were different.

When she got home, Leia called her mom and dad just to say hi. Both seemed a little reserved, leaving her to her wonder what was wrong.

Later, she sat on the sofa and turned on the TV. A hundred channels, she mused, and not a single thing she wanted to watch. She finally settled on an old Western...

The wagon train stopped for the night when the sun started to go down. Leia climbed down from the seat, one hand massaging her sore back. Some of the men went hunting, returning with a deer, which was split between the five families who were heading West to Colorado. She was traveling with a family she didn't know. For some reason, it seemed perfectly normal.

It was almost dark when the Indians attacked. It happened so fast, she saw everything in quick glimpses—painted warriors armed with bows and arrows or rifles. Confusion reigned. Men fought. Women screamed. Children cried and hid their faces. The scent of gun powder and blood hung heavy in the air. It was over in moments. The men had all been killed, the women and children taken captive.

Leia trembled with fear as one of the warriors lifted her onto his horse and then swung up behind her. His name was Shadow Dancer. She didn't know how she knew that, or why he seemed familiar. They rode until well after dark, then made camp along a shallow river. Shadow Dancer lifted her from the back of his horse, letting her body slide intimately against his own as he set her on her feet.

Later, after everyone had eaten, he spread a blanket on the ground away from all the others and gestured for her to lay down. Her fear left her when he stretched out beside her and drew her into his arms.

"Who are you?" she asked. "Why do you seem so familiar?"

"We have met before," he said, lightly stroking her hair. "We will meet again."

A shiver of excitement danced down her spine as he undressed her, removed his breechclout, and rose over her, a tall, handsome man with ebony hair and midnight eyes. He whispered to her, telling her not to be afraid. She cried his name as she lifted her hips to receive him, sobbed with pleasure as he possessed her...

Leia woke abruptly to find Rohan standing beside the sofa, gazing down at her. "Did you do that?" she asked, sitting up.

"Do what?"

"Put those images in my mind?"

He shook his head as he dropped down beside her. "Your cry woke me. What were you dreaming about?"

"The Old West. I was on a wagon train and you and some other warriors attacked us. You carried me away. You said we'd met before and would meet again. And then you made love to me."

He grunted softly. "Sorry I missed it."

"What do you think it means?" she asked, looking troubled.

"It was just a dream, darlin'. I'm not sure it means anything."

"Do you believe in reincarnation?"

"No." He put his arm around her shoulders and gave her a squeeze. "Do you?"

"I didn't, but now I'm not so sure. It all seemed so right, so familiar. I felt like I was really there, that I had seen it all before."

He grinned as her stomach growled. "Why don't you get something to eat while I shower and get dressed?"

Her gaze ran over him, openly admiring his broad shoulders and long legs. She loved everything about him—his scent, his touch, the sound of his voice, the tenderness she heard when he whispered her name, the way he looked at her, the masterful way he made love to her, branding her his. She was sure there were some women who would find that offensive, but she gloried in his possession. It made her feel loved, cherished, protected.

She slid her fingertips down his arm. "It seems a shame to cover up that gorgeous body."

His laughter filled the room. "You can take my briefs off later, but right now, you need to get something to eat. And so do I. Meet you back here in an hour."

With a sigh, Leia shuffled into the kitchen. She hadn't been to the store recently and her choices for dinner were few. She settled on breakfast for dinner—French toast, bacon, and a glass of milk. She watched the news as she ate, but found her mind wandering to Janae. She wondered if Trent would give her Janae's phone number, or at least let her call Janae on his phone. She couldn't help worrying about her friend and the boys. Problem was, she didn't have Trent's phone number.

She cleared the table, loaded the dishes into the dishwasher, and put the pans in the sink to soak. As often happened when there was food around, she found herself thinking about Rohan. What would happen if he ate a hamburger or a slice of pizza, or drank a Coke?

"I'd be violently ill," he said, coming up behind her. "My body can no longer process mortal food."

She turned in his arms and linked her hands behind his neck. "Have you tried?"

He nodded. "Soon after I was turned." He recalled the incident all too clearly. He'd been with a lovely young thing in Italy when she offered him a bite of lasagna. Foolishly, he had taken it. Minutes later, he'd fled the restaurant and been violently ill for two days. He's sworn never again then and there.

"Maybe it would be different now."

He grunted softly. "Maybe. But it's not a risk I'm willing to take."

"That bad, huh?"

He shuddered with the memory. "You have no idea."

"What are we going to tell my parents when we cut the cake and you don't eat any?"

"Just tell them I'm allergic to eggs or whatever else cake is made of."

"I guess that would work. You weren't gone very long."

"I couldn't wait for you to undress me," Rohan said with a sly grin. "Have you ever made love on a kitchen table?"

"No. Have you?"

"No. It'll be a first for both of us."

Leia glanced at the table, which was round and made of solid oak. "Sounds uncomfortable."

"You can be on top."

Laughing, she began to undress him, only to pause when she saw the bite mark on his neck. "It's not healing," she remarked, everything else momentarily forgotten. "It's black and blue around the edges."

Rohan ran his fingers over the ragged wound Josiah's bite had left behind. It was about an inch wide and just as deep. During performances, he'd had to cover it with stage make-up. Occasionally, it hurt like hell.

Leia shook her head. "It looks bad."

"Forget about it," he growled.

She would have argued, but when he whisked away their clothing, he somehow managed to whisk away her concern as well.

With Rohan on the bottom, she discovered that making love on a table wasn't bad at all.

Chapter Thirty-Three

Leia had intended to go lingerie shopping first thing Monday morning, but after making love to Rohan until the wee small hours of the morning, she got a rather late start. By the time she left the apartment, it was almost one when she reached the mall.

There were so many lovely nightgowns to choose from, so many styles and fabrics—long and slinky, short and sexy, silk and satin and nylon. Nighties that hid nothing at all, others made of soft flannel that hid everything.

It took her a while to choose. Even though she was no longer virginal, she picked out a long, filmy white gown for her wedding night, a sexy black satin one with a provocative slit on the side, and a hot-pink baby doll set. She bought slippers to match each nightie. She also bought a robe, as well as a very sexy bra and matching bikini panties.

After paying for her things, she wandered into the Ladies' Department and spent an hour trying on dresses but couldn't find anything she really liked.

Her next stop was the food court where she bought a decadent chocolate doughnut and a pint of milk. How did Rohan live without chocolate? she wondered. But then, a love for chocolate seemed to be more of a female thing.

She had to pass through the Men's Department on the way to the parking garage. She paused in the underwear aisle. Rohan tended to wear a lot of black, she mused, as she looked at the briefs. Grinning inwardly, she bought him several pairs to match her nightgowns—a couple pairs of skimpy black briefs, a pair of white ones, and a pair in hot-pink.

Pleased with her purchases, she left the store, surprised to see that the sun was low in the sky. She hadn't realized she'd been in the mall for so long.

Leia had just put her shopping bags in the trunk and closed the lid when she had the uneasy feeling she was being watched. Suddenly wary, she glanced over her shoulder, felt a trickle of alarm when she saw a tall man with brown hair standing a few feet from her car. She tried to look away and found that she couldn't draw her gaze from his, nor could she move.

Fear sent a cold chill racing down her spine as he strode toward her. She recognized him then. It was the man who had been sitting behind her during two of Rohan's performances in San Diego. The vampire who had turned him. *Josiah.*

"Leia, how nice to see you again." His voice was without inflection.

She shivered violently as the wintry chill running down her spine turned to ice. "What do ... do you want?"

"I merely wished to meet the woman who has stolen my fledgling's heart." Lifting his hand, he stroked his long, narrow fingers lightly over her cheek and down the length of her neck. "I wonder," he mused. "Are you as tasty as you are lovely?"

Leia's gaze darted wildly from side to side, desperately hoping to find help, but the parking garage was empty save for the two of them.

Her fear turned to horror when his hands folded over her shoulders, his nails digging painfully into her flesh. He smiled wolfishly as he leaned forward, his tongue laving the soft skin below her ear. *Oh, Lord,* she thought. *He's going to bite me.*

The thought had no sooner crossed her mind than she felt the sharp prick of his fangs at her throat. There was no pleasure in his bite, merely a sharp pain that was quickly over.

The vampire licked her blood from his lips. "I can see why Rohan is so entranced with you," he remarked. "I haven't had a human companion in decades. Perhaps you and I…"

She never knew what he'd been about to say. One minute they were alone, the next Rohan was there.

Fangs bared, he stepped between her and Josiah. "What the hell do you think you're doing?" he snarled.

Josiah lifted one shoulder in a negligent shrug. "Merely taking a taste. Surely you don't object?" he said, his voice thick with warning.

Leia bit down on her lower lip as the tension between the two vampires grew palpable.

"She's mine, damn you!" Rohan growled. "Back off."

Leia felt the power around Josiah grow stronger. It raised the hair along her arms and made her stomach churn.

"I'm your sire," Josiah said. "Surely you remember that what is yours is also mine?"

"Go to hell."

"Are you willing to fight me for her?"

Rohan nodded curtly. "Right here. Right now."

Josiah glanced around. "Alas," he said, with a wry grin. "We are no longer alone. Perhaps another time, in another place."

Leia blinked and Josiah was gone. She gasped as all the strength went out of her legs. She would have fallen if

Rohan hadn't quickly turned and threw his arms around her. The next thing she knew, they were in her apartment.

She sagged in his arms.

"Shh, love, it's all right now," he whispered.

"He...he wanted me...to be his...his companion."

"No way in hell," Rohan said, and then swore a crude oath. "He bit you! Dammit, I'll kill him for that." Cradling her in his embrace, he sat on the sofa and rocked her back and forth until her trembling ceased.

"My car..." Leia said.

"I'll get it later. Right now, you could use a drink." He settled her in a corner of the sofa, covered her with a throw, and went into the kitchen but found nothing stronger than soda. A thought took him to the nearest liquor store where he bought a bottle of port wine. He was back in the apartment before she knew he'd been gone. In the kitchen, he poured a glass of port, then carried it out to her. "Here, love, drink this."

She sipped it slowly, then frowned. "Where did you get this? I don't remember having any wine in the apartment."

He shrugged. "I made a quick trip to the liquor store."

"You're so thoughtful," she murmured, leaning against him.

"Drink it all, love."

She did as he asked, sighed as a delightful warmth spread through her. "His bite wasn't as nice as yours," she murmured, her eyelids fluttering down as he spoke to her mind, willing her to sleep.

Rohan held her close, his hatred for his sire swelling within him. There was an unwritten law that vampires did not prey on humans who had been claimed by another. He swore again. "All that crap about what's mine is his," he growled, "I don't think so. Not by a long shot."

He stretched out of the sofa, content to hold Leia close to his side.

Sometime later, Leia woke to find herself alone on the sofa. She glanced around the room but there was no sign of Rohan. No doubt he had gone hunting

Sitting up, she lifted a hand to her neck, felt a wave of revulsion as she remembered Josiah biting her, drinking her blood. She had felt violated, unclean. Something she had never felt with Rohan. She had never been so frightened in her whole life. One thing for certain—Rohan's sire was scary with a capital S.

What if Josiah came after her? She knew Rohan would fight for her, but could he win? Josiah was older, therefore stronger, according to what Rohan had told her. And like Rohan, Josiah could be awake during the day.

She put the troubling thought out of her mind. They were getting married in a few days. Rohan needed a tux. She needed to rent a hotel room for her parents. So much to do, she thought. So little time to do it. She shouldn't have left everything until the last minute

Slipping off the sofa, she went into the bathroom to shower, hoping she could scrub away the memory of Josiah's vile touch. She was drying off when her cell phone rang. Wrapped in a towel, she dashed into the living room and scooped it up. "Hi, Dad."

"You sound out of breath," Brian Winchester said. "Are you all right?"

"Of course I am. What's up?"

"What are you doing?"

"I just got out of the shower."

"We need to talk."

The words poured over her like ice water. "Is something wrong? Is Mom all right? Luke?"

"They're both fine," he said, curtly. "Get dressed. I'm waiting out front."

Leia's hands were trembling as she pulled on a pair of jeans and a sweater, stepped into a pair of sandals. Her father had sounded so serious, all she could think was that something terrible had happened to her mom, or maybe her brother, and he didn't want to tell her the bad news over the phone.

She found her father parked in front of her apartment. She took a deep breath as she opened the passenger door and settled into the seat. "What's going on?"

Her father put the car in drive and pulled out of the apartment complex and into the street.

"Dad, you're scaring me."

He drove for another few minutes. Leia's heart was pounding when he pulled up in front of the small park located not far from her apartment building. He switched off the engine, then turned in his seat to face her. "What do you know about this guy, Rohan?"

Leia frowned. "All I need to know. Why?"

"I had a friend of mine do a background check on him." He held up his hand when he saw the protest in her eyes. "He checked the DMV records, birth records, voting records and LAPD's database. All Rohan's information is fake. Date of birth, parents' names, social security number, driver's license. There are no records of anyone known as Shadow Dancer, or Rohan Stillwater."

Leia blinked at him. In the back of her mind, she heard Rohan's voice telling her the police didn't even know he existed. Apparently, neither did anyone else. It wasn't surprising, she thought. He'd been born over three hundred years ago in an Indian village. It was likely that even Rohan didn't know the exact year or date of his birth. Still, in this day and age, it was hard to believe even a vampire could stay under the radar. How did he get a driver's license, credit cards? And then she frowned. She didn't know if he had a license. She'd never seen him use a credit card. Only cash.

"You can't marry him," her father said flatly. "For all you know, he could be a serial killer, a rapist, who the hell knows what else. I'm taking you home with me."

"But..."

"There is no but," Brian said as he put the car in gear. "I'm taking you home now."

"This is kidnapping, you know," Leia muttered irritably.

"So have me arrested," her father retorted. "I'd happily go to jail to keep you from marrying that man until I know who he really is, and what he's after."

It wasn't *who* Rohan was that had her worried, Leia thought. But *what* he was. There was just no way to explain that he was a vampire, let alone expect her parents to believe it. Or accept it.

Josiah grinned as he dissolved into mist and followed the blue Subaru. He had been determined to have the woman since that first taste only hours ago, and this seemed as good a time as any to take her and make her his.

Trent swore under his breath as he watched the vampire disappear. Dammit all to hell! He'd been so close to taking the bloodsucker's head and now the chance was gone. Who knew when he'd get another?

He frowned as he got into his car and pulled out of the park behind the blue Subaru, curious to know where Leia was going and who she was with. It sure as hell wasn't Rohan.

Trent took a deep breath and let it out in a long, slow sigh. What difference did it make who Leia was with? His whole world was falling apart. Janae was threatening to divorce him if he didn't quit his job. They'd had a hell of a fight, with her screaming that she couldn't live with a man who made his living killing other men. He should have lied when she asked if he'd ever killed anyone. Instead, he'd refused to answer and that had just made it worse. He had been sorely tempted to tell her the truth—which was, of course, forbidden—and in her current state of mind, it probably would have sent her over the edge. When she locked him out of the bedroom, he gave in and promised to quit, but only after he'd finished his current assignment, which meant destroying Rohan and his sire, no matter how long it took.

He swore long and loud. He was angry and frustrated with the day's events. And horny as hell.

Sensing Leia's anxiety, Rohan released his prey from his thrall and willed himself back to Leia's apartment. He stood in the middle of the living room, every sense on alert. Leia had left the apartment a short time ago and she had been upset at the time, though he couldn't determine why. Lifting his head, he closed his eyes, his senses moving outward from the apartment.

Her father had been here.

What the hell?. Why had Winchester spirited his daughter away?

He considered a moment, then grunted. He'd been well aware of Winchester's suspicions, but that was to be expected. The man had been a detective for over twenty-five years. Being suspicious was second nature. A deep dive into his identity probably set off a lot of alarm bells in Winchester's mind.

As soon as he stepped out of the apartment, he caught the lingering scents of both Josiah and Frumusanu.

Muttering an oath, he opened the blood link between himself and Leia.

Chapter Thirty-Four

Leia paced the floor of her old bedroom, her irritation rising with every step. What right did her father have to interfere in her life? She was a grown woman, for goodness sakes, not a child. She didn't need her father to make decisions for her.

She glanced at the big old oak tree outside her window. She had often used it to sneak out of the house when she was a teenager. Why not now? She eased the window open and slipped out. It was an easy climb to the ground. Once she was away from the house, she would call Rohan to come and get her.

She had just reached the edge of the side yard when Josiah materialized in front of her.

"Well, well, well," he drawled as his hand closed firmly over her forearm. "I was wondering how to get you outside and here you are."

"Let me go!" she shrieked.

"I don't think so."

Heart pounding with fear, Leia opened her mouth to scream. And the world went black.

Rohan muttered an oath as the link between himself and Leia was abruptly cut-off. He froze in mid-stride. Both his sire and a hunter had been on her trail. Either one could have knocked her unconscious. Or killed her. Those were the only two things that could keep him from contacting her.

For a moment, fear held him immobile. And then he followed the blood link that bound them together, until it, too, disappeared. What the hell? How was that even possible?

Rohan glanced at the large white house where she should have been, but she wasn't inside. He was about to knock on the front door when Trent Frumusanu pulled into the driveway and stepped out of the car.

"What the hell are you doing here?" Rohan growled.

"Looking for Leia. I've been following her. I was at her house earlier and just missed the best chance I've had yet to take Josiah's head. She drove away in a blue Subaru with a man I guessed is her father. I figured she'd be here."

"She isn't. Josiah's got her."

"The hell you say!"

"That's not the worst of it. I can't connect with her." Rohan didn't want to think about what that might mean. He tried to connect with Josiah but to no avail. The link between them had been closed.

Rohan glanced at the house as the front door opened and Brian Winchester stepped out on the verandah, a revolver in his hand.

"Get the hell off my property, Stillwater, or whoever you are. My daughter's not marrying you."

"Your daughter's gone," Rohan growled.

Winchester snorted. "She's in her room."

Rohan shook his head. "Not anymore."

With a frown, Winchester went back into the house. He returned mere moments later, his brow furrowed. "Where did you take her?"

"I didn't take her anywhere." Damn, he was wasting time standing here, yet he was at a loss to know what to do next. He was helpless if he couldn't connect with her. She could be scared, in pain, and he'd never know it. She had to be with Josiah, he thought. That was the only answer that made sense. It filled him with a cold sense of dread.

Winchester stared at the man standing beside Rohan. "Who the hell are you?"

Trent glanced at Rohan. "Should I tell him the truth?"

"Not if you want to see tomorrow."

"I'm Trent Frumusanu. My wife is a friend of Leia's."

Winchester looked at Rohan again. "Dammit, where's my daughter?"

"If I knew, I wouldn't be here."

Winchester's eyes narrowed ominously as his finger curled around the trigger. "I'll give you just three seconds to tell me where she is."

Rohan sucked in a breath. The man wasn't bluffing.

Just then, Cynthia pushed the screen door open, hitting her husband's shoulder.

Inadvertently, Winchester squeezed the trigger.

Rohan reeled back as the slug slammed into his chest, just above his heart.

Trent swore.

Cynthia screamed.

Winchester's face went white as he realized what he'd done, and whiter still when Rohan remained standing, apparently unhurt. "What the hell? Cynthia, get in the house!"

Looking like she was about to faint, she ducked inside and slammed the front door.

Rohan looked down at the dark, red stain spreading across his shirtfront and then, in a move too fast for either man to follow, he sprinted forward and snatched the pistol from Winchester's hand.

Winchester stared at him. "What the... who the hell are you?"

Rohan shook his head. Leia's father was either the bravest man he'd ever met, or a complete idiot. "You should have used silver bullets," he drawled as he bent the barrel of the gun in half and dropped the weapon at Winchester's feet.

Winchester blinked at him. "Who do you think I am, the Lone Ranger?" His eyes narrowed. "Vampire." He hissed the word. "I should have known. When I was a rookie cop back in the day, L.A. was plagued by a serial killer. The press nicknamed him *The Vampire Killer* because he drained his victims of blood..." He took a deep breath. "It was you, wasn't it?"

"Don't be any more of a fool that you already are," Rohan muttered. "It was Josiah."

"Who the hell is that?" Winchester asked.

"He's an old, old vampire who happens to be my sire."

Winchester frowned. "What in tarnation does that mean?"

"I'll give you a lesson in vampire lore some other day," Rohan said curtly. "We're wasting time here." Pulling off his shirt, he used it to wipe the blood from his chest before dropping it beside the pistol.

After a moment, he walked around to the side of the house. Winchester and Trent trailed behind him.

Lifting his head, Rohan scented the air. Leia had been here not long ago. And so had his sire. It was obvious that Josiah had taken Leia and transported the two of them out of the area, leaving no trace and no trail to follow. Dammit! If he couldn't connect with her, if he couldn't follow the blood link that bound them together, he might never see her again.

Damn and double damn, he had to find her before it was eternally too late. The thought of never seeing her again was unthinkable. He forced down the rage pulsing inside him. He needed to stay calm, to think clearly. He needed to find her, because without her, life wouldn't be worth living.

"What now?" Winchester asked, his voice rock-steady.

The old man must have been one hell of a cop, Rohan mused. He winced as his injury began to heal, leaving no trace behind.

He heard Trent mutter, "I guess the stories about vampires healing rapidly are true."

"So it seems," Rohan said. "Winchester, go look after your wife."

"My wife's fine! What the devil are you going to do about finding my daughter, you damn, dirty bloodsucker?"

"Everything I can. Now go inside before I break your fool neck."

Brian Winchester glared at him, but wisely turned around and made his way back toward the front of the house.

Rohan shook his head as he heard Winchester bolt the front door. As if a lock could keep him out, he thought, as he glanced at Frumusanu. "You wanna take a shot at me, too?"

"Not right now," Trent replied with a wry grin.

"Smart man," Rohan muttered.

"How are you going to find Leia?"

"I don't know." Dammit, in three hundred years, he'd never felt this helpless.

"I'd like to lend a hand."

Rohan snorted. "As if I'd trust you."

"I don't trust you, either," Trent retorted. "But maybe we could have a temporary truce?"

"I thought you were itching to take my head?"

"Yeah, well." Frumusanu shrugged. "I'm not doing it for you. Leia is Janae's best friend. I'd hate to see anything happen to her."

Rohan lifted a skeptical brow "But?"

"Janae threatened to leave me if I don't give up hunting."

"Isn't that supposed to be a secret?"

"I didn't tell her I was hunting vampires, just collecting bounties on ordinary people. She thinks it's wrong. Now, about that truce…"

Rohan thought it over and then said, "What the hell, it's a deal. At least until we find Leia."

Trent nodded and held out his hand. "Truce."

Rohan stared at the hunter's hand, then shook it. "Truce."

"So, where do we start?"

Rohan shook his head. "Beats the hell out of me. Just one thing—when we find Josiah, I'll kill him. You can collect the reward."

Chapter Thirty-Five

Leia might have thought she was in hell if she wasn't so cold. She couldn't see anything but blackness, hear anything but her own rapid breathing. Worst of all, she couldn't move. Was she tied down? Paralyzed? Dead? Where was Rohan?

She froze when she heard scratches on the floor. Rats?

With a sob, she closed her eyes and tried to pray but she couldn't speak, couldn't think coherently.

Rohan. Rohan. Rohan. In her mind, she screamed his name. But there was no answer. Had he abandoned her?

Her eyes flew open as light flared. Afraid to look for fear of what she might see, she squeezed her eyes shut again. And heard coarse laughter.

"Wake up, sleeping beauty," urged a familiar voice. "I feel like a snack."

She shuddered at the sound of Josiah's voice. In the faint light, she saw that she was tied to a bed in a small, dark room made of concrete. There were no windows, no furniture other than the hard cot beneath her.

Josiah stood beside her, his lips parted in a wolfish grin that revealed gleaming, white fangs. In a sudden move, he was bending over her, his fangs at her throat.

Please, she prayed. *Please let me die.*

Lifting his head, the vampire shook his head. "No death for you, girl, at least not the kind you want."

Leia stared at him. "Wh...what do you mean?"

He licked her blood from his lips. "There's death," he said, with a wolfish grin. "And then there's death."

Her eyes grew wide as she grasped the meaning of his words.

"I'll give you the same choice I gave Rohan. Life or death? It's up to you."

I'm dreaming, she thought. *Having a nightmare. I'll wake up in Rohan's arms soon and we'll have a good laugh.*

But she wasn't dreaming. There was no pain in dreams, she thought, as Josiah sank his fangs into her throat once again.

She must have fallen asleep or passed out, because the next time she woke, she was alone. A small candle provided a modicum of light. Best of all, she was no longer tied to the bed. Sitting up, she saw a wooden tray on a stool. Her mouth watered at the scent of fresh coffee.

She rose stiffly and walked toward the tray where a cup of coffee waited, along with a tuna fish sandwich, a small bag of potato chips, and a banana.

Ravenous, she gobbled down the sandwich, took a breath, and ate the chips and the banana. She saved the coffee for last. It was lukewarm and black. She preferred hers with sugar and cream, but she was in no position to be picky.

With her hunger assuaged, Josiah's proposition jumped to the forefront of her mind. *Life or death?* How did anyone make a choice like that? she wondered. Josiah said he'd given Rohan the same choice. Rohan had obviously chosen life as a vampire. But that wasn't really life, was it? Just a different kind of death. One she didn't want to think about it.

Was it day or night? How long had she been here? Was Rohan looking for her? If so, why couldn't he find her? He always had before. Why was this different? What if he'd stopped looking? Her parents must be frantic, wondering where she was, if she was dead or alive. She would never see them again, she thought sadly, no matter what choice she made. They would never accept having a vampire for a daughter. She remembered Rohan saying he'd had no control over his hunger when he was first turned. Would she prey on her own parents?

Lost in a mire of despair, she threw herself on the cot and cried herself to sleep.

Rohan stalked the night, his fear for Leia like a living thing inside him, clawing at his vitals as one day turned into two. Where the hell was she and why couldn't he find her? He had known Josiah was powerful, but he'd never known a vampire who could block a blood bond between vampire and mortal. He refused to admit she might be dead. Why would Josiah kill her?

He came to an abrupt stop as a new thought crossed his mind. What if his sire had turned her? As Josiah's fledgling, the blood bond between Leia and himself would be destroyed, replaced by the new bond of fledgling and sire.

The idea that she might have been turned by Josiah was beyond bearing. He groaned deep inside. *Not that*, he thought desperately. *Never that.*

Once again tied to the bed, Leia stared at the ceiling. Was it day or night? And why did Josiah insist on tying her up? Even if she were free, she couldn't escape. She didn't even know where she was, although she had the feeling she was deep underground. No sound penetrated the room. The air was cold and damp, musty. There were no windows, no door that she could see. Tears leaked from her eyes and she couldn't wipe them away.

Life or death? The words played over and over in her mind. She had to give him an answer tonight. Rohan had told her only old vampires could be up and about during the day. One hundred years of never seeing the sun. What would it be like? She imagined sleeping all day, existing on the blood of others, alienated from her friends and family. Never teaching again, always hiding the truth of what she was.

Maybe death *was* better.

She froze as she sensed she was no longer alone. Hopelessness and fear enveloped her as she caught Josiah's scent. How she hated him. She blinked against the pale light when he lit the candle.

"It's time to make your decision," he said. "If you choose death, I will oblige you. If you choose life, I will make you my fledgling and you will love me."

"I'll never love you! Never!"

"Oh, yes, you will. You will have no choice in the matter. You will do whatever I wish. I will treat you well, give you anything you desire. And when I tire of you, I will let you go. So, what will it be?"

"I'd rather be dead than spend another minute with you."

"I feared that would be your answer," Josiah said, with a shrug. "And I fully intended to kill you, but..." He took a deep breath. "You smell so damn good, and your blood is so sweet. Death will have to wait another day."

She cringed as he bent over her, shivered as his eyes went red, flinched when he sank his fangs into her neck and drank and drank. As she felt herself slipping into oblivion, she screamed Rohan's name.

Rohan's head jerked up as Leia's desperate cry broke the barrier between them. In an instant he knew where she was, and that Josiah was going to turn her.

Praying that he wasn't too late, he transported himself to the ancient graveyard behind an old Catholic church in England, and flew down the broken, stone stairs that led to the forgotten crypt that lay far below the earth.

"What the hell?" Josiah sprang to his feet when Rohan materialized inside the tomb.

"What the hell is right!" Rohan snapped, his gaze darting momentarily to Leia, who lay on a cot, her face deathly pale, her heartbeat barely audible.

"Get out of here," Josiah demanded. "She's mine now."

"No way in hell. I'll see her dead first."

A wide smile spread over Josiah's face. "She is almost there now. Such a tasty little morsel. You'd better get a drink while you can."

Fury erupted inside Rohan. Loosing a Lakota war cry, he flew at his sire and slammed him against the wall. Before he could rip out his sire's heart, Josiah sank his fangs into Rohan's throat. There was an ugly tearing sound as Rohan broke free. Blood sprayed Josiah's face as Rohan darted back. Grabbing the candle, he drove it into his sire's eyes.

Josiah let out a bellow as the flame scorched his skin and singed his eyes, temporarily blinding him. The stink of burnt flesh soured the air.

Knowing he had only moments before Josiah recovered, Rohan lifted Leia, cot and all, and transported the two of them to her parents' home.

Brian Winchester sprang out of his easy chair when Rohan suddenly materialized in the living room carrying a cot, which he gently placed on the floor. Winchester gasped when he saw Leia, her neck stained with blood, her face deathly pale. He couldn't tell if she was breathing.

"What the hell have you done to her?" he asked, barely able to speak for the fear burning inside him. "And what the hell happened to you?"

"There's no time to explain now," Rohan said. "Hopefully, I saved her life."

Winchester moved closer. Reaching down, he checked his daughter's pulse, which was barely discernable.

"Lock all your doors and windows," Rohan said, his voice sharp. "And then bring me a wet rag and some whiskey if you've got any. Dammit, Winchester, do it now! I'll explain later."

Spurred by the urgency in Rohan's voice, Brian hurried to do what he'd been told.

Pulling his phone from his jeans, Rohan made a quick call to Frumusanu. "I'm at Leia's parents' house. Stop whatever you're doing and get here as fast as you can," he said curtly, and ended the call.

While waiting for Winchester, Rohan untied Leia's hands and feet. Speaking to her softly, he removed her clothing down to her underwear, smoothed the hair away from her face. After wrapping her in a blanket pulled from the back of the sofa, he lifted her into his arms and carried her to the sofa where he cradled her in his arms. Biting into his wrist, he held it to her lips. "Drink, love," he murmured.

Compelled by the power in his voice, she suckled the wound.

Rohan watched, pleased when a little color returned to her cheeks. He wondered idly where her mother was. A moment later, Winchester returned with a wet washrag, a bottle of Jack Daniels, and a shot glass. "What the hell is she doing?" he exclaimed.

"She's drinking my blood."

Winchester stared at him, mouth agape, eyes wide.

After a moment, Rohan withdrew his arm. He took the rag from Winchester and wiped the blood from Leia's neck and offered her a little whiskey. Gaining his feet, he carried her upstairs to her room and tucked her into bed.

Winchester trailed behind him, stood in the doorway as he watched Rohan make Leia comfortable. "What's going on? What happened to my daughter? Why was she drinking your blood? Who the hell *are* you?"

Rohan turned to face Winchester. "You said it. I'm a vampire. Another vampire kidnapped her and held her prisoner. He drank from her. She was near death when I found them. I gave her my blood to strengthen her. Now, she needs to rest."

He didn't tell Winchester how very near death she'd been, or that she wasn't yet out of danger. If she started to slip away, he was going to have to make a decision that would change her life forever.

Chapter Thirty-Six

Leia wandered in an unfamiliar world. She had lost track of the time, didn't know if it was day or night. Sometimes she was alone. Sometimes Josiah was there, taunting her, demanding that she choose between life and death. Sometimes Rohan was there, begging her to live, his voice soft as he whispered that he loved her, would always love her, vowing that he would never let her go. Once, she imagined that she was drinking his blood. It was hot and thick and should have been disgusting, but she swallowed it eagerly and wished for more.

She was warm now, drifting on a red velvet sea. Voices came and went. Her father's, filled with anger and confusion, her mother's, filled with tears.

Nothing mattered anymore, not life or death. Only Rohan's voice, filled with fear as he begged her to come back, and the taste of his blood on her tongue. Why did he keep pleading for her to come back? Back from where?

And what was that ghostly white light flickering in the distance?

Chapter Thirty-Seven

"Winchester, go down and answer the door," Rohan said, never taking his gaze from Leia. He'd taken a quick shower earlier and noticed that the nasty bite in his neck still wasn't healing, but he'd worry about that later. Right now, his only concern was Leia.

"No one's knocking."

"Frumusanu will be here in a minute. Let him in and send him up here."

"Who the heck is that guy, anyway?"

"He's a vampire hunter. Now, go let him in."

With a shake of his head, Winchester went to do what he'd been told.

Rohan stroked Leia's cheek. Her mother had come in minutes ago and gone into hysterics again when she saw her daughter. Rohan had spoken to the woman's mind, calming her, promising her that everything would be all right, because any other outcome was unthinkable. When Mrs. Winchester had regained a semblance of calm, he'd sent her downstairs.

He heard Frumusanu's footsteps on the stairs a few moments later.

"What's going on?" the hunter asked when he entered the room.

As quickly as possible, Rohan brought him up-to-date. "If Josiah comes here, I might need some back-up, although he shouldn't be able to enter the house uninvited, but, with him, you never know."

Frumusanu nodded. He was armed with a pair of pistols loaded with silver, a dagger with a wicked silver blade, and a wooden stake sharpened to a fine point.

The hunter had come prepared, Rohan mused. Between the two of them, they should be able to destroy Josiah. He hoped.

"Go back downstairs and keep watch," Rohan directed. "Don't let the Winchesters go outside for any reason. Tie 'em up if you have to. Just keep them inside. And don't let them answer the door. All Josiah needs is an invitation. I'll be up here, with Leia. Holler if you need me. Questions?"

Frumusanu shook his head. "I just hope to hell you know what you're doing."

"Yeah," Rohan said, lightly stroking Leia's cheek. "So do I." He didn't know what the hell Josiah had done to her, but he'd never seen anyone react to a vampire's bite like this. Her heartbeat was irregular and faint, her face pale. Sitting on the bed beside her, he spoke to her mind. *Leia?*

Rohan? Where am I? Why is it so dark?

You're unconscious, love. Josiah bit you. Do you remember that?

Yes. It was awful. He told me to choose between life and death, but he refused to kill me when I chose death. He said he was going to turn me... that he could make me love him. Did he change his mind? Am I dead? Is that why it's so dark, why I don't feel anything?

Rohan swore under his breath. Taking her hand in his, he said, *I don't know what he did to you, love, but I'm afraid it's fatal. If you don't wake up soon, I'm going to offer you the same life or death choice he gave you.*

She was quiet for a long moment, and then, in a panicky voice, she said, *It's getting darker. Rohan! I'm so afraid...*

Pain speared through him as her voice trailed off and he felt her slipping away. Dammit, he had to act fast or he was going to lose her.

Life or death, love? I can give you a life like mine, if you want it. It's not so bad once you accept it. Leia? Leia! She was too far gone to answer, leaving him only moments to decide.

A thought closed and locked the bedroom door. Whispering, "Forgive me, love," he cradled her in his arms and made the decision that would leave her forever in the shadows of eternity.

Rohan looked up when someone pounded on the door. It was Winchester, demanding to see his daughter. Reluctantly, Rohan tucked Leia under the covers. A thought unlocked the door.

Winchester burst into the room, his face an angry mask. "That man downstairs refuses to let me out of the house."

"You should thank him."

"I'm not going to listen to any more of this vampire crap. I want you to..." Winchester broke off in mid-sentence as he approached the bed. "She looks better," he said, looking confused.

Rohan nodded. "Yes."

"How? Why?"

"Maybe you should sit down."

Frowning, Winchester stared at him, his eyes dark with suspicion. "Why?"

"Leia was dying."

Winchester shook his head. "I don't believe you. She looks fine."

"I don't give a damn what you believe. She was dying and I did the only thing I could do to save her."

"And what was that?" Winchester asked warily.

Rohan thought briefly of fabricating a lie, but her family had to know sooner or later and now was as good a time as any. "I made her what I am."

Winchester stared at him, fists tightly clenched, his face mottled with rage. "What on God's green earth gave you the right to decide my daughter's fate? We should have taken her to the hospital if she was that bad off."

"She would have been dead before you got there."

Winchester sat down hard on the desk chair in the corner. "I don't believe in vampires," he murmured. "And now you're telling me my daughter is one." He shook his head in denial. "It can't be true."

"Should I have let her die?"

"Yes! It would have been better than turning her into a monster."

"Do I look like a monster to you?"

Winchester's narrow-eyed gaze moved over him. "No," he admitted reluctantly.

"She won't be one, either. She'll still be your daughter."

Winchester blew out a ragged breath. Rising, he moved to Leia's side and gazed down at her for a long moment. A single tear slid down his cheek. "When will she wake up?"

"Tomorrow, when the sun goes down."

Bending over, Winchester brushed a kiss across his daughter's forehead. Moving to the door, he paused and then turned. Staring at Rohan, he hissed, "I hope you burn in the hottest circle of hell for all eternity."

Cynthia was waiting for him in the living room. "How is she? Brian?"

He dropped onto the sofa beside her, hands dangling between his legs, his head bowed.

"Brian? Answer me."

"He said she'll be okay. That she'll wake up tomorrow night."

"How does he know that? He's a dancer, not a doctor."

Winchester blew out a sigh, then lifted his head to meet his wife's eyes. "He's a vampire."

Cynthia stared at him, open-mouthed, and then shook her head. "This is no time for bad jokes, Brian Thomas Winchester."

"Believe me, honey, I'm not joking."

"Vampire!" she murmured, and fainted dead away.

Trent walked through the house, peering out the windows before drawing the curtains, checking to make sure all the doors and windows were locked. As it grew darker, he turned on all the downstairs lights, the front porch light, the lights in the patio. From time to time, he checked his weapons.

Standing at the foot of the stairs, he tapped his fingers on the banister, wondering what Rohan was doing up there. An hour ago, Leia's parents had gone up to their bedroom and shut the door. He hadn't heard a peep out of either one of them since.

Feeling hungry, Trent went into the kitchen and rummaged around in the refrigerator. Mrs. Winchester must have been shopping recently because there was a lot to choose from. In the end, he made a ham and cheese sandwich. He pulled a beer from the back of the fridge, poked around in the cupboards until he found a bag of chips, then settled at the kitchen table, one of his pistols close at hand.

It was going to be a long night.

Josiah prowled the perimeter of the girl's house. He was a powerful creature, able to do amazing things. It galled him that something as ordinary as a threshold could repel him. Yet no matter how many times he tried to enter the house, he couldn't breach that flimsy barrier, nor could he go through any of the windows or down the chimney. The damn threshold protected those entrances, as well. He could burn the place down, he mused. That might be fun. It would drive the whole damn family and the vampire out into the night. And the hunter, as well. He hadn't forgotten his vow to kill the hunter who had destroyed Magdalena. But there was no hurry. Right now, he was focused on getting his hands on the woman again. New blood. A new conquest.

He paused abruptly, muttered every curse word he knew in a dozen languages. As clearly as if he were in the room, he could see Rohan bending over the girl, drinking her close to point of death, then giving her some of his blood. He could feel the transfer of preternatural power, sense Rohan's blood flowing through the girl's veins, strengthening her, reviving her. *Changing her.*

Hell and damnation, his troublesome fledgling now had a fledgling of his own. A fledgling that should have been his, Josiah thought irritably. Dammit to hell, perhaps, after all these centuries, it was time to put an end to Shadow Dancer.

And then he smiled. All was not lost. He was Josiah, a master vampire. As such, he could still make her his.

⚜ ⚜ ⚜

Leia woke abruptly. A glance at the edge of the curtains showed it was dark outside. Had she slept the day away? Odd, she could see everything clearly even though the room was almost pitch black. Just as odd was the fact that she knew her parents and Trent Frumusanu were down in the kitchen having dinner—her mother's pot roast, carrots, potatoes, and chocolate cake for dessert. The scent of the food made her feel faintly queasy.

She smiled as she heard footsteps on the stairs and knew they belonged to Rohan. She sat up as he opened the door and stepped into the room.

"How are you feeling?" he asked, somewhat warily.

"Wonderful." She held out her arms, frowned when he stayed by the door. "Is something wrong?"

"How do you really feel?"

"Fine," she repeated. "Why?"

Rohan took a deep breath, unsure of how his princess would take the news of her changed state. They had never seriously discussed the possibility of Leia becoming a vampire.

When he didn't speak, Leia frowned. "You're scaring me. Has something happened?"

"You could say that. What do you remember of yesterday?"

As if his words had unlocked her memories, she had a clear recollection of Josiah threatening to turn her, of his fangs savaging her throat, of Rohan bursting into the room and spiriting her away.

She bit down on her lower lip, her eyes wide and afraid. "Did he... did he turn me?"

"No."

She frowned. Someone had given her blood. She could still taste it on her tongue. Rohan's blood. In a voice thick with accusations, she asked, "Did you?"

"You were dying," he said quietly. "I couldn't let you go."

"You said you would *never* turn anyone against their will."

"I tried to ask what you wanted me to do, but you were too far gone to answer."

Leia sat very still, afraid to move for fear she would go mad and start throwing things. Rohan had made her a vampire. She stared at him, trying to absorb the meaning of his words.

A few days ago, she had been an ordinary woman who loved her parents and her job, who had fallen head-over-heels for a Native dancer. And now she was a vampire and nothing would ever be normal again. And yet, her life hadn't been anywhere near normal since the night they met. She didn't want to be a vampire, she thought dully. She just wanted to be Leia.

Vampire. She should have felt something, she thought. Anything. Fear. Terror. Anger.

Vampire. Hadn't she known all along that this decision lay somewhere in her future when she decided to stay with Rohan? As he'd once said, any changes made would have to be made on her part. Hadn't she known, deep inside, that sooner or later she would have to become what he was? Still, she had hoped to put it off for ten or twenty years. And yet, maybe it was better this way. She wasn't sure she would ever have found the courage to ask him to do it, or agreed if he'd asked her.

Troubled by her silence, he said, "Leia, I know this is difficult for you."

"You wanted to kill the vampire who made you," she remarked, feeling numb inside.

Rohan nodded. Until last night, he had decided to give up his quest for vengeance against Josiah. What was the point? What was done, was done. And, as he'd told Leia, being a vampire wasn't so bad once you got used to it.

But last night had changed everything. Josiah had laid his hands on Leia and for that there could be no forgiveness. He wouldn't rest until Josiah was dead. Or he was. "What are you trying to say?"

"I don't know." She toyed absently with a corner of the bedspread. "I don't want to be a vampire, but I guess life of any kind is better than death." She glanced up at the ceiling and sighed. "Do my parents know?"

"Yes."

"They'll never look at me the same way again, will they?"

"They took it pretty well, all things considered." It was mostly true.

"Why is Trent here?" She lifted a hand to her throat. "He'll be hunting me now!"

Rohan laughed in spite of himself. "We have a truce."

"You and Trent?"

"He agreed to help me protect you, for Janae's sake, not mine."

Leia met his gaze. She saw him differently now. Oh, he was still outrageously handsome and sexy. He always would be. But she was aware of more than just his looks or his physique. She saw the preternatural power that hovered around him like an invisible cloud. Was that the dark aura Janae had sensed? She could feel that power brushing against her skin. A portion of his power was now hers. It was a startling thought, but she knew it was true. She could feel it inside her, knew she could pick up her bed and tear it to shreds with no effort at all. It was frightening. And exhilarating.

"Do you hate me now?" he asked. "Want to take my head?"

"Of course not." She hesitated before asking, "Do you still love me?"

"Until the day I die." He studied her a moment, confused that the first thing on her mind hadn't been blood. Some new vampires went into a feeding frenzy, others couldn't function until they fed the first time. But that didn't seem to be the case with Leia. He thought about it a moment, wondering if it was because he had been turned by a powerful vampire and now he was a powerful vampire in his own right. Although why that should matter, he couldn't begin to guess.

Leia took a deep breath. "Do you still want me now that I'm a…" She couldn't bring herself to say the word out loud. To do so would make it all too real.

"I don't care what you are," he muttered. A thought locked the door and then he was beside her. Pulling her down on top of him, he kissed her.

It was a long, almost brutal kiss, but Leia gloried in it. He had been holding back before, she thought, afraid of hurting her. What would their lovemaking be like now? she wondered. Sliding her hand under his shirt, she raked her nails down his back and shoulders. They were writhing on the bed when someone knocked on the door.

Rohan muttered an oath as he stood and tossed the covers over Leia. A thought unlocked the door.

Leia quickly sat up and tucked the covers under her arms. "Come in."

Her father glowered at Rohan. "I want to talk to my daughter. Alone."

With a nod, Rohan left the room, quietly closing the door behind him.

Feeling afraid and vulnerable, Leia glanced at her father. What would he think of her now? Would he see a monster every time he looked at her?

Winchester cleared his throat. "The vampire told us what he did," he said bluntly. "It's a terrible thing and he had no right to do it, but…" He took a deep breath. "Your mother and I would rather have a daughter who's a vampire than no daughter at all. We love you, honey. We'll help you in any way we can."

"Oh, Daddy," she murmured, and burst into tears.

"There, there, it'll be all right," her father said as he sat on the edge of the bed and gathered her into his arms. "You can stay here as long as you like. The vampire says we're all in danger as long as that other vampire lives. But once this is over, I never want to see him again."

"He saved my life."

"He took your life, Leia. I can't forgive him for that. I'm grateful you're still here, but none of this would have happened if it wasn't for him."

"Dad…"

"I don't want to talk about it." He kissed the top of her head. "The vampire said you might need some time to… to adjust, so come downstairs when you feel up to it."

She might never be up to it, Leia thought dolefully as she watched her father stride out of the room. How was she going to face her mother, Janae and Trent? Her brother? She felt the sting of tears in her eyes when she realized she wouldn't be able to teach kindergarten next year, or spend the summer days at the beach. She would never go out to lunch with Janae again, or watch the sun rise, or share dinner with her family, or open presents on Christmas morning. Until she had survived a hundred years, she would be trapped in a death-like sleep until the sun went down. It wasn't fair.

She couldn't live like this, didn't want to live like this. She didn't want to be a vampire and exist on nothing but the blood of others. She just wanted to be plain old Leia again.

Railing against fate, she buried her face in her pillow and let the tears flow, wishing all the while that Rohan had just let her die.

Chapter Thirty-Eight

Trent looked up as Rohan entered the kitchen. "What the devil's going on?"

Rohan shrugged. "Leia's trying to adjust to her new life. It's not easy. Sooner or later, she's going to be craving blood and she'll be embarrassed and sickened by it. I'm a little surprised that feeding wasn't the first thing on her mind." He had listened to her conversation with her father, ready to intervene if she suddenly attacked him.

"Were you?" Trent asked, obviously curious about the whole vampire thing. "Embarrassed the first time?"

"Not really. But I came from another culture, a different time. Death and killing weren't viewed in the same way back then as they are now. In ancient times, the Scythians drank the blood of their enemies."

"Nice."

Rohan shrugged. "It will be normal for Leia now. If she views it that way, it will be easier to accept. She'll think it's repugnant the first few times because she knows she's supposed to feel that way. But after a while, she won't think anything about it. So, have you seen any sign of Josiah?"

"No, but I could feel him lurking around outside, no doubt looking for a way in."

"Yeah." Rohan dragged a hand across his jaw. What the hell were they going to do about Josiah? He opened his preternatural senses. Leia's parents had gone to their room. Leia was feeling restless. In a few minutes, she would start to feel discomfort and then pain. He expanded his senses, searching for Josiah, but found nothing.

Rohan?

He felt the onset of panic enhanced by her pain. "It's started," he told Trent. "I'm going to take her hunting for an hour or so. Stay here and look after the Winchesters."

"Are you crazy?" Trent exclaimed. "You can't go out there."

"I'll take her far away from here, don't worry. You just stay alert and keep her parents safe while we're gone."

"Now I'm babysitting," Trent muttered. "Be careful."

"You, too."

Leia let out a startled gasp when Rohan suddenly appeared beside her.

"Get dressed," he said. "We're going out."

"Out? Are you crazy? Josiah is out there."

"He won't see us."

Her hands shook as she pulled on a pair of jeans and a sweater, tugged on a pair of low-heeled boots. "Where are we going?"

"Some place far away."

Rohan wrapped his arm around her waist and the next thing she knew, they were in an alley that opened onto a busy city street.

Leia glanced around, blinked at the bank across the way. The name on the building read St. Louis National Bank.

Rohan reached for her hand and led her to the sidewalk. "You okay?"

She moaned softly. "I hurt all over. What's wrong with me?"

"You need to feed." He said it bluntly.

Her eyes grew wide. "You don't mean..."

"Exactly."

"I can't!" Just the thought of it was revolting. "I won't, and you can't make me!"

"You can and you will, or the pain will get worse and worse."

Leia shook her head. She couldn't bite someone's neck like some rabid animal and drink their blood. She just couldn't. Civilized people didn't do that. But even as the thought crossed her mind, the pain grew sharper and more intense. She bit down on her lower lip to keep from crying out.

"Most female vampires prefer to drink from men," Rohan said matter-of-factly. "Do you have a preference?"

She looked up at him, her face pale and twisted with pain. "Help me."

Shit. Pulling her behind a tree, he bit into his wrist and held it out to her. "Drink."

She didn't argue. With a wordless cry, she suckled the dark-red blood oozing from the twin punctures in his arm. And the pain magically went away. She had expected to feel repelled but she would gladly have taken it all. And that troubled her greatly.

She let out a little growl of protest when he pulled his arm away.

"Vampires only drink from another vampire in an emergency," he said, licking the tiny wounds in his wrist to seal then. "You need human blood to survive. Come on."

Taking her hand again, Rohan led her down the sidewalk until he saw a young man striding toward them. He captured the man's gaze and compelled him to follow them down a side street, out of sight of passersby.

Leia looked at the man. He was probably in his twenties, with brown hair and gray eyes. And he smelled so good, her mouth watered.

Rohan grinned. He had worried about his little fledgling for nothing. She was a natural. He bit into the man's neck, then stood back and let Leia's vampire nature take over. When he judged she'd taken enough, he spoke to her mind, telling her to stop. He was somewhat surprised when she did. "You okay?"

She licked her lips. "I should be ashamed, repulsed, disgusted. Why aren't I?"

He shrugged. "Some people are born to be vampires. I think you're one of them."

She tilted her head to the side, curious to know how it had been for him. "Were you?"

"Maybe. I never gave it any thought." Becoming a vampire had been easy for him once the initial craving for blood had passed. He had hated Josiah for centuries, he mused, when he should have been thanking him. But that had changed when his sire bit Leia. Taking her hand in his, he said, "Come on, let's go home."

Moments later, they were back in her room. "Will you teach me how to do that?"

"Yes, but I don't think you'll need much instruction. I have a feeling you'll know instinctively what to do."

Her gaze moved over him. "Are you repulsed by me, by what I've done?"

"Hell, no, I'm proud of you," he said with a grin.

"What'll we do now?" she asked. It was hours until dawn.

"I've got a few ideas," he said, drawing her into his arms. "But not until we're out of your father's house. Let's go downstairs and see how Frumusanu's getting along. He could probably use some sleep."

Leia felt unaccountably embarrassed and uncomfortable when Trent looked at her. What did he see? Did she look different? Was he thinking he had one more vampire to dispose of? Would he still let Janae be her friend? Lordy, would Janae even want to be friends with a vampire? Probably not. Come to think of it, she had never heard Rohan mention any friends—vampire or otherwise—save for the members of the dance troupe. And they seemed more like acquaintances than friends. She wondered suddenly if they knew what he was. "Aren't you supposed to be dancing tonight?" she asked.

Rohan shook his head. "I called Deer Killer. Told him there was a death in the family and I couldn't make the rest of the engagement."

"A death in the family," Trent muttered, with a sidelong glance at Leia. "That's rich."

"All right, you two, that's enough," Rohan said. "Trent, stop looking at Leia as if she'd suddenly grown two heads and a tail. She's the same as she always was. She isn't going to turn into a ravening monster or try to turn you or drink your blood. And, you, Leia, stop being ashamed. You haven't done anything wrong. Aside from having to sleep during the day and surviving on blood, you're the same as you always were. If you want to work, you can teach night school or hold online classes from home, or, hell, I don't know. There are a lot of night jobs. Right now, our main concern is Josiah. He wants to kill Trent, he wants to make you his, and I'm pretty sure he'd like to take my head even more than Trent does."

Trent scowled at him. "Very funny. I'm gonna go call Janae and then get some sleep."

"Good idea," Rohan said.

"You can use the guest room upstairs," Leia offered.

"Thanks." Trent glanced from Rohan to Leia, muttered something unintelligible under his breath, and headed for the stairs.

"Well, that was fun," Leia remarked.

Rohan settled on the sofa and motioned for her to join him. "It'll get easier," he said as she snuggled against his side. "I know you're confused now, but it'll pass."

"What *are* we going to do about Josiah?"

"I don't know. It's doubtful he'll just give up and go home, wherever the hell that is."

"Maybe we could leave the country?" Leia suggested.

"It wouldn't do any good. He's my sire. He'll be able to find me wherever I go."

She sat up and stared at him. "Does that mean you'll always be able to find me?"

"Exactly. You can run, but you can't hide." He lifted one brow. "You don't want to hide from me, do you?"

"Of course not."

His gaze searched hers. And then he said, quietly, "If you ever want to leave me, I'll let you go. I won't like it, but I won't hold you against your will."

"Josiah said he could make me love him, so I guess that means you could, too."

"But I didn't. And I won't."

She snuggled against him again. "We were supposed to get married on Sunday. I guess that's off now that Josiah's prowling around."

"I'm afraid so."

"My father would never have approved anyway," she said with a heavy sigh. "He wasn't too crazy about the idea in the first place."

Chapter Thirty-Nine

Trent sat on the edge of the bed in the Winchester's guest room and stared at his phone. Then, with a sigh, he called the number of the burner phone he'd given to Janae. It was late, but she answered on the first ring.

"Hi, honey, it's me. How are you doing?" he asked.

"We're all right. The boys miss you."

"What about you?"

There was a pause before she said, "I miss you, too. When can we come home?"

"I don't know. Hopefully, soon. Listen, I've got something important to tell you, and I don't want you to say anything until I'm finished. Okay?"

"What's wrong?" she asked anxiously. "Something's wrong, isn't it? I can hear it in your voice."

"Janae, just listen! That dancer, Rohan, is a vampire and—"

"Oh, Trent, this is no time for jokes."

"It's not a joke. It's the truth. I know it's hard to believe, but I've seen the proof with my own eyes."

"But... there's no such thing."

"Yeah, well, I'm afraid there is. And that's not the worst of it. He's made Leia one, too."

"Oh, no! Trent, if you're kidding me, I'll never forgive you. Never!"

"It's the truth. I swear it on the life of our boys. It's one of the reasons you can't come home now. I wasn't going to tell you, but I thought it would be best if you heard it from me. That's why I sent you and the boys away. You can't tell *anyone* about this. It could put Leia's life in danger. And yours and the boys, too. Do you understand?"

"Not really."

"Just promise me you won't breathe a word of this to anyone. Not your parents, not anyone."

"I promise. Oh, poor Leia."

"She seems to be doing all right, I guess. Listen. I need to get some sleep. I love you, sweeting. I'm sorry for this mess and I'll come and get you as soon as I can."

"Be careful, Trent. I don't know what I'd do without you."

"I'll call you again when I can. Stay close to home. Don't invite anyone you don't know into the house. Vampires can't enter a home unless they're invited. Warn your parents, too. You can't tell them the vampire part, just warn them to be wary of strangers. And whatever you do, don't go out at night. And remember, you can't tell anyone what I've told you. Not a word, not a hint."

"All right. I love you, Trent."

"Love you, too. Good night, sweeting."

Chapter Forty

Leia woke abruptly. Momentarily confused, she stared at the ceiling. Funny, she had never noticed that hairline crack in the corner before. Odd that she could see it now, when the room was dark.

And then she remembered. She was a vampire. She had no memory of falling asleep. One minute she'd been talking to Rohan and the next, nothingness. Apparently vampires didn't dream.

Sitting up, she glanced around the room, looking for Rohan, but he wasn't there. Of course he wasn't. Her father would have a fit if she dared share her bed with a man while under his roof.

As soon as she thought about Rohan, she knew he was downstairs with Trent, just as she knew her parents had eaten an early dinner and taken refuge in their room. With a sigh, she wondered if things would ever be remotely normal between herself and her parents again. Would they always look at her with pity and a little fear?

Slipping out of bed, she changed out of her nightgown into a pair of jeans and a sweatshirt, pulled on her boots, washed her face, combed her hair. She frowned when she brushed her teeth. Where were her fangs? Did they only come out when she was feeding? She certainly hoped so!

Squaring her shoulders, she opened the bedroom door and marched resolutely down the stairs.

Rohan and Trent both looked up when she entered the kitchen—Trent with an odd mix of sadness and curiosity. Rohan smiled at her. "Hungry, love?"

She wanted to deny it, but what was the point. She nodded curtly.

Rohan unfolded from his chair in a fluid movement. "Keep an eye on things, hunter," he said, before wrapping his arm around Leia's waist and transporting the two of them out of the house.

In the blink of an eye, Leia found herself at the beach. The water beyond the waves reflected a full, yellow moon. Small fires made little splashes of light along the shore. She wrinkled her nose against the suddenly odious smell of roasting hot dogs and mustard. "What are we doing here?" she asked.

"Getting you something to satisfy your hunger," he said, taking hold of her hand. "And then I thought we'd make out on the sand like a couple of randy teenagers."

She laughed in spite of herself. They strolled along the shore for a while. Everything looked different somehow. The moon seemed brighter. The sand seemed to sparkle even in the darkness. Even the air felt different.

Rohan came to a halt as they passed a young couple. Tugging on Leia's hand, he turned around and followed them. She watched, fascinated, as he called the people to him, then led them into the shadows. "You want him or her?"

"We're going to ... to feed here?"

"No one's watching and they wouldn't see anything if they were."

"Him, of course." Drinking from the girl just didn't seem right. Leia let out a startled gasp when she felt an ache in her gums as her fangs lengthened. So, she mused, they only come out when needed.

Expecting to feel repulsed, she bit the man's neck. She took only a small sip. The blood was warm as it slid over her tongue. Suddenly famished, she took a little more, and then a little more. Never had anything tasted so good! It troubled her that she wasn't disgusted by what she was doing.

Laying a hand on her shoulder, Rohan said, "Enough."

Leia licked her lips as Rohan released the couple from his spell.

"Are you all right?" he asked.

She nodded, wondering how soon she could feed again.

Rohan caught her hand in his and gave it a squeeze as they continued along the shore. Leia let out a little gasp of pleasure when he drew her into his arms and kissed her.

She leaned into him, frantic for his touch, his kisses. She pulled him down on the sand, her hands all over him in her haste. She stopped abruptly when she reached for his belt. What was she doing? They were on a public beach, for goodness sakes.

"All your senses are heightened now," Rohan said quietly. "Taste, touch, smell. It's like living in a new world where everything is enhanced. The air smells different, the world looks different. You feel different inside. Your sense of touch is sharper, as is your vision. It takes a little while to get used to it all. In the meantime," he said, hoping to lighten the mood, "feel free to touch and taste to your heart's content."

She stared at him, too embarrassed by her wanton behavior to speak.

Siting up, he took her in his arms again, one hand stroking softly up and down her back. "You'll learn to control it," he said. "Like everything else. I ... *shit*!"

Before she could ask what was wrong, Josiah materialized in front of them.

Rohan swore as he stood. Pulling Leia up with him, he thrust her behind him.

"What do you want?" he asked brusquely.

"That's a stupid question, even for you," Josiah retorted. "Now hand her over."

"Go to hell."

"After you," Josiah hissed. Darting forward, he reached around Rohan and grabbed Leia's arm, let out a harsh cry when she buried her fangs in his shoulder.

Josiah released her immediately, muttered an oath as Rohan sank his fangs into his back. And then he was gone.

Leia stared at Rohan. His eyes were red and angry, his lips stained with Josiah's blood.

"Are you all right?" he asked.

"Are you?"

He regarded her through narrowed eyes. And then he grinned. "We make a hell of a team, you and I."

"We do, don't we?" she said, linking her arm with his.

"He's not going to give up. You know that, don't you?"

"Yes, But I'm not afraid anymore. Tomorrow's supposed to be our wedding day," Leia remarked. "I think we should run away and get married. Oh!" she exclaimed. "I have to call Rosemary and Bonnie and Helen and tell them tomorrow isn't happening. How could I have forgotten? I hope Rosemary didn't spend a lot of money on a new dress."

"Too late to worry about that now. What about your folks?"

"We won't tell them, or anyone else. It'll be our secret."

"Sounds good to me," he said, wrapping his arms around her. "Maybe I'll ask Trent to be my best man."

"I don't guess it would be a good idea to invite Janae as long as there's a chance Josiah might show up."

"Probably not."

"What if he does show up?"

"We beat him once. We'll beat him again," Rohan said with a careless shrug. And then he laughed. "It'll be the most unusual wedding of the century. A hunter being a vampire's best man."

They were walking back the way they'd come when Rohan caught the scent of fresh blood. They found the young couple they had fed on earlier under a pile of seaweed.

"He loved her very much," Leia murmured. "He proposed to her earlier tonight and she said yes. She was pregnant."

"How do you know all that?" Rohan asked. He knew it, too, having read the girl's mind.

"I don't know. I just do."

"You're pretty powerful for a fledgling," he remarked. "You read his mind while you were feeding without even realizing what you were doing. I'm not sure why, but I think it's because I carry Josiah's blood and you carry his through mine. I think that's why you didn't crave blood the moment you woke up. Why you've accepted all of this so well."

"Why did he kill them?" she asked, her voice tinged with sorrow. Three lives lost for no good reason. Tears stung her eyes as she thought about the baby that would never be born. "Why?" she asked again.

"It's what he does."

"You won't ever let me do that, will you?" she asked, her eyes haunted.

"No, love," he said, drawing her into the comfort of his arms. "But I doubt you'll ever want to."

"It's so sad," she murmured. "Shouldn't we notify the police or something?"

"No. Someone else can do it."

"I'd hate for a child to find them like that."

Rohan grunted softly. "You're right. I'll give the cops a call when we get back to the house."

After an anonymous phone call to the police, Rohan joined Trent in the Winchesters' kitchen. Taking a seat across the table from the hunter, he said, "How would you like to be the best man at my wedding?"

"Are you serious?"

Rohan shrugged. "I don't see it as a problem unless there's some kind of hunter code that forbids it."

Trent snorted. "I'm pretty sure there isn't. No one would have ever considered the possibility. But what the hell? Count me in. When is it?"

"It was supposed to be tomorrow, but, all things considered, we've decided to elope."

"Janae's going to be almighty upset when she finds out Leia got married without her."

"It's too dangerous for her to be here now."

"I know."

Rohan slapped Trent on the shoulder. "We'll probably get married again when this is all over so Leia's parents and her brother and Janae can be there."

Trent blew out a sigh as Rohan left the kitchen. His life hadn't been this complicated until he met Rohan Stillwater. Before then, he'd been sure all vampires were monsters, merciless killers with no moral values, no thought other than death and destruction. He had to admit Rohan seemed like a decent guy. If things had been different they might have been friends. And then he laughed. Hell, he thought with a wry grin, they *were* friends.

Leia called the church to cancel the date, took a deep breath, and called Rosemary and the others to let them know the wedding was off. She apologized profusely for the short notice. When that was done, she went upstairs and knocked on her parents' bedroom door. Her father called for her to come in.

Leia took a deep breath before stepping into the room and closing the door behind her.

Her father was sitting in the big old easy chair in the corner. Her mother was sitting up in bed, pillows at her back, a paperback book in her lap. Fear flickered in her eyes when she saw Leia.

"Is something wrong?" her father asked.

"Everything is wrong," Leia said. "Why are you two staying in your room? Are you so afraid of me that you can't face me?"

Her parents shared a glance, then her father said, "Your mother isn't comfortable having Rohan and that hunter in the house."

"He hasn't changed, Mom," Leia said. "He's the same man you thought was so wonderful just a few days ago. The same man I intend to marry."

A faint blush rose in her mother's cheeks. "It isn't just him. It's you. I don't know you anymore."

"I haven't changed, either. Well, a little, but I'm still me. And I still love you."

Her mother stared at her, then stood and walked toward her. "How can you be the same? You're a vampire now."

"But you wouldn't know that if Rohan hadn't told you. Do I look different? Sound any different? Act any different?"

"Well ... no."

"Please don't be afraid of me. I'd never hurt either one of you. But you're hurting me." Leia's heart swelled with emotion when her mother took her in her arms and held her close.

"I'm so sorry," Cynthia murmured. "Hurting you is the last thing I want to do. I should be helping you adjust in any way I can."

Her father gained his feet and wrapped his arms around both of them. Voice thick with unshed tears, he said, "We're still a family, Leia. Welcome home."

Although reluctant to spoil the mood, there was one thing she needed to know. "Will I still be part of the family when I marry Rohan?"

Her father sucked in a deep breath while Leia held hers, waiting for his answer.

"I'll accept him," her father said after a tense moment. "I always said like should marry like and I guess now the two of you are, well, you know."

"Mom?"

"As long as you're happy and safe, I'll do my best to make him feel welcome."

"I love you guys," Leia said, relieved that her parents hadn't put up a fuss. Feeling as if all was right in her world again, she hugged her dad and kissed her mother on the cheek. "I've got to go tell Rohan the good news!"

She found him in the living room, staring out the window.

"Did you win the lottery or something?" Rohan asked when he saw her. "You look like you're about to burst with happiness."

"I am!" Smiling hugely, she said, "My Mom and Dad still love me."

"Hell, I could have told you that," he said dryly.

"And they don't have a problem with us getting married."

"So, I guess that means we don't need to elope."

"I guess not. You don't mind waiting a few days, do you? I canceled the church, so we'll have to find another date."

"I don't think we should get married right now."

"Why not?" she asked. And then frowned. "Josiah."

"Yeah. Probably not a good idea to make any plans while he's around," Rohan remarked, and then he grunted softly. It might not be a good time for a wedding, but it might be the perfect time to set a trap.

He discussed his idea with Leia, who seemed doubtful but was willing to go along with it. After Leia went up to her room, he roused Trent.

"What the hell do you want?" the hunter growled. "It's the middle of the night."

"Prime time for vampires," Rohan said. "Listen, I need your help. I have an idea."

Leia was by turns nervous and scared the next night as the details of Rohan's plan were worked out. Her only part was to call the church and find a date. She didn't tell her parents what was going on.

It took several calls before she found a small, non-denominational church that had several nights available during the week.

The night of the wedding, Leia told her parents that she and Rohan were going out for a while. Knowing that if things went wrong she would never see her parents again, she hugged and kissed them both before she left the house.

Trent waited for them on the sidewalk.

Once outside, Rohan dissolved into mist and went to Leia's bedroom to retrieve her wedding gown and his suit. They quickly changed clothes in the garage.

The skies were cloudy when Rohan transported the three of them to the church.

Leia took a deep, calming breath when they arrived. Clinging to her future husband's hand, they walked up the stairs and into the foyer, with Trent trailing behind. Leia took another deep breath when Rohan gave her hand a squeeze and murmured, "Here we go."

The couple playing her parents sat in the first row. Another eight or nine "guests" were scattered on both sides of the aisle. A spray of bright yellow daisies adorned the center of the altar. White candles flickered on either side.

Whispering, "Good luck," Trent moved down the aisle to take his place as best man.

Hand-in-hand, Leia and Rohan walked down the white runner to where a tall man clad in a long black cassock waited, Bible in hand. His gaze moved over the congregation and then he opened the book. "Dearly beloved," he intoned in a deep, deep voice. "We are gathered here..."

Leia let out a gasp when she heard Josiah's voice in her mind. *You foolish girl. Did you really think I'd let you marry someone else?* She cast a frantic look at Rohan. "He's here!"

Rohan opened his preternatural senses, searching for his sire, but either Josiah wasn't nearby or he was blocking his presence. Speaking to Leia's mind, Rohan murmured, *Relax, love. We're ready for him.*

Before she could reply, Josiah burst into the chapel.

Chapter Forty-One

Rohan immediately put Leia behind him. The minister dropped his Bible and darted out the side door.

The remaining men and women—vampire hunters all—stayed where they were.

Josiah chuckled as his gaze moved over the "guests" and then settled on Rohan. "You think this pathetic bunch can take me?" he asked, his voice heavily laced with disdain.

Rohan shook his head. "No. This is just between you and me."

Josiah made a sweeping motion with his hand. "Then why are they here?"

"Wedding guests."

Josiah snorted. "Maybe I'll leave a couple of them alive to witness *my* wedding. What do you say, Leia, my dear?"

"In your dreams, you creep," she retorted, her fear momentarily swallowed up in her hatred.

Eyes narrowed, Josiah glared at her.

Leia felt his power move over her, dark and heavy. It raised the hair on her arms and made her stomach churn with revulsion.

"Come to me!" he commanded.

She felt a faint pull in his direction, but that was all.

Rohan grinned at his sire. "Your power seems a little weak tonight."

Leia flinched as she heard Josiah's voice in her mind again. *You will come to me now!*

With an impudent grin, she sent him her answer. *What are you going to do if I don't?*

Outraged by her ability to defy him, Josiah launched himself toward her, his outstretched hands like claws, his fangs extended.

Before she could move out of the way, Rohan sprang forward, blocking Josiah's attack. The two vampires slammed into each other with a sound like thunder. Preternatural power blasted through the room, driving Trent and the other hunters to their knees.

Leia sensed the hatred between Rohan and Josiah like a palpable presence in the chapel as they came together time and again, fangs ripping into flesh that healed almost immediately. Dark-red blood sprayed across the walls, the ceiling, the stained-glass windows. Leia gasped as several drops slid down her cheek.

Both men were liberally soaked with blood now. Their taunts and growls echoed off the walls, sending icy shivers down Leia's spine. With a savage cry, Rohan tore a chunk of meat from Josiah's shoulder and gouged a deep gash in his right arm, while Josiah raked his nails down Rohan's back, ripping through cloth and flesh, splattering blood over the pews and the floor. It was like watching two jungle cats fight to the death, and yet Leia couldn't look away.

She glanced fleetingly at Trent and the other hunters. One and all, they were transfixed, seemingly incapable of movement. Trent could have been of help, if necessary. Why had Rohan incapacitated him?

Leia was on edge, poised to strike if the opportunity presented itself, but when it came, she discovered she couldn't move. Rohan had rendered her powerless, so that, like the hunters, she could only watch, unable to interfere. She felt a sudden rush of anger. She wasn't a puny mortal anymore. Why wouldn't Rohan let her help? After all, Josiah was *her* enemy, too.

The fight seemed to go on forever. There was blood everywhere, leaving Leia to wonder how much longer the confrontation could last. She had never seen anything so violent, or so brutal. Their clothing was in rags, their bodies streaked head-to-foot with crimson. Both were breathing hard now, but they didn't seem to be tiring.

Rohan, let me help. He's my enemy, too.

No way in hell, love, was his quick reply.

The end, when it came, came quickly. Rohan feinted left and lowered his guard. Confident of victory, Josiah darted forward, let out an unearthly howl of pain and disbelief when Rohan plunged his hand into Josiah's chest, ripped out his heart, and threw it across the room, where it landed on the floor with a sizzle like that of frying bacon.

Josiah stood there a moment, his eyes blazing with hatred before he slowly spiraled to the floor. He made a last, feeble attempt to rise, and then lay still.

With the end of the battle, the preternatural power in the room faded and disappeared. The hunters glanced around, muttering among themselves.

Heaving a sigh, Rohan stared at the body of his sire.

Leia, freed of his hold on her, hurried toward Rohan, only to let out a shriek when one of the hunters drew a pistol and shot him.

She screamed, "No!" when he collapsed.

The gunshot echoed in the air as Trent drew his own weapon and fired at the hunter who had shot Rohan. His gaze moved to the others. "I'll kill the next man who makes a move," he warned. "We had a deal. No killing except for Josiah."

Leia glanced at Rohan. He wasn't moving. Was he dead? As much as she longed to go to him, something warned her not to move.

"When did you become a vampire lover, Frumusanu?" asked one of the hunters.

"We had a deal," Trent repeated. "A deal that included Rohan."

"We don't make deals with vampires," another said scornfully.

"So now we'll collect double," a third man remarked with a shrug. "Let's pick up the bodies and get the hell out of here."

"We might as well take the girl while we're at it," the lone female hunter said.

Leia froze as two of the hunters started toward her.

Hardly aware of what she was doing, Leia gathered her power around her and sent it outward, leaving all the hunters except Trent immobile. She blinked, startled by what she had done with just a thought.

Rohan lay as before, unmoving.

Dear Lord, he couldn't be dead! With a strangled cry, Leia ran to his side and dropped to her knees beside him.

He wasn't breathing!

Glancing over her shoulder, she called, "Trent, help!"

He came quickly to her side. Kneeling, he peeled what was left of Rohan's shirt away from the bloody wound in his chest.

"He's dead," Leia wailed, and burst into tears.

"I don't think so," Trent replied. "Look. The bullet missed his heart. I reckon the silver burns like hell. That's probably why he isn't moving."

"But he's not breathing!"

Cut the damn thing out.

She heard Rohan's voice, thick with pain, in her mind. "We have to get it out!" she exclaimed. "Now!"

Trent muttered an oath. "Of course. I should have thought of that." Reaching into the pocket of his trousers, he pulled out a switchblade. "I'll do it."

Leia bit down on her lower lip as Trent began to probe the ugly wound for the slug. She tried to look away but some unwanted sense of morbid curiosity made her watch.

Rohan groaned once, a gut-wrenching sound that brought fresh tears to her eyes.

After what seemed like an eternity but was likely no more than a minute or two, Trent let out a cry of victory as he dislodged the slug. Sounding resigned, he muttered, "Now for the hard part."

Leia stared at him. What could be worse than what he'd just done? Comprehension dawned when Trent rolled up his shirt sleeve. "He needs fresh blood. Don't let him take too much."

"How will I know when enough is enough?"

"If my complexion turns as white as my shirt, it's too much," he said with forced good humor.

"Maybe I should do it," Leia suggested.

"No. He needs human blood right now. You can give him a little of yours later. One thing you *can* do," Trent said, holding out his arm. "Bite me."

Leia gazed at his arm. What if she bit him and *she* couldn't stop? Taking a deep breath, she bit into his left wrist. His blood was warm and sweet and oh, so, tempting. She had thought all blood would taste the same, but she'd been wrong. Some was better than others. Exerting all her self-control, she lifted her head and held Trent's bleeding wrist to Rohan's lips.

In an instant, he buried his fangs in the hunter's arm and drank. And drank.

"Enough!" Trent cried.

Rohan growled at Leia when she tried to pry him away from Trent. "Rohan, it's me. Let him go."

He stopped at the sound of her voice. A long shudder ran through his body and then he opened his eyes. And grinned at her as he ran his fingers over his neck and felt the nasty bite Josiah had inflicted on him shrivel up and disappear.

"What are you grinning at?" Leia asked.

"It's gone," he said.

"What's gone? Oh." Her brow furrowed. "Did it heal because you killed Josiah?"

Rohan nodded.

"One more reason to be glad he's gone," Leia muttered.

In a single, fluid movement, Rohan stood. Taking hold of Leia's left hand and Trent's right, he pulled the two of them to their feet.

"What now?" Leia asked, raking her glance across the hunters who stood as still as statues.

Rohan jerked his chin toward the hunters. "What happened?"

"I'm not sure," Leia said with a shrug. "One of them said they should take me along with you and Josiah and when two of them started toward me, I... I don't know what I did. But they've been like that ever since."

Rohan threw back his head and laughed. "Damn, girl, you beat all, you know that?"

"What are you gonna do with them?" Trent asked, sorely afraid of the answer.

"Well," Rohan drawled. "We've got two choices, either kill 'em all, or erase their memories."

"I vote for the second one," Leia said.

Rohan shook his head. "I was afraid you'd say that."

She stared at him, wide-eyed. "You wouldn't really kill them all?"

"That's why they came here," he reminded her. "To destroy me. And they came damn close. You've got to know they wouldn't have spared you, either."

"I know, but to kill them in cold blood...that...that's murder."

"Isn't that what they tried to do?" he asked dryly. "Kill me in cold blood?"

He was right, Leia thought. "It just seems wrong, when they can't defend themselves," she argued, knowing it was a weak argument at best. "But you do what you have to do."

Shit! He couldn't do it with her standing there looking at him like he was about to drown a sack of helpless puppies. Had he been alone, he would have disposed of them without a second thought, but he couldn't do it now, couldn't bear to have her think he was a cold-blooded killer. She would understand how things were after she'd been a vampire for a couple of years. But this time, for her, he would let the hunters go.

"Rohan?"

"You win, love. I'll erase their memories of you and Trent and this night and send them on their way."

It didn't take long. Leia watched, astonished, as he led the hunters outside where he spoke to each of them in turn, wiping the memory of what had happened and replacing it with a new, different memory for each man and woman, and then sent them away.

Leia glanced over her shoulder. "What are we going to do about the awful mess in the church?"

"I know a guy who makes his living cleaning up this kind of thing," Trent said. "I'll give him a call. By morning, this place will look as good as new."

Rohan nodded. "It's been a busy night," he said, slipping his arm around Leia's shoulders. "Let's go home."

Rohan transported the three of them to the front yard of the Winchesters' house.

"Listen," Trent said, not quite meeting Rohan's eyes. "I'm sorry about tonight. I thought I could trust those guys. They promised all they wanted was Josiah. I should have known better than to believe them."

Rohan shrugged. "Things go wrong. The main thing is, Josiah is no longer a threat to you or Leia or anyone else."

Trent held out his hand. "As of tonight, I'm out of the vampire hunting business."

Rohan grinned as they shook hands. "Good to know."

"We'll call you and Janae when we set a real date," Leia promised.

"Do that," Trent said as he unlocked his car. "It's been...interesting."

"Interesting," Rohan muttered. "Right."

"You look like one of the walking dead," Leia remarked. He was covered with blood, his shirt and jacket were shredded, there was a long rip down one pantleg. "You can't go inside looking like that. You'll give my mom a heart attack."

"Yeah. Come on," he said, slipping his arm around her waist. "Let's go to my place. I can get cleaned up there."

Leia wandered around Rohan's apartment while he showered. She hadn't paid much attention to her surroundings the first time she'd been here. Now, she noted that the furnishings all looked expensive. The gray walls were bare save for one large painting over the sofa, and what looked like an Indian war shield and lance over the fireplace. The real deal? she wondered. Or replicas?

Standing in the bedroom doorway, she listened to the water run in the shower while an image of Rohan naked and covered in soapsuds played across the screen in her mind. Feeling suddenly bold, she undressed and opened the shower door.

A slow grin spread over Rohan's face as she stepped inside and closed the door.

"I have some blood on my face," Leia said, with a shrug.

"Uh-huh."

"I wondered if you'd wash it off for me."

"It looks like war paint," he said, with a grin. "Seems a shame to remove it."

When she scowled at him, he grabbed a washcloth and scrubbed the dried blood from her cheek. "As long as you're in here," he drawled, and proceeded to wash her from head to foot. And then he handed her the cloth.

Washing Rohan was an amazingly erotic sensation. She started at his shoulders and was nearing his waist when he turned the water off, lifted her into his arms, and carried her into the bedroom.

They didn't make it as far as the bed.

It was late when they finally made it back to her parents' home. Leia ducked into the garage to retrieve the clothes she'd left the house in. The interior of the house was dark, save for one lamp burning in the living room. Feeling well-loved and drowsy, Leia sank down on the sofa and closed her eyes.

Sitting beside her, Rohan draped his arm around her shoulders. "You okay, love?"

"Better than okay," she said, snuggling against him. "You're alive, Josiah is gone." She grinned at him. "All my hungers have been fed."

Rohan chuckled. "It's been one hell of a night. Worst wedding I've ever been to."

"The next one will be better," she murmured, sleepily.

"I sure hope so."

"Let's find a different church." She was going to need a different dress, too. The one she had worn tonight was ruined and had too many bad memories attached to it. She wasn't sure how she'd explain it to her mother. "Why am I so tired? It's hours until sunrise."

"You're a fledgling. You've had a busy night, lots of stress, not to mention some rather, ah, acrobatic sex."

She laughed softly. They had made love three times. Rohan was an energetic and imaginative lover, to say the least. She sighed with the memory. He had taken her to places she'd never dreamed existed, but hoped to visit again, soon.

Rohan brushed a kiss across the top of her head as the dark sleep claimed her. Lifting her into his arms, he carried her up to her room, undressed her, and tucked her into bed. "I love you, darlin'," he murmured.

He stood there a moment, debating where to spend the night. They had better get married soon, he thought, as he left the house, because he was getting almighty tired of sleeping alone.

Chapter Forty-Two

"A new wedding dress?" Cynthia asked with a frown. "What's wrong with the one you already bought?"

Leia glanced at Rohan, who was lounging against the door jamb in the kitchen. She could hardly tell her mother the truth, that it had been ruined fighting off a bunch of vampire hunters.

With a grin, Rohan spoke to her mother's mind, erasing the memory of their previous shopping trip. For good measure, he wiped any memory of it from her father's mind while he was at it.

"I was thinking of going shopping tonight," Leia said, sending an appreciative glance at Rohan. "Would you like to go with me, Mom?"

"What a silly question," Cynthia said, her voice laced with excitement. "I've always dreamed of this day."

"Me, too. How soon can you be ready?"

"Just let me tell Dad we're going."

Leia sighed as her mother hurried upstairs. Turning to Rohan, she said, "Thanks. I couldn't think of a plausible lie."

"No problem, although you could have done it yourself."

"I know, but... it just didn't seem right to use my power on my own mother."

"Have fun," he said as Cynthia returned. "I'll see you later."

"Leia, how are you, really?" Cynthia asked as they pulled out of the driveway.

Leia grimaced inwardly. This was a conversation she had been dreading. "I'm fine, Mom. Honest."

"Do you feel...you know, different?"

"Sometimes. But mostly I still feel like me."

Cynthia fell silent for a moment. Taking a deep breath, she asked, "But what about the...the blood?"

"Oh, Mom, do we really need to talk about this?"

"I'm sorry, hon. But I can't help being curious. Becoming a vampire isn't like changing your hair color or rearranging the furniture. You can't change it back."

Leia laughed in spite of herself. And then she sobered. She couldn't blame her mother for having questions when there were still things she wanted to know. "It's like being me, only more so. I'm physically stronger. Everything looks the same, yet different. Colors are brighter. I can hear sounds I couldn't hear before, see farther. I thought I'd be repulsed by the blood, but I'm not. Rohan has made the whole transition easier for me."

Thankfully, they reached the mall before Cynthia could ask any more questions.

As she had before, Leia walked up and down the aisles in the bridal shop. To her surprise, she found a gown she liked even better than the first one. The clerk said they had ordered a new one several weeks ago for a client who had then changed her mind. The gown was scheduled to arrive on Friday, along with a matching veil.

"Well, that was lucky," Cynthia said as they left the store. "It's a beautiful dress and except for being a little too long, it fits perfectly."

Leia nodded. "All we need now is a church and a wedding date. And flowers."

"And a cake," her mother said.

"And a cake," Leia repeated. She knew a moment of regret, thinking that Rohan wasn't the only one who couldn't eat it now.

"Oh!" Cynthia's eyes widened. "You can't have any, can you?"

"No. But everyone else can."

"Do you miss food?"

"Not really. I thought I would, but I don't."

Her mother was unusually quiet on the drive home. No doubt pondering all the things she'd learned about vampires, Leia mused. It must be hard for her parents to relate to her the way she was now. She considered herself fortunate that they had accepted her, even though she knew they weren't happy about her new and unusual lifestyle. She wondered how her brother would react when he found out. His shoot in Italy had ended and he would be home within a few days.

Staring out the window, Leia pondered her future. What would life be like once she and Rohan were married? Would they live in her apartment? Or Rohan's lair? Or buy a new house?

Would he continue to dance? She hoped so, although he had talked of quitting. They wouldn't get old, wouldn't have children or grandchildren... Of course, if Rohan were agreeable, they could adopt a baby, but she would never feel a child of her own move within her womb, never know the wonder of creation.

She put the thought out of her mind. Human or vampire, there was no point in fretting over the future.

⚜ ⚜ ⚜

Leia was in her bedroom when her phone rang. She felt a surge of hope followed by a sudden sense of uncertainty as she answered. "Janae! How are you? Where are you?"

"I'm fine and I'm at home. How are *you*? Trent told me what happened..." Janae's voice trailed off. "Maybe you don't want to talk about it."

"No, it's fine. I hope we can still be friends."

"Well, to be honest, I wasn't sure, at first. But, well, like I told Trent, I'll just have to learn to accept it."

"I hope so. I've missed you."

"I miss you, too. I guess we can always go to the mall after dark," Janae said with forced cheerfulness. "And go out for dinner instead of lunch, and see midnight movies."

"Yes."

There was a long silence.

"I'm so glad you called," Leia said. "Rohan and I are getting married soon and I was hoping you'd be my matron of honor."

"You know I will. How soon is the wedding?"

"I'm not sure yet. We still have to find a church."

"A church!" Janae exclaimed. "Won't you go up in flames?"

"Not to worry," Leia assured her, with a laugh. "That only happens in horror movies."

"Good to know. Are you home?"

"No, I've been staying with my parents," Leia said, and then frowned. Why was she still here when the danger was past? "I should be going home soon, though. I'll let you know."

"Okay. I'm so glad you're all right."

"Me, too. Bye for now."

Home, Leia thought. It was time to go home. Why had she been putting it off? Leaving her room, she went in search of Rohan.

"Hey, I'm ready to go whenever you are," he said when Leia mentioned going back to her apartment.

"I don't know why I've stayed here so long."

"This is home," he said quietly. "Your memories are here. You feel safe with your parents. Not many places make you feel that way."

How many places had he lived? she wondered. Did he have a place where he felt warm and safe? Welcome?

Her parents were disappointed when she said she was going home that night, yet she couldn't help feeling they were also a little relieved, mainly because Rohan would be going with her. Her parents made every effort to make him feel welcome, but she sensed their discomfort at his presence. She might be a vampire, too, but she was their daughter. Rohan was a stranger and they couldn't help being a little afraid of him. She could understand that. Even when he wasn't trying, there was no ignoring the power that clung to him like a second skin, the sense of being other.

By nine o'clock, they were ready to go. Her mother and father hugged her longer than they usually did.

"Remember," her father said, "we're here for you, no matter what."

"I know." Going up on her tiptoes, Leia kissed his cheek. "I love you, too."

Cynthia gave Rohan a brief hug. Brian shook his hand.

Rohan breathed a sigh of relief when they left the house. It had been an effort being with her parents, constantly reining in his power so as not to frighten them, although he wasn't sure he'd succeeded.

Leia sensed the change in him immediately. His preternatural power filled the air around them. "Is it hard, not letting people see you for what you really are?"

He shrugged. "A little. Most people don't feel it, but your father picked up on it right away."

"He never said anything."

"He wasn't sure what it was. Some people are extra sensitive to the supernatural."

Holding Leia's hand, he transported them to her apartment.

Inside, she kicked off her shoes, then wrinkled her nose as the stink of rotten food assailed her nostrils. "Whew! I need to clean the fridge."

Rohan laughed softly as he gathered her into his arms. "Later."

"But the smell!"

"Later," he said again, his voice softly entreating.

"Later," she agreed, and gave herself into his keeping.

Leia stared at her reflection in the mirror, pleased beyond words that she could see herself. All the myths and legends said vampires had no soul and therefore cast no reflection. Another old wives' tale, Rohan had assured her.

It had taken two weeks to find a church and a suitable date, and another week after that to have her dress altered. Ordering a cake and flowers had been easy, since she didn't need a huge, fancy cake or any exotic blooms.

But, finally, the day—or night—arrived.

"You look gorgeous," Janae said.

"Thanks. So do you."

"I can't believe my little girl is getting married," Cynthia said, sniffling.

"Mom, please don't cry."

"You look so lovely," her mother said, setting Leia's veil in place. "You've always been beautiful but now there's something about you... a kind of glow." She bit down on her lower lip. "Does it have anything to do with what you've become?"

"I don't know, Mom, but I think it has more to do with the man I'm marrying."

There was a knock at the door and an unfamiliar voice advised them it was time.

"I wish you every happiness," Janae said. She picked up her own flowers and handed Leia the bridal bouquet.

There was another knock and her father and brother poked their heads in.

"Are you ready?" her father asked.

Leia nodded.

"You look pretty good," Luke said, with a wink. "Try not to trip on your way down the aisle."

Leia made a face at him as he took their mother's arm and left the room, followed by Janae.

"I'm so nervous," Leia remarked, taking a last glance in the mirror. "And I don't know why."

"Brides are supposed to be nervous," her father said, with a faint smile. "Are you sure about this?"

"A hundred and ten percent."

"All right, then," he said, a note of resignation in his voice. "They're waiting for us. Remember, if it doesn't work out, your room is always waiting."

Knowing he meant well, Leia kissed him on the cheek. "I love you, Dad. Please be happy for me."

"If you're happy, I'm happy," he said, as he took her hand and gave it a squeeze. "Here we go."

The chapel had been decorated with flowers and ferns. A white runner stretched from the foyer to the altar, where long, white tapers burned. An organist played softly as Luke seated their mother. The minister stood in front of the altar clad in a black suit and tie.

A side door opened and Rohan and Trent took their places beside the minister.

Butterflies went crazy in Leia's stomach when she saw Rohan. Had there ever been a more handsome man in all of creation? She melted inside when he winked at her.

The organist broke into the *Wedding March* and Janae started down the aisle.

"This is it," Brian said, giving Leia's hand a reassuring squeeze.

They hadn't taken more than three steps when all hell broke loose.

Feeling as if she were reliving a nightmare, Leia watched half-a-dozen men carrying rifles and wooden stakes charge down the aisle. She gasped as she recognized the man in front. It was the minister from their sham wedding, the man who had run out the side door when Josiah burst into the chapel.

Janae let out a scream when one of the intruders hissed, "traitor" as he twisted Trent's arm behind his back and shoved a pistol into his belly.

Leia glanced at Rohan as she felt his preternatural power gather around the hunters, stealing their ability to move.

Leia's father muttered, "What the hell's going on?"

Her mother fainted and only her brother's quick reflexes kept Cynthia from sliding to the floor.

Luke's eyes lit up. Leia had no doubt that her brother was imagining the mayhem they were watching as a scene in a future horror movie. She had been somewhat nervous about telling Luke about herself and Rohan, but he'd been excited to learn his sister and future brother-in-law were vampires. Considering his fascination with super-hero movies, she probably shouldn't have been surprised.

Janae grabbed Leia's hand and held on tight.

The minister seemed unaffected by the intrusion.

Rohan took a few steps forward, his angry gaze sweeping over the hunters. "I'm getting damn sick and tired of this," he snarled. "So I'm giving you clear warning. I suggest you tell whoever the devil your leader is to leave me the hell alone. I haven't killed anyone in a long time, but if you don't stop harassing me and mine, I'm coming after you. All of you. There's nowhere you can run, nowhere you can hide, that I can't find you."

Eyes blazing red, he unleashed more of his power. Helpless, the hunters stared at him. One man fainted. Others dropped to their knees. A keening cry filled the chapel as pain ripped through them, one and all.

Withdrawing his power, Rohan said, "That's but a taste of what I can do. If I ever see any of you again, you won't like what happens next. Now get the hell out here."

In less than a minute, the hunters were gone as if they had never been there.

"Well, damn," Luke said. "That husband of yours sure knows how to put on a show."

His words broke the tension in the room. When all was in readiness again, the minister smiled at the guests.

Leia stared at him, startled to see a hint of fang, and only then realized that he was a vampire.

The ceremony was brief. An exchange of vows, an exchange of rings and a heartfelt pledge to love each other forever. Leia couldn't help but notice that everyone let out a relieved sigh when the minister declared, "I now pronounce you man and wife. Rohan, you may kiss your bride."

Leia smiled as Rohan lifted her veil and took her in his arms. "Forever and always," he murmured.

"Always and forever," she whispered. Her eyelids fluttered down as he claimed his first husbandly kiss and she knew she could endure anything as long as he was there beside her.

The wedding party returned to the Winchesters' house after the ceremony. Her mother had arranged for a caterer and there were sandwiches and salads and champagne for those so inclined, and a chocolate cake with white frosting with the customary bride and groom on top.

While her mother and Janae were busy in the kitchen, Leia took Rohan aside. "I have to know," she said. "Were the hunters who showed up tonight the same ones who attacked us before?"

"No." He caressed her cheek. "After tonight, I don't think we'll have any more trouble with any of the hunters in this area. Now, stop worrying. Brides are supposed to be happy and carefree."

"I am happy," she said.

He kissed her, hard and fast, before they returned to the party.

"Well," her brother said as they entered the living room, "that was the damnedest wedding I've ever seen. Lucas and Spielberg would have loved it."

"Here's to the bride and groom," Trent said, lifting his glass. "May happiness follow you wherever you go."

Rohan smiled at him. "It's often said that politics makes strange bedfellows. So, it seems, do vampires and hunters."

"Except I'm not a hunter anymore," Trent reminded him, slipping his arm around Janae's waist. "Maybe I should become a vampire. What do you think, Rohan? Think I'd make a good bloodsucker?"

"Trent!" Janae exclaimed, a look of abject horror on her face. "Don't even think that!"

"I'm only kidding, sweeting," he said, with a wink at Rohan.

Leia grinned, thinking what fun it would be if Trent and Janae were vampires, too.

Catching her thoughts, Rohan shook his head. Leia laughed as his words whispered in her mind. *Stranger things have happened, love.*

Later that night, when the two of them were alone in her apartment, Shadow Dancer danced for his bride. Clad only in the hot pink briefs Leia had bought for him, he dipped and swayed, every movement mesmerizing, erotic, his copper-hued skin glistening in the light of the candles beside the bed. Almost, it was as if he was making love to her.

She couldn't take her gaze away from him, or help noticing the way his briefs outlined his masculinity. He was wild and beautiful, a law unto himself as he bent and twisted and spun, his body as fluid as water, his muscles taut. His power filled the room as he performed the intricate steps. It was a dance she had never seen before and she knew in her heart that no one else had ever seen it, either. It was just for her, his unique way of telling her he loved her.

He danced closer, tempting her touch, and she reached out to him, her fingertips trailing boldly over his muscular chest, his hard, flat belly. A seductive smile played over her lips as the bulge in his briefs grew larger.

With a low growl, he slid under the covers and drew her into his arms. Leia snuggled against him, fervently praying that the man who had danced his way into her heart would never let her go.

~finis~

Dear Reader ~

I hope you enjoyed reading this story as much as I enjoyed writing it. Some characters quickly become favorite. Rohan is one of them. Shadow, from the Reckless *series, is another one. I couldn't bear to say goodbye to him, so after* Reckless Heart, *I wrote* Reckless Love, Reckless Desire, Reckless Embrace, *and the short story*, Reckless Destiny.

Mara, from the Night *series is another favorite. She started out as a minor character in* Night's Kiss, *but I liked her so much, I wrote* Night's Touch, Night's Master, Night's Pleasure, Night's Mistress, Night's Promise, *and* Night's Surrender.

Rylan Saintcrow is another favorite of mine. I fell in love with Rylan Saintcrow while writing As Twilight Falls, *so I wrote* Twilight Dreams, Twilight Desire, Twilight Destiny *(which holds another of my fav heroes, Jason Kincaid). I recently finished the fifth book,* Twilight Longings, *and I'm currently working on the sixth.*

All the Best,
Amanda

About the Author

Amanda Ashley started writing for the fun of it. Her first book, a historical romance written as Madeline Baker, was published in 1985. Since then, she has published numerous historical and paranormal romances and novellas, many of which have appeared on various bestseller lists, including the *New York Times* Bestseller List and *USA Today*.

Amanda makes her home in Southern California, where she and her husband share their house with a Pomeranian named Lady, a cat named Kitty, and a tortoise named Buddy.

For more information on her books, please visit her websites at:

www.amandaashley.net
and
www.madelinebaker.net
Email: darkwritr@aol.com

About the Publisher

This book is published on behalf of the author by the Ethan Ellenberg Literary Agency.
https://ethanellenberg.com
Email: agent@ethanellenberg.com
Facebook: https://www.facebook.com/EthanEllenbergLiteraryAgency/

www.ingramcontent.com/pod-product-compliance
Lightning Source LLC
LaVergne TN
LVHW011800060526
838200LV00053B/3640